Darren O'Sullivan is the author of five psychological thrillers. He is a graduate of the Faber Academy and his debut novel, *Our Little Secret*, was a bestseller in four countries. When Darren isn't writing, he is found directing theatre or with his eight-year-old son, which is his happy place.

You can follow Darren on Twitter and Instagram @Darrensully or on Facebook/DarrenO'Sullivan-author.

Also by Darren O'Sullivan

Our Little Secret
Close Your Eyes
Closer Than You Think
Dark Corners
The Players

THE
PRICE

DARREN O'SULLIVAN

ONE PLACE. MANY STORIES

HQ
An imprint of HarperCollins*Publishers* Ltd
1 London Bridge Street
London SE1 9GF

www.harpercollins.co.uk

HarperCollins*Publishers*
Macken House, 39/40 Mayor Street Upper,
Dublin 1, D01 C9W8, Ireland

This edition 2023

1

First published in Great Britain by
HQ, an imprint of HarperCollins*Publishers* Ltd 2023

Copyright © Darren O'Sullivan 2023

Darren O'Sullivan asserts the moral right to be identified as the author of this work. A catalogue record for this book is available from the British Library.

ISBN: 9780008342074

This book is for my Nan, Francis Mullis,
who was always a believer . . .

PROLOGUE – 26TH JULY 2023

George

The high-pitched alarm screeched above the sound of falling rain. Its shrill piercing noise made it difficult to hear any movement coming from inside the building, but I knew he was there, somewhere. The side door to the garage was smashed open and the shards of glass scattered over the floor shimmered in the reflection of the streetlights. He was there. He was inside, and he would have to come out through the broken door I was standing next to; I just had to be patient and wait for him to make a run for it. He would come to me, and I would use the cover of night to surprise him. However, even knowing I had the advantage, I was nervous. He was proving to be slippery, resourceful. If I screwed this up, I knew I'd likely not get another chance. If I fucked this up, I might get hurt, or worse.

Forcing myself to steady my breathing in the hope it would lower my heart rate, calm me, and stop me from acting on impulse, I stepped back against a wall ten or so feet from the door and pressed myself against it, feeling safe in the knowledge that no one could sneak up on me.

I looked into the building, trying to make out any movement

in the darkness, hoping I wasn't mistaken in the belief he was still inside. For too long I had wanted this man – he represented the keystone to bringing down Henry Mantel, the man who had caused so much pain and suffering, the man I had fought to bring to justice for over a year. Right now, Mantel's associate didn't know I was here, waiting. Finally, I had the upper hand.

Just as I began to doubt myself, I heard a noise coming from inside the garage. It was nothing more than a shuffle, but it was enough. Moments later I saw movement and the surge of adrenaline flooded from my stomach, into my arms, legs, head, readying my muscles for a fight. For so long I had wanted to find a way to Mantel, and the person who was the crucial link to enable an arrest was about to step out of a crime scene in front of me. As a police officer I didn't often feel on edge, but as I waited, I struggled to contain my nerves. The man, the thief, climbed through the broken door and out into the rain. I sprang out of my concealed spot and tried to grab him, though he twisted out of my grip and began to run.

I had to stop him escaping.

'Stop! Police!' I shouted, stepping out into the light, blocking his way. The man looked back, his face obscured by a baseball cap and a shroud of mist from the pouring rain.

'I said stop!' I shouted, giving chase.

But the man kept running, and he was fast, the distance between us continuing to grow. In a straight sprint, I wouldn't stand a chance – but this was no ordinary race. I'd been to this garage many times, and I knew that the thief was heading towards a dead end, a self-made trap. I would catch him, arrest him, and finally I'd have Henry Mantel for his crimes. For too long Mantel had been one step ahead, for too long he'd acted like he was untouchable. But not any more. Once I had the thief in custody, the truth would spill about Mantel and the robberies, the drugs and – more recently – the murders he had committed. Who this guy was, beyond a thief, I didn't care. I only needed him as leverage, to land the bigger fish.

Although the wall behind the building did form a dead end, I knew the man would likely be able to scale it, but to do so, he would have to slow down. I'd gain a crucial few seconds to close the gap, grab him, and drag him to the ground. This man, this thief, was the key to it all, every single crime, every single death.

Soon I would finally have my answers.

Soon, it would all be over.

16TH JULY 2023

10 days earlier.

CHAPTER ONE

Clara

Every morning, just as I woke, for the briefest of moments I would forget that my daughter had cancer. Then, as I remembered the sickness and tests and treatments, the pain would hit me, and break my heart all over again, like it was the very first time.

Today was no different. As the pain settled into the continuous gnaw in my gut that I had become accustomed to, I focused on taking deep measured breaths and remembering all the things I was doing to help her. These were the things I could control, I reminded myself. When she felt sick, I comforted her, when it was time for treatment, I took her to appointments and held her hand. I showed her only positivity, even when I was struggling to find it myself. I wouldn't say I was coping, but I was hanging in there, determined to get through it so she would ring the bell that meant she was cancer-free. And once this ordeal was over, hopefully, in time, I would recover too.

The pain subsided and Tabatha stirred beside me. As I sat up to reach for her in the cot that I kept beside my bed, I looked at the time. It was just before four; she had slept only a handful of hours, which wasn't enough. I wondered if she knew today was a big day for her. First we had the support group, and then the hospital appointment I had been both dreading and desperate for. It was going to be tough on so little sleep, for us both.

'Hey baby, did you sleep well?' I said, picking her up and giving her a cuddle. She cooed and I nuzzled her closer, speaking to her in a sing-song tone. I fought back the tears forming at the sight of how ill she looked. She was clearly exhausted; the dark patches under her eyes were like those of an adult, one with the stresses only adults should have. She was too small, too young, too innocent for this, but I continued to sing, to chat, to smile, all for her. From my position on the edge of the bed, I looked across the hallway into the spare room. George still wasn't back from his late shift. When he came home late from work, he often slept in there, but, the covers of the single bed lay undisturbed. My first instinct was to worry something had happened to him because, after all, in our line of work, there were risks. But I stopped myself. I had enough to worry about with Tabatha. George was fine. I would know otherwise. He was likely just working a double shift, which he'd been doing a lot recently. We all had to find a way to cope, I supposed.

During her illness and treatment, I'd noticed that Tabatha's appetite suffered, but it was usually best when she first woke, when she was a little refreshed by a brief sleep. So despite it being before dawn, I took her across the hallway into the kitchen, sat her in her highchair, and spoon-fed her some Weetabix. We'd started weaning only a few weeks before, so as I tried to get the spoon into her mouth, food ended up on her chin, her nose, her cheeks. And as I was tired, I didn't have the energy to stop her when she grabbed a handful of the mushed-up food and threw it on the floor. She smiled, delighted with herself and I smiled back. For a brief moment it almost felt like nothing was wrong. Despite the mess we made, she'd managed to eat a little, and some food was better than nothing. Once she finished, I cleaned her up, put her in her favourite bouncy chair and made myself a much-needed cup of coffee. As I flicked on the kettle, I saw a Post-it note with George's scrawl stuck to the kitchen side.

Morning my girls,
I love you,
Daddy x

It made me smile. It was something so small and yet so thoughtful; it made me feel like he still cared in the way he once did before the diagnosis had changed everything. The note didn't say when he would be home, or if he was coming to the support group – as he had promised for the last three meetings and yet still hadn't turned up – but he still cared. I had no doubt he loved Tabatha; the pained expression he carried since finding out our daughter was unwell showed as much. But at times I wondered if he still loved me. Having a baby should have brought George and I even closer together, made us even tighter as a couple. We had become a nuclear family. Yet the distance between us was wider than ever before.

After I poured my coffee, I put on some early morning TV and mentally prepared myself for the day ahead. Tabatha dozed at around six, and sitting beside her, Netflix quietly playing in the background, I did too. When we both woke just before eight, George still wasn't back.

Where are you? I wondered.

Even though it was still early, hours before the support group I had found comfort in started, I began to get myself and Tabs ready. Soon Mum would arrive at the bookshop below our flat, the bookshop that belonged to her, and I needed her in the absence of my husband. I needed an adult who understood how hard this was.

Once she was dressed, I looked at my daughter. If you didn't know she had cancer, it was almost impossible to tell. At just over six months old, she was young enough that her bald head wasn't automatically associated with cancer treatments. Her skin was a little paler than usual, her eyes a little darker, however, she smiled, played, and looked pretty much like any baby of that age. It's funny, most parents want their children to be special, to shine, but I was desperate for my child to go unnoticed, to blend in, and for the most part, she did. But I knew that time was borrowed. They'd warned us that before she started getting better, she would likely get worse, and soon people would start to question why she was so thin, and so pale. Strangers we passed on the street would know my baby was ill.

With Tabs settled, I quickly showered and dressed myself, then carried her down the flats' internal stairs that lead directly into the bookshop.

I walked through the small stockroom-cum-staffroom and opened the keypad-secured door between the stock room and the shop floor.

'Mum? Are you here yet?' I called out, but the shop was quiet.

Placing Tabatha in a highchair at one of the new tables in the café area, I switched on the coffee machine to make myself another drink. I'd need all the caffeine I could stomach.

A few years back, when things were rough and the lockdown seemed never-ending, I suggested that she used a part of the government bounce-back loan to turn the rear of the shop into a café, with a small play area for little ones. In recent years, the high street book trade had been hit hard – thanks in no small part to online shopping – but in Buxton, coffee shops seemed to be doing better than ever. So by dedicating a space for coffee lovers in the hope they'd also buy books and up the profit seemed like a perfect solution, and we all jumped at the opportunity to help Mum who had worked tirelessly in her business for years. George and I helped renovate the space, and when we found out we were expecting Tabatha, we pictured our baby there, playing in the children's corner. We imagined Mum reading books to her, and Tabatha happy and laughing and clapping – a delight for customers. We had planned it all out; once I had finished my maternity leave, I would go back to being a police officer, working the opposite shift to George, and Tabatha would become a regular in the bookshop, with either mum or one of us by her side. The three of us making it work. I dreamt of a version of life where we were all happy in this café, in this shop. It was bright, it was hopeful, though as I looked at the barely-used children's area, it hurt. I had pictured this beautiful future. Now I understood how naive I had been; seldom do plans play out as we hope.

I made myself an Americano and sat down with Tabatha,

playing, singing and tickling her little feet until I heard the familiar bell as the shop door opened, and Mum walked in.

'You look terrible, Clara, is everything all right?' she asked when she saw me.

'Yeah, Tabs didn't sleep well.'

'Is she okay?' Mum came over and took her from me to give her a cuddle.

'She was just unsettled.'

'I see,' Mum said. I could see she was trying to work out what that meant.

'Mum, I promise, she's fine, we're both fine.'

'And George?'

'He's still working.'

She nodded. 'You know you can call me. I could stay over, be there when she wakes, so you can sleep a little.'

'I know, thanks Mum. It's fine though, really.'

'Sorry, I'm fretting, ignore me,' she waved it off and gave me a kiss on the cheek. 'What time is the hospital appointment today?'

'Twelve.'

'Will you ring me after?'

'I always do.' I smiled.

'Sorry, love, you know I only worry.'

Leaving Tabs with mum, I made her a cappuccino and as she took a sip, moaned in appreciation.

'You're getting good at making these now.'

'Yeah, finally learning how to do the milk properly. Figured if I can perfect it, we might get more people through the door.'

Mum smiled. 'Clara, don't get too used to being here. As

soon as Tabatha is better, you'll be going back to your proper job, all right?'

'Sure.' This was exactly why I needed her around; she still saw that bright future I once could.

Mum chatted to Tabatha, played peek-a-boo, sang nursery rhymes, and I watched, remembering Mum doing similar things with me when I was a little girl.

'This is the best part of my entire day, the best part, yes it is, yes it is,' Mum said, in the way that made Tabatha smile. 'What are you doing until the appointment?' she asked when she noticed me watching.

'We've got our support group.'

'Oh, nice,' Mum said, but didn't offer any more. She stood up, Tabatha still in her arms, and began to prepare for the shop opening. Like George, she hadn't been to the support group either. Unlike George, she would if I asked her. But I didn't feel that was right. No one else at the group took grandparents, it was only mums and dads I doubted there was a rule against it, but regardless, I didn't offer. I was holding out hope that George would walk through the door, smile at me and Tabatha, and come with us to the group. He didn't say it out loud, at least not to me, but I understood why he was hesitant to come to the sessions and why, until now, he hadn't been. The group could be upsetting. Hearing so many people talk about their pain, worry and grief was difficult to listen to, and I knew that although George didn't really talk to me about how he was feeling, he was already struggling not to be overwhelmed as it was. But I wanted him to come, despite how hard it was, because amongst the grief and worry was hope. I had heard stories of children going into remission, beating the disease, ringing that victory bell. It helped me focus on Tabatha doing that one day too, and I wanted that for my husband. I wanted him to have hope.

When we first discovered Tabatha was sick, our oncologist, Dr Bhari, gave us a pamphlet for the group. I was sceptical, but a few days later I felt so low, so afraid, that I forced myself to go. And there I met Sadie, and within minutes I knew I had made the right decision to go along. Sadie's daughter had the same cancer as Tabatha, but she was optimistic, proactive, positive, and we quickly bonded and exchanged numbers. She went to the group alone as she was a single mum and she assumed I was too, until I told her about George, and how he was reluctant to come. She understood, saying it was hard to take that step, and I guess she was right. But I still didn't like the fact that George couldn't bring himself to try at least once.

Thinking of Sadie, I grabbed my phone and pinged her a quick message.

Hey, are you coming today?

True to form, she messaged back within a few minutes.

Of course. Everything good your end?

Yes, fine, restless night but all fine. How about you?

All good here, and the same, but then we don't get much sleep do we? See you and Tabatha later X

Finishing my coffee, I joined Mum and greeted the first of the customers that had already started browsing. I began to get ready to leave, loading the buggy with the changing bag, bottles and snacks before placing Tabatha in the seat. I messaged George, thinking that maybe he was on his way or would meet us there. Hoping today was the day he would take that leap.

14

Hey, love, Tabs and I are ready to go to the group, are you still coming?

Three dots pulsated on my screen; he was messaging back. Still, I hoped he would come as he had promised.

Sorry, something's come up at work. I'll be back for the hospital appointment.

'Love?' Mum asked, no doubt seeing my disappointment. I needed George for this, and again, he wasn't there. I was sure part of the reason he didn't come was because he would appear vulnerable, and he didn't cope well with that. He didn't like asking for help or support. At times he was old-school in his masculinity, needing to shoulder things alone, and as much as I tried to tell him that it wasn't healthy, he couldn't seem too change it. I needed him to show his vulnerability, I needed him to admit he was struggling, so we could talk properly about how we were both feeling and shoulder the burden together. Like a couple should.

'Clara?' Mum asked again when I didn't reply.

'Yeah, sorry, I'm fine. See you later,' I forced a smile – one Mum saw straight through. And before she could press me further, I kissed her on the cheek and left.

As I felt the rays of the warm morning sun, I pulled out my phone and messaged George back in hope.

I'm leaving for the group now, can you try and make it? We'll wait for you outside the church. I really want you there with me. Please? x

He messaged back quickly.

I can't. I'm sorry, I promise I will next time.

Sighing, I put my phone away and walked towards the town's church where the group was held. On my own, again. Feeling abandoned by the man I loved, again.

CHAPTER TWO

George

Putting my phone away, I took a moment to bury the guilt I was feeling about letting Clara down and pulled myself together. The guilt was always there, when I worked, when I was at home, it didn't matter. It was now a constant companion. One I couldn't quite push away, no matter how much I tried.

'George? Everything all right?' Mike asked.

'Yes, fine mate,' I said, before I looked through to the man – the boy, really – in the hospital bed in the room I was standing outside. Mike had been in earlier to speak with the doctors about his condition, hoping to speak to him too, but the boy had been unconscious. Now he was awake, and staring at the ceiling. We didn't know a lot, only that he was on our radar because of his link with Henry Mantel. He might have been a drug runner or cash handler, or any other illicit part of the Mantel regime, but regardless of his role, he was on our ever-growing list of names and faces connected to Mantel and the drugs empire we knew he ran, even if we hadn't yet been able to prove it. The kid was involved somehow, though, and had been found in a heap, almost beaten to death, between a takeaway and pub in the town centre in the early hours of the morning. He'd been there all night.

'Shall we go in?' Mike asked.

'Nah, let's leave it a little longer. Kid's still coming to terms with what happened to him. He knows we are stood here waiting. When he looks at us, we'll know he is ready to talk.'

I looked at my phone again, thinking Clara would have messaged back, but she hadn't and I knew that she was pissed off at me for not being there when I promised I would. Again. I would never miss a hospital appointment, regardless of what came in at work, but the group was just people sitting around and sharing their stories of misery, of how their children were dying. I could think of no worse place to go. Besides, I needed to be here. This could be an important lead in the Mantel case. For over a year, he had always been one step ahead, but now I couldn't help feeling we were finally catching up. This kid, who was still refusing to meet my eye, could have information that would finally allow us to pin something concrete on him, be it money laundering, drug distribution, assaults or worse. People knew, just as we knew, what kind of man Henry Mantel was, but they didn't speak ill of him. They didn't dare. But the kid in front of us now was a sitting duck and if we could persuade him that police protection was the best thing for him, we could get some solid evidence. I didn't know why he had received his beating. Maybe he fucked something up. Or perhaps Mantel might have felt like he was close to cracking, wanting out – and if that was the case a good beating was a warning. And it wouldn't end with this attack; the kid would be watched, and probably murdered, in time. If I could reassure him he was safe, if I could convince him that Mantel couldn't get to him now, maybe he might give us something that would push us one step closer to being able to catch the man I have tried to arrest for far too long.

'George, I've been wondering. How's she doing?' Mike asked, breaking into my thoughts.

'Tabatha? She's fine.'

'Is the treatment working?'

'We think so, she seems a little brighter now the side effects have faded.'

'That's great news.'

'Thanks. We're meeting with the doctor today to look at the latest scans. Literally two floors below us.'

'Well, they do amazing things now, the C-word doesn't have the same fear as it did twenty or thirty years ago. They're finding treatments and cures all the time, and if she's feeling brighter, I'm sure it will be good news.'

'They tell us her type is ninety-five per cent curable,' I said, not for the first time either. I had convinced myself the more I spoke of it being all right, the more likely this would be true.

'That's good, I'm sure it will be one hundred per cent before you know it.'

'Thanks mate. Anyway, let's talk about Connor,' I gestured to the kid who was now sipping water a nurse had handed to him before she left the room. 'Think he will talk?'

'Hopefully.'

'We need him to.'

'George, isn't it fucked up we're even talking about this? Look at him, he's just a kid. He shouldn't be caught up in any of this.'

'Yeah, they get younger and younger.'

Connor put down his water, then turned his head and

looked directly at me, with his one good eye that wasn't swollen shut.

'That's our cue.'

Mike and I walked into the room.

'Hey Connor,' I smiled. He didn't return it.

'What do you want?' he asked, his voice barely a whisper, too hoarse for any more. The kid was in a lot of pain, but he didn't need to speak for that to be clear. The broken jaw and swollen face said it all.

'Firstly, we are making sure you're okay. You took one hell of a beating.'

'I'm fine.'

'Connor. We need to know who did this to you.' Mike looked at him in a way which told him we all knew the answer.

'No one, I slipped.'

'Connor, we can help you.'

The kid laughed, a quiet, painful laugh, one that morphed into a cough that made him double over, clutching his ribs. I reached for the cup of water and once he stopped coughing, he took a sip before lying back and closing his eyes. 'Sure, you can,' he managed to say.

'We can protect you,' I added.

'I have nothing to say to you.'

'We can help you.' Mike tried again, repeating the offer.

'I'm tired.'

'We know Henry Mantel did this. Tell us what happened, and we can stop him.'

'You can't, though, can you? You need to go now. I can't have him see you here with me.'

'Connor . . .'

'He'll kill me if he thinks I've talked.'

'We won't let him. We can protect you,' I repeated.

'No, you can't.'

'Let us help you.'

'You can't help me. If anyone finds out you're here . . .'

Connor pressed the alarm attached to his bed to get the attention of a nurse or doctor, and turned his head away from us.

'Connor,' Mike said quietly. 'Kids are getting hurt. Three students ended up in this very hospital last week because of the stuff Mantel pushes. He's cutting the drugs he sells with other chemicals, cheap and dangerous. It's making people really sick. We need to help them. You've all but told us it's Mantel who did this to you. We need more. Please mate?'

Connor didn't respond, just pressed the alarm again.

'Come on, George.'

I paused, still hoping that Connor might tell us something that could help him and us.

'Come on,' Mike repeated, and reluctantly we left the room, just as a nurse walked in to check on the boy.

'What do we do now?' Mike asked.

'I don't know mate,' I said, downbeat. 'We are so close to Mantel.'

'I know, we'll get to him. Come on, the kid won't talk.'

I looked back through the window at Connor, who was looking back at me hesitantly, though he held my eye this time, like he wanted or needed to say something. And so I slowly approached his bed once more.

'Connor?'

'Are kids really getting sick?' he asked.

'Some are dying.'

'And Mantel won't know I've said anything?'

'No, not a thing.'

'If he finds out—' Conner started.

'He won't.'

'He might be watching. He has people everywhere.'

'Not everywhere. We can and will look after you.'

'He might even have someone watching right now.'

'Then when we leave, we will talk about how you refused to speak to us. If anyone is watching, they will feed back that you have kept quiet.'

Connor closed his one working eye and took a deep breath. 'Talk to Reece Hunter.'

The name didn't ring a bell. I looked at Mike and could see he didn't know it either.

'Thank you, Connor.'

'If he ever finds out—' he slurred again, blinking a fat tear.

'He won't. When you're well enough, we'll make sure you leave the area, we will help you get out.'

'You promise?'

'I promise. Connor, you have done a good thing today.'

Leaving him to rest, Mike and I made our way off the ward and into the lift.

'Have you heard that name before? Reece Hunter?' I asked.

'No, mate.'

'No, me neither.'

As we descended, the lift stopped on the third floor, the oncology department, and I felt Mike looking at me.

'Funny, I'll be back here within a few hours.'

'Can you just stay here? Have a break before your appointment?'

'No, I've got to pick up Clara and Tabs.'

'I see. I can get them, and bring them to you?'

'No, Mike, thanks anyway, but I need to do this.'

This morning I was here as a copper, working and trying to solve a case. This afternoon I'd be back here as a father, scared for his baby. The same building, but everything would be different. I could see Mike wanted to say something, but thankfully the lift door closed and we continued down to the ground floor in silence. At the main entrance, we made our way outside. As we walked past various patients and visitors, I spotted a newspaper stand outside a small confectionery shop. On the top was a magazine called M1. A community magazine that showcased news from Manchester and surrounding areas. I had heard that inside was an article about Mantel. I picked it up, scanned the pages and sure enough, on page 15, there he was. The headline read '*New salon opens, generating employment opportunity for the locals of Buxton.*' Underneath was a photo. There, smiling smugly, stood Henry Mantel.

'Look at this, Mike,' I said, handing Mike the magazine.

'Seems crime does pay,' he replied.

'It's just another front to clean his drug money.'

Mike turned the page over. 'Have you seen this?'

'*Three critically ill in Stockport following suspected "party drug" overdose*'.

The irony wasn't lost on me that on the page before, the very person behind these drugs was being fêted as a pillar of the local community. But then that was his MO; hide in plain sight. For those who didn't know any better, Henry Mantel was a community-focused man who brought jobs to the town and supported charities. He was kind and generous, using his 'good fortune in business to give back.'

Mantel had operated like that for years, hiding behind charitable gestures. But just over a year ago, his name had surfaced in connection to a string of ODs in nearby Stockport. With a little digging, we could see something in his financial portfolio wasn't making sense. Although the numbers added up, taxes were paid and income/expenditure was balanced, it didn't seem right. He would have periods of drought, and then large profits would funnel through his many businesses. After watching those businesses, which all had consistent foot flow, we couldn't see where this extra money, declared as customer trade, was coming from.

It was clear that Mantel was doing something illegal and cleverly covering his tracks, and when we spoke to criminals who were already known to us, no one would say a bad word about him. They would either call him charitable or, in most cases, they wouldn't say anything at all. We could all see they were afraid of him.

'I can't fucking wait to bring him down,' I spat, throwing the magazine back onto the stack of others.

Mike got on his phone, and rang the office.

'I need you to find a Reece Hunter. He must be in the system somewhere, and then call me back.'

Hanging up, he turned to me. 'I'm gonna head back to the office, do some digging. If anything looks promising, I'll let you know.'

'I'll come back with you.'

'No, go, get your family and have something to eat. You gotta look after yourself, mate. You have that appointment, your family need you well.'

'You're right.'

'We might not find anything out for days,' he added.

'It's just we're so close now,' I said.

Mike understood. He knew the reasons why I wanted Mantel off the streets, beyond the fact it was my job. He knew about my brother. About how he slipped away from our family, how he died because of people like Henry Mantel getting their claws into him. He knew I wanted Mantel because I wanted to vindicate my brother. But he was right; I had somewhere to be, and Mike could carry on in my absence.

I didn't know anything about this Reece Hunter, but I also felt that Connor wouldn't feed us anything we couldn't use. He was a brave kid, maybe even a good kid who was too easily led and manipulated. And as much as I tried to remain objective, I couldn't help but think that maybe this Hunter character would open the door on our investigation.

For now, I needed to put the case to the back of my mind, and focus on my daughter. As I was driving towards town, to drop Mike off at the station before heading home, I couldn't help but be haunted by the newspaper headlines about the teenagers hospitalized, feeling a pang of loss for my own brother. I'd been too young to help him and I'd lost him. But I was determined not to let history repeat itself. I would help my daughter through her recovery, and I'd bring down Mantel for good, so she'd have a safer world to live in.

CHAPTER THREE

Clara

Summer had fully set in, and the trees held their lustrous green hues, alive and bold. I found myself watching the slender ends of branches dancing in the breeze, and I was thankful for it; summer made everything feel better with its long warm days, the life everywhere. But still, as I looked at the foliage I wondered, did the leaves know that they would one day wilt and fall, and die? Did it even matter? I answered for them; yes. Life always mattered. Always. I hoped.

I stopped several times to show Tabatha a flower or a bird in a tree, and when we arrived, both she and I were calm. Even though this was now my forth session, I felt nervous before walking into the group meeting. I knew the reason why, of course. In that moment between opening the door and joining the circle, I would see who was there, and who wasn't. Every time a family was missing, I would fear the worst. Most of the time it was just an appointment, or another commitment. But sometimes it wasn't.

I opened the door and as I struggled to get Tabatha's buggy in Gary, who led the sessions, saw me and dashed over to help.

'Hi Clara, so glad you could make it.'

'Hi Gary.'

As he helped me lift the buggy over the small step into the building, I could see several familiar faces with their babies, standing around the edges, unloading their little ones from buggies, waiting for the session to begin. On the floor in the middle of the room were colourful foam mats that connected like a giant jigsaw puzzle. I watched for a moment, focusing on some of the parents. Most looked as tired as I felt, some lost, too. Only one person looked optimistic, as she did every week, and I smiled at her when she saw me. Walking over, I gave her a hug.

'Hi Sadie.'

'Hey. How are you doing?'

'You know. It's bloody hard, but we're trying to stay upbeat.'

'That's all any of us can do. How's Tabatha been since we last spoke?'

'Sleep is a struggle, but you know all about that, too.'

'I swear, when Sophie is better, I am going to sleep for a month.'

I laughed. 'How's she been?'

'You know what, she's been good. She's eating better than she has for a long time and she's sleeping in a little more.'

'Oh Sadie, that's great to hear,' I said, pulling her into a fresh embrace. Sophie also had neuroblastoma but she was turning the corner towards health. It was only a matter of time before my daughter joined her.

'Your appointment is today, isn't it?' Sadie asked, wanting to move the conversation along; I could see the relief she felt was close to spilling over. I was surprised she remembered as

26

I'd only mentioned Tabatha's hospital appointment in passing the week before.

'Yep, it's today.'

'I'm sure everything is going to be all right. I can feel it, you'll get good news.'

'Thanks, Sadie.'

Gary took his place in the circle and all of the families drew in to sit and begin the session. I had known Gary for maybe a month, and knew he lived close by in town, but despite his pleasant manner and his leadership of the group, I didn't really know anything about the man. He carried our grief, he understood what we were going through, that he had been there himself and that was why he wanted to help, but he didn't offer any more as to the outcome of his struggles. He didn't need to, though. It wasn't written on his face, etched into the crow's feet around his eyes, where most carried the burden of deep sadness, where I could see my own husband carried his. It was in the way his shoulders sat, the way his fingernails were bitten short, to the point of being raw. It told a story about him, a sad one. Sadie thought it too, though like me she didn't really know anything about Gary's life outside of the sessions. I didn't want to ask, though. It was enough that he'd been on this road, and we all could sense where it had ended for him. We all saw how sometimes he would look at Tabatha or Sophie or one of the other babies with such longing. Gary knew that spring didn't always follow winter. While I was living my life in the shadow of my daughter's disease, he was a man who had the look of someone living in perpetual night. I was sure, if I could see inside his chest, I'd see a scorched brand mark in the place where a heart once sat. As much as my own heart ached for him, I hoped to never experience what he clearly had. I guess that was another reason why I came back; Gary was resilient, hopeful, even after what Sadie and I had assumed was his story. I wanted to learn from that.

As Gary asked how we all were feeling, the general consensus, besides Sadie, was that everyone felt lost. One by one, parents spoke of their hopes, fears and news. We all listened to one another without pity or feeling the need to comment. We all knew there were no words to help, but having people to listen meant everything. Throughout this, parents played with their children to keep them occupied; if you took away the discussion around illness and hospital visits, it would look just like any other parent and baby group. I understood why people came back over and over. I understood why *I* did. If only George would keep his promise and come too, then he would see it for himself and feel the hope I felt after each session. He would see that despite him saying the group was for hopeless people, it was the very antithesis of that. We talked of treatments, of victories, of research we were all doing in our spare time. I had found a friend through the group, someone who I trusted and who understood what I lived through day to day. Sadie and I would be friends for life – better, stronger, together. As the conversation moved on to what stage everyone's child was at with treatments, so that those who had been through them already could offer support, one parent mentioned some research they had been doing into treatments being offered in other countries. Again I didn't comment, just listened to what they spoke about, interested in what they'd learned. I hadn't looked that far afield, as Tabatha was responding well to the treatment she was on, but I understood why a parent might. One way or another, we were all researchers, night-time Google wanderers. Worst-case scenario-ers.

As people broke into smaller groups, Sadie and I grabbed a coffee and found a quiet corner to speak. We put Tabatha and Sophie in their buggies, ready for their mid-morning naps.

'Sadie, have you done much research into this experimental treatment stuff?' I asked.

'Oh yeah, I've researched loads!'

'Really?'

'Yes.'

'Oh,' I said, now wondering if I was failing my daughter for not doing the same. 'Anything stand out as being something to think about?'

'At the Children's Hospital of Philadelphia, they are trialling a treatment with a drug called Floxiline.'

'Floxiline?'

'It's specifically for childhood neuroblastoma.'

'Oh wow. And?'

'They are getting some incredible results.'

'Are you thinking of pursuing it as an option. Christ, where would you even start?'

'No, not at all. Sophie is doing so well. It's just . . . I'm on my own, and when she's asleep my mind wanders and I need something to keep my spirits up. It's always so positive to hear there are new treatments being developed that work to help beat the cancer.'

'Yeah, I understand that. You can always call me, you know.'

'I know, but you're going through this too. I don't want to

keep you up if it's a night you and Tabatha have are managing to get some sleep.'

'What's it called again?'

'Floxiline.'

Before I could forget, I typed a note into my phone. I would look it up, but only for the same reasons as Sadie – to keep my spirits up when they dipped. Because despite being married, I felt alone in this, just like her.

'I should warn you though,' Sadie continued. 'It's bloody expensive.'

'Dare I ask?'

'With the cost of the treatment, travel, insurances and accommodation to stay out there, it's around £230,000.'

'Shit, that's a lot.'

'I know, but it still gives me a lift when I need it. Because if things started to go wrong, which hopefully they won't, but *if* they did, there is always a plan B.'

I agreed, understanding how important it was to keep positive, even when it felt like the world was trying to crush me alive. 'She's asleep.' I smiled, looking down at my baby.

'So is Soph.'

'It's almost like they aren't unwell when they sleep,' I said, my eyes firmly on my daughter, thinking of the life she should be having.

'Clara, today, at the hospital, it's going to be all right.'

'Thanks, Sadie. I don't know how you stay so upbeat.'

'I visualize. I see everything being okay, and if I believe it, it will be.'

Gary, who was floating around chatting to everyone, made his way over to us, and for a while we spoke of other things, of life before, and what we hoped life would be after cancer. He asked if I missed my job and I almost lied, saying I didn't, but I realized that if I lied here, of all places, it was pointless coming, so I told him the truth. I missed it terribly. When he wandered off, Sadie turned to me.

'Clara, you know, I still can't see you being a copper. I mean, the uniform.'

'I hated the uniform bit but thankfully, I didn't wear it for long. I was, I mean, I am a detective.'

'That is so cool. Do you think you'll ever go back to it?'

'Still on maternity leave, so having to think about it a lot, and I've concluded, I don't know.'

Sadie laughed, as did I but saying it aloud for the first time, I realized how I hadn't really thought about it properly at all. Despite my head saying I would go back one day, my heart was saying I wouldn't be a copper ever again. I wouldn't give any time away that I could be spending with my daughter. I loved the force, but the hours were long, the shifts a challenge. And I wasn't sure I could do that to her. Time was precious.

Gary announced it was time to wrap up, and thanking him, I gave Sadie a hug and left.

Since I'd discovered my daughter was sick, I'd had a small candle of hope inside my chest that I kept burning, although it flickered every now and then. After seeing Sadie, the candle always burnt a little brighter, it was always a little easier to protect. Now, as I walked home, I visualized Tabs being well, George and I happy once more, close once more, just as Sadie told me to.

My phone rang, bringing me back to reality. I could see from the display it was George. Despite trying to feel positive, the feeling of abandonment from this morning came rushing back.

'Are you on your way back?'

'Yes, just left, we'll be home in ten minutes.'

'Want me to come get you?'

'No, it's fine. Have a cuppa, you've had a long night. We'll be back soon.'

'I'll make us both one to take on the drive,' I noticed his voice was tight, clipped.

'George, are you all right?'

He sighed. 'I think so. I mean, she's doing so well, she's having the right treatment.'

'She is.'

'And we caught it early,' he continued. 'I don't wanna say it out loud, but . . .'

'I know, I feel it too,' I told him. 'I think we're going to get good news.'

'You really think so?'

'Yeah, I do.' And I did. Tabatha was going to be okay, I could feel it. Sadie's optimism was contagious. 'See you in ten.'

As I put my phone away, I felt myself lift. Seeing Sadie did that anyway, but it was also good to know that my husband was feeling just like me, quietly optimistic. We were eye to eye on this and somehow we'd get through it. We were going to get the news that our daughter was on the road to recovery.

CHAPTER FOUR

Henry Mantel

Standing in his office overlooking the garage workshop floor, Henry Mantel watched as his staff worked away, drilling bolts to remove wheels from their axles, lifting cars onto ramps. Bonnets up, the radio on, grease and dirt and graft. His worker bees. At the other end of the workshop, closest to the small reception area where two customers waited, he saw Tony heading his way. Henry already knew why he was coming to see him.

Moving away from the glass, Mantel took a seat behind his desk, asserting his power, and waited for the three familiar taps on the door.

'Come in.'

'Hi Henry,' Tony said, stepping inside and closing the door behind him.

'Tony,' Mantel replied, holding his cards close.

'Boss, the kid is awake.'

'Well we assumed he wasn't going to die.'

'I've been told he had two visitors earlier. From the description given, I think one of them was George Good—'

'I know,' Mantel cut in before falling into silence. Tony waited patiently.

Mantel wasn't shocked the police had been to see Connor. The kid had been assaulted and they'd want to know what happened. But, when he was informed that it was George Goodwin who'd been there, he paid more attention. Goodwin would only have gone if he knew Connor worked for him.

'He's becoming a real thorn in my side,' Mantel said, still not looking at Tony.

'Who, the kid? I can sort that.'

'No, Goodwin.' Mantel looked at Tony. 'Do we know how the police were when they left?'

'I've been informed they looked disappointed.'

'What about Reece Hunter?'

'He's at home. Everything is quiet, as it should be.'

'Then it seems everything is fine.'

'Henry, what if the kid talked?'

Mantel smiled. 'No. He's not stupid, he knows what would happen if he did. The kid understands how this all works.'

'I can sort it.'

'No, leave him.'

'So what should we do?'

'Nothing. We carry on as normal.'

'But the police, they must be pretty close if Goodwin went to see Connor today.

'Maybe they know something about the assault, but they don't know anything else.'

'Henry, if the kid snitched about what we are doing, about things we've done before—'

'Enough!' he shouted, making Tony's eyes flicker. Mantel

took a breath, smoothed his hair and when he continued, his voice was calm once more. 'We keep going. Stay on course. We have a lot coming in, a lot to distribute. And with our business associates being new clients, bringing a lot of money to the table, we cannot have delays. Connor was . . . unfortunate, but business is business and we have a deadline to hit.'

'Sure thing, boss.'

'Hunter is ready. We carry on and we don't worry about George Goodwin; he's way out of his depth. Once Hunter has distributed and we've provided the returns, cleaned legitimately as we promised, we can re-evaluate what happened with Connor so we don't have another blip like this.'

Tony nodded, absorbing his boss's instructions. 'Henry, you know George Goodwin is gonna start hanging around more now.'

'He's a fucking nuisance, and you're right, he will be snooping, but let him. As far as I'm concerned, I'm just running this business, tending to my others. We are pillars of the community, offering jobs and apprenticeships, giving to charity. The trade will happen right under his nose but he'll be so busy watching me doing all of my wonderful things through my many businesses, he'll never know.'

'You sound so sure.'

'I am. I have people everywhere, Goodwin can't do anything or go anywhere on official business without me finding out. That's why I knew he was going to see the kid. He doesn't know anything about Hunter, because if he did, I would have been told already. Hunter has been in our back pocket for a long time now, keeping his nose clean, keeping a low profile for exactly these reasons. Hunter and me, there is no link.'

'But what if . . .'

'Tony, relax. We've planned for these things. This is why we are careful. Connor was a mistake, but as I said, he knows better than to speak. He knows what we do to those who go behind our backs.'

'You're right.'

'So we keep going. Let Hunter go to work and do what he's being paid to do.'

With nothing more to say, Tony left the office, closing the door behind him. Mantel kicked his feet onto the desk. He put his hands behind his head and closed his eyes, reassuring himself that Goodwin knowing about the connection to Connor was just a small blip in an otherwise full-proof plan.

CHAPTER FIVE

George

With Tabatha asleep in the back of the car, Clara and I sat in silence as we made our way towards Manchester. Our daughter needed her rest, but more than that, I wasn't sure what either Clara or I could say that would help with the anticipation of the appointment. We both hoped for positive news, of course, but until a doctor held our eye and told us she had beaten it, the doubt still crept in. So we sat quietly with our own thoughts, sipping the teas I had made for us both. I knew I should apologize for not coming to the group as I'd promised I would this time, but I couldn't. It wasn't just because work was busy. I just couldn't face seeing sick children. I couldn't face their struggles; I wasn't tough enough. And I couldn't tell Clara this was the reason why. If she thought I cared more about being at work it was easier to explain away. It wasn't true, of course. I wished I had felt able to be at the group, just like I wished I could be at home with them both the rest of the time. But I had to stay strong, didn't I? If I went, if I allowed myself to open up, I knew I would fall apart. I had no idea how to be strong unless I was at work. But instead of explaining this to her and saying sorry for my failings as I knew I should, I turned the radio on instead and it quietly played behind our thoughts and the hum of tyres on tarmac. It cut through the silence between me and my wife, the silence that seemed to be growing as the weeks went on. And I felt a small relief for it.

We ate up mile after mile in silence, until it was almost unbearable. Then my phone pinged. As it was connected to CarPlay I tapped the screen and the message played through the speakers in Siri's automatic voice.

'Hey, it's me, we have an address, setting up surveillance and requested CCTV from the area. More soon. Send my love to Clara.'

Siri then asked if I wanted to reply, and I said no.

'Was that about the Mantel case?' Clara asked.

'Yeah.'

'How's it going?'

'We had a new name come into it this morning. A new lead. Mike is doing the legwork now.'

'I see.'

I could see that Clara was stopping herself from asking more; she didn't want me talking about any of the bad things I had going on at work in front of Tabatha, asleep or not. That was a rule we had put in place when we discovered we were having a baby. We could talk about work; it was important for her to know that Mummy and Daddy were both in the police force. But the details stayed out of her earshot. The world was a tough place, and our job was to shield her from it for as long as possible.

'It's funny,' Clara said after some time.

'What is?'

'All these people we're driving past are getting on with their lives, like today is just any other day. Do you ever think like that? Like how someone can be happy and calm on a day like today? How can everyone carry on like nothing is happening?'

'I've never really thought about it,' I lied. The truth was, I thought of little else. I hoped by denying I'd had the same thoughts, we would stop talking about how frightening this all was, but as I kept my eyes on the road ahead, I was aware she was watching me, looking at me, trying to work out all the things unsaid in a way only Clara could.

'George, talk to me, tell me what you're thinking.'

'I'm not thinking anything, I just want to be there, you know?'

'George—'

'I'm fine. Let me concentrate.'

Clara looked at me for a little longer and then returned her attention to the world outside her window.

'Sorry, I just . . .'

'No, it's okay, I understand,' she replied, and I knew she really did.

'How was the group?' I offered, hoping she would sense my apology.

'It was fine, I saw Sadie.'

'Who?'

'My friend there. Sadie, with her baby who has the same —'

'Oh yes, her. How's she doing?'

'She's so optimistic about it all. I'm glad I met her.'

I looked over at her and smiled. She smiled back, and we returned to our silence, however now it felt lighter. I reached over, took her hand in mine and gave it a squeeze. She squeezed mine back and let go again.

'Clara, once this is all over, once Tabatha is well, I think we need to get away.'

'Really?'

'Yeah, the three of us, somewhere warm, with a beach.'

Clara smiled again. 'Crystal clear waters.'

'Warm breezes.'

'Sunsets.'

'Tabatha playing in the sand. Or us walking through the tide.'

'The three of us, just enjoying the long days of doing nothing. George, it sounds perfect.'

'Let's do it then. When this is all over, let's book something.'

'I'd like that,' she said.

***

Arriving at the hospital we made our way to the oncology department, and I felt like a different person to the one who'd been here only hours earlier. Like the work version of me and the father version of me were disconnected.

Entering the consultation room, Dr Bhari – the man who first told us about Tabatha's condition– greeted us and asked us to take a seat. I tried to read him, looking for the micro expressions that give people away, that Clara had taught me when we first started dating – the ticks, flicks of the eye, touching of various parts of the face that showed the truth of what a person might be thinking – but I couldn't work him out. To me Dr Bhari seemed completely neutral, completely unreadable. I guessed that being a doctor on a cancer ward, you had to stay neutral to protect your own sanity. I didn't dare look at Clara to see if she could see anything I couldn't. I suspected she already knew what he had to say, she had a gift for these things. Dr Bhari didn't waste time, and got down to business.

'I have the results of the scans we did on Tabatha last week. As we know, we hoped that we had caught Tabatha's neuroblastoma early enough for her to make a full and swift recovery. But I'm afraid . . .' He hesitated, took a deep breath. It felt rehearsed. 'I'm afraid this isn't the case.'

'What are you saying?' I asked confused.

'The tumour hasn't shrunk as we had hoped.'

'It's the same?' Clara asked.

'No. There is no delicate way to say this, so I'll be direct, but it has grown.'

I opened my mouth to say something, but the words wouldn't come. I was aware Clara was speaking, understanding, processing, her mind sharp even at the worst of times, three steps ahead of everyone else. I could hear her voice reverberating, however, I couldn't place what she was saying. It was like she, and everything else, was underwater. Not the water you would find in a swimming pool; this was dark water, deep water. Cold water. The noise in my head was too loud, it dulled all of my other senses and the conversation around me was muffled.

'Mr Goodwin? Mr Goodwin?'

Clara squeezed my forearm, snapping me back into the room as I tried to focus. Clara looked so pained that I had to turn away from her and towards Dr Bhari who had obviously said something to me, and was now waiting for an answer.

'Mr Goodwin, the treatment approach is very much the same. We will begin a tougher course of chemotherapy. Let's get on top of this, what do you say?'

I swallowed and found my voice once more. 'Doctor, what's the prognosis?'

Dr Bhari shot a look at Clara, then turned back to me. I realized he had already told us what the prognosis was, and I hadn't heard. I looked at my wife; her eyes were brimming.

'It's impossible to say without beginning treatment, however, as I have said, although it is rare for the cancer to spread, it does happen, and it usually treatable.'

'Clara, you read somewhere that there is a ninety-five per cent survival rate for stage one and two, didn't you?'

'George . . .' she said quietly.

'So what is it now?'

'Mr Goodwin, I don't think—'

I cut him off. 'What is it? Please.'

'George,' Clara said again. She took my hand, but I moved it away.

'Dr Bhari. I need to know,' I insisted, my words tight and my voice threatening to crack.

'Forty per cent, maybe fifty per cent.'

I looked at Tabatha who was asleep and my stomach lurched, my jaw felt slack, and from deep inside me a quiet rage began to build. I needed to get out, I needed to step away, because I knew if Clara offered any kindness or the doctor tried to offer any hope, I would fall apart. I needed to be a man, someone who was stoic, someone who was strong. And I was failing.

'I need a minute.'

'George,' Clara pleaded. I looked at my wife but I couldn't

stay, as much as I wanted to, as much as I needed to. I couldn't stay.

'I just need a minute,' I said again, my eyes blurring with tears. Clara didn't look at me, her disappointment in me palpable. She had every right to feel that way; she was coping and I was letting her down once again by not being as strong as she was.

'I'm sorry, I'll be back in a minute.' I mumbled, unable to look at her.

Leaving the room, I made my way down the corridor towards the exit.

CHAPTER SIX

Clara

I watched George leave, unable to show or share what he was thinking or feeling. I wished he'd stayed, I wished he'd cried or even held my hand as he did briefly in the car. I wished he'd fought. We should have been together to face the news, a team, and he left me alone once more. He was giving up; he would never say it, but I could see it in his eyes.

'Mrs Goodwin,' Dr Bhari continued. 'I know this is a shock, there are still things we can do. We have some of the best doctors here and survival rates are improving all the time. I want to start some more aggressive chemo, but before, I want to collect some stem cells, which we will freeze and then administer after the next round of Chemo is complete.'

'Um, sorry, besides this, is there anything else we should be doing?'

'Right now, no, but Mrs Goodwin, I want you to know we have tools, and we will use them all to help Tabatha.'

I nodded, and Sadie's comment about the options overseas came to mind. 'Doctor, I have been told about this drug they have in America, specifically for this type of cancer. Flonine,

44

no, that's not it, hang on,' I said. Grabbing my bag, I began to look for my phone to see the note I made.

'Floxiline,' Dr Bhari said.

'Yes, that's it, Floxiline. My friend told me they are getting amazing results.'

'Yes, it's looking very promising.'

'Is it available here?'

'No, the drug is still at trial stage. It can take a long time to go from there to it being readily available.'

'How long? I mean, could we consider it?'

'No, I'm afraid not. We are talking years.'

'Oh,' I said feeling deflated once more. 'Couldn't we at least explore getting a place on the trial? I need to help my daughter.'

'Mrs Goodwin, I know you do, and you are, and we are doing everything we can, too. By all means research the trial programme, understand the options and risks, but right now, we need to focus on what we can do for her here. I want to keep Tabatha in hospital and start her treatment this evening.'

'Yes, of course, sorry, I just—'

'There is nothing to apologize for.'

Tabatha woke, and in the unfamiliar environment, she cried out. Wiping tears I didn't want her to see, tears I hadn't realized until then had fallen, I unclipped her from the buggy and picked her up, bobbing her gently until she soothed. George must have heard her cry as he came running back into the room.

'She just woke up confused.'

George lowered his head, his wall was up again, protecting him from breaking down. I could see he wanted to cry, yet he hadn't managed to.

45

The doctor escorted us to the room, told us to wait, as someone would be along shortly to begin the stem cell extraction, and we did as instructed. There was a lot George and I needed to wrap our head around and discuss.

Dr Bhari left, giving us time to compose ourselves before someone came in to tell us what was happening next. Despite him saying Tabatha was in good hands, I couldn't help thinking about the reality of her having a fifty-fifty chance of survival. In any other context they weren't bad odds, but not when it came to my daughter. A flip of a coin – heads you win, tails you lose. It wasn't good enough, not when – if Sadie had done her research properly – there could be a treatment, a wonder drug that could do incredible things. Dr Bhari told me I could look into it, and I was going to. If there was anything at all I could do to increase her odds to something more hopeful, I just had to give it a shot.

By the time someone came to begin the extraction, withdrawing her blood which was then processed, removing the stem cells before recycling them back into her body, a thankfully painless process for Tabatha, I had made my mind up; I wouldn't stop Tabatha getting treatment here, of course not. But I wouldn't wait either. I would research, speak to whoever I needed to speak to, and if the drug really was getting incredible results, I would find a way to get a place in the trial programme. I would raise the money needed and I would take Tabatha to America. I didn't care what it cost, or what I had to do. It might not be needed, but if the treatment here stopped working, I would be ready to take Tabatha on a plane to that programme whatever the cost. I knew I was running before I was able to walk, but this idea gave me hope. And I needed hope, we needed hope more than ever.

With Tabatha asleep in the hospital cot, George and I sat in silence. I was waiting for him to say something, to have an outburst or say it wasn't fair or declare he was afraid. He didn't. He sat white-knuckled, jaw clenching, his eyes fixed out of the hospital window.

'George,' I offered quietly, reaching out and touching his tensed forearm to try and start a conversation.

He opened his mouth as though he was about to say something, but closed it again.

'George. Can we talk about this?'

'Clara, I can't right now.'

'We need to talk about it, about what's next.'

'What do you mean, what's next? We do what the doctors tell us, and then we wait.'

'George, she has a fifty-fifty chance. Are you telling me you're happy to leave it at that?'

'Of course I'm bloody not. I wouldn't be happy if it was a ninety-nine per cent chance that she would be okay. I need it to be one hundred.'

'Don't shout at me, George.'

'Don't ask such stupid questions, then.'

I knew what he was doing, he was deflecting his pain, and I should have let it go. But I couldn't. George needed to know what I wanted us to do. Not me, us.

'George, Sadie told me something today and—'

'Please, Clara, stop for a minute. I just, I just need some time.'

'George, listen for a second, please?'

He looked at me and took a deep breath. 'Sorry.'

'Don't be, I understand, I know you don't mean it. It's terrifying to think what could happen if the treatment doesn't work again. But George, there might be a different option.'

'What do you mean?'

'This morning, Sadie told me about a trial that's happening in America for Tabatha's type of cancer. It's early stages, but it's working.'

'Really?' he said, looking up at me hopefully.

'I need to do the research, but it might be something to consider, just in case treatment doesn't work.'

'Clara, I don't want to think like that.'

'Nor do I, but we have to, don't we?'

'I guess.'

'It's called Floxiline. I'm going to look into it. Just, just don't lose hope.'

'Would we even be able to get a place?'

'I don't know.'

'And even if we did, is it expensive? It's not free in the US.'

'It's around £230,000.'

'£230,000? How Clara? How are we going to raise a fortune on one full-time salary and your maternity leave pay?'

'The radio, the papers, we could set up a "fund my cause" page. We could . . .'

'Clara, don't. You're giving me false hope and it's not a healthy way to think about this. We need to focus on what we can actually do. The doctors seem confident that more treatment could work.'

'George, I'm not saying we are going to go for it, we might not even be able to, but we need to look into other options. Just in case,' I said.

'We have help here, we need to let the doctors do their job. We need to focus on actual plans, not pipe dreams.'

'I'm not saying we don't focus on what we're doing here, of course we do, but George, Tabs has . . .' I couldn't finish my sentence.

George started to reply and then stopped himself.

I was about to plead my case once more, but I was cut off by the sound of George's work phone pinging. Before I could tell him to ignore it, he pulled it from his pocket and read the message. Afterwards he locked it and held the phone in his hands.

'You shouldn't have read that,' I whispered. I was furious at him, partly for looking at the message, partly for not listening to what I was trying to tell him.

'I can't ignore the phone when it's work.'

'You can, you're not on shift. You've been at work all the time lately, they know what's happening this afternoon.'

'Mike knows to only message if it's about the Mantel case.'

'He shouldn't have sent it then. It can wait until morning.'

'Clara, don't blame him, I asked him to.'

'Then you're both in the wrong.'

'Clara, have you forgotten what it's like being a copper? You don't switch off, you don't have days off.'

'Don't patronise me George.'

'Clara.'

'So don't raise your voice, George,' I hissed.

'You know how deep I am with this case. I don't have a choice.'

'You do, George, today you do. We've just been told our daughter is really sick. She is hours away from beginning new treatment. Today you could switch your fucking phone off!'

My outburst startled Tabatha and she began to cry. It killed our heated debate and I turned to comfort her, apologising to her for shouting.

'I'm sorry, Clara. I just, I don't know how to cope with any of this, and with work I have . . .'

'Power,'

'Yeah, I have some power over what happens.'

'I know, I do. But I need you, George, *we* need you.'

He didn't reply.

'Running from this won't help.'

'I just don't know any other way to cope right now.' His voice so fragile I was sure it would break.

'This Mantel case, it might help you feel better, George, but it doesn't help her.'

He turned to face me. 'Love, I'm not as strong as you are with this. I'm trying, I really am. I'm just . . .' He trailed off, too vulnerable to finish the sentence. I went over and wrapped him in a hug, one I so desperately needed. He didn't hug back but kept his arms limp by his side. I wanted him to hold me, to reassure me, but he didn't even have the strength for that.

'I'm scared, too,' I said.

'You cope so well.'

'I don't want to cope, believe me,' I replied, letting go of him and stepping back. 'But hiding from it, running away won't help our baby. And this thing in America, this drug, it might.'

'I understand, Clara, but can we just focus on what we can do for her right now?' he sounded broken, and I knew not to push it any more. For now.

'I'm guessing that message from Mike, it was important?'

'Yes.'

'Do you need to ring him back?'

'Don't hate me.'

'I don't,' I said, my anger towards him like a cloud that was parting. George didn't say anything else, nor did he look at me, but stepped outside the room, the phone to his ear before the door was closed. I went back to sit with Tabatha, and from the other side of the door, I heard George's muffled voice, quietly talking. I tried to listen but couldn't hear the words he said. I did, however, hear his tone back in work mode, his vulnerability, his honesty now gone. The call lasted for only a few minutes before he came back into the room.

'Clara, something has come up. I need to go.'

'Sure,' I said, trying to not sound hurt. 'It's fine.'

'It's really not, we both know that, but still.'

'Just promise me you'll think about what I've told you.'

'I promise. Clara, if I really shouldn't leave, if you need me to stay, just say.'

I thought about it for a moment as I looked at my husband. I could see he was torn. I looked back at Tabatha who was sleeping soundly again. We'd be all right without him. I needed him to stay, but I wouldn't make him, that was for him to decide.

'Promise you will keep in touch, keep me posted?' he said.

'I promise.'

George kissed Tabatha on the head then came and planted a light kiss on my cheek. It was so gentle it almost didn't exist. Like a dream that vanishes as soon as you wake. Even with that, I was painfully aware it was still the closest we had been in weeks, and I suspected guilt drove him to kiss me more than love. He told me he would be back as soon as he could, and then he left.

As the silence took hold I opened my phone and began to research the trial. I googled 'Floxiline programme, USA' and started reading the hits. It didn't take long to discover that the Children's Hospital of Philadelphia was running two trial programmes. I knew I needed to look further into what the drug actually was and how it worked, but there would be no point if it wasn't going to be an option. So my first job was to find out if it was even possible to try and get a place. Did they offer it to people from the UK? Was there space? Again, I was running at this, but I knew that if I stopped or slowed, I'd probably fall. On Google, via a search of the hospital, I found a research tab and tapped it, scrolling down to find the Floxiline programme. Through that link was a number. Standing up, I moved towards the window where I saw George, head down, walking away from the hospital in the direction of the car park. With my hands shaking, I dialled. It took a while to connect.

'Good morning, Children's Hospital of Philadelphia, Audrey speaking. How may I help you?' a woman with a cheerful American accent said.

'Um, hi, I was wondering if I could speak to someone about the Floxiline trials you have going on?'

'Of course. Putting you through now.'

The woman transferred me to someone called Clarke, and we spoke for twenty minutes. I explained who we were and what was happening to Tabatha and he was sympathetic and understanding. I told him that we were just looking at options right now, and he went into more detail about the Floxiline programme and how it worked. Then, just before the conversation ended, I asked hypothetically what the chances were of Tabatha being accepted. I wasn't ready for his answer. I assumed that if this was something we needed to do, we would have weeks, months to sort it out. But he told me that if we acted now, we could potentially get her into the programme a lot sooner than I expected.

CHAPTER SEVEN

George

'Shit!' I shouted into my steering wheel as I drove away from the hospital and my daughter. 'Shit, shit, shit.'

I swerved into the outside lane, narrowly missing the car in front of me. The driver looked at me, shaking his head at my recklessness.

'Screw you, Henry Mantel.'

A tear managed to escape and I blinked it away before I punched the steering wheel in frustration.

I should have stayed.

'And fuck you, George Goodwin.'

With my heart galloping uncontrollably and my rage unable to release itself, I felt pressure building in my head. I needed to pull over before I crashed. Swerving into a layby, the car behind blaring its horn as it shot past, I put the handbrake on and got out. Walking around to the passenger side, I leant against the door and looked out into the fields that lined the road. I forced myself to take deep, measured breaths; anger wouldn't help my daughter, it wouldn't help with work either. Anger was not my friend, as much as it wanted me. So I ignored it, taking in the view, and after a few minutes, I felt it begin to quieten down. It didn't leave, it never left, but it wasn't controlling me any more. Then clearer, calmer, I was able to think. I needed to keep going, I needed to keep trying to bring Mantel to justice. With my daughter, I was powerless to change what was happening, but with him, I could. I could make the world a slightly better place for her. I could make sure that when she was well, Mantel had been put away. I could make my world fair again. People would be helped, people would be saved, and I would be owed a debt in return. And that had to be repaid, didn't it? Good deeds ensured more good deeds, didn't they? Otherwise why would anyone want to do anything for other people? Why would there be good at all?

It wasn't the most rational idea I had ever had, but for the first time in months I was starting to see a way through this. If I stopped Mantel, there would be justice in the world and then Tabatha would have to get to better.

By the time I arrived at the office, my anger had subsided into a quiet determination to bring him down. Walking in, I saw that Mike was in the conference room with DCI Mercer and a few other officers. As I approached, Mike spotted me and stepped out.

'Everything okay at the hospital?'

'Yeah, it was fine.'

'She all right?'

'Yeah,' I repeated, forcing a smile. I didn't want his pity, I didn't want anyone's. 'She is going to be fine; everything is going to be fine,' I lied. I couldn't face telling him, or anyone, the truth. I thought if I said it out loud, that she was getting worse, I would somehow seal her fate. Besides, she would get better, I was going to make sure, in my own way. 'What developments have I missed?'

'Not much. Mercer is setting up a briefing, think she was hanging on for you.'

'Thanks mate,' I smiled, walking into the conference room, nodding to Mercer before taking a seat.

'Right, team,' Mercer commanded from the front of the room. She was wearing her trademark dark grey suit. Beside her was an interactive white board, the remote for it in her hand. 'Here's what we know. This morning, a new lead has come to light in connection with the investigation.' She looked at me and Mike. 'This is Mr Reece Hunter.' Behind her, a photo, likely taken from Facebook, came up on the screen.

Mercer continued, 'A known address was quickly found and we have CCTV footage showing Hunter in conversation with Mantel.'

Around the room officers smiled our way.

'Yes, yes, well done,' Mercer went on. 'But we have more to do.'

'Can we see the footage?' I requested.

'I had a fiver on it being you to ask,' Mercer replied, making everyone in the room chuckle.

She pressed a button on her remote and stepped away so we could all see the screen clearly. The camera pointed at a row of shops, an independent baby clothes store and a Colemans. At the edge of the frame, there was a door that looked like it led up to a flat above one of the businesses.

The footage was grainy but clear enough, and after a minute, the shape of a broad, heavy-set man, a little under six foot tall, approached, a bag in his hand. Henry Mantel. He walked into the screen from the left, the direction of the town centre. He stopped just shy of the door, leant against the window of the clothes shop, and lit a cigarette.

Another minute passed, and the door on the right of the screen opened. A smaller man, the same rat-like man Mercer had shown us, stepped into shot. I moved closer to try and read what was being said, but it was impossible, though I could see that the two men were discussing something.

'What do you think they're talking about?' I whispered to Mike.

'It won't be good things,' he replied.

The conversation lasted only a minute or so, then Hunter nodded and Mantel walked away. Leaving the bag at Hunter's feet.

Reece Hunter then picked it up and went inside, and the video stopped.

'When was this from?' I asked.

'Two days ago,' Mercer replied. 'It seems that Reece Hunter, who was unknown to us until now, is involved with Mantel. What I want to know is, what is in that bag?'

'I think we all know, Ma'am,' I said.

'Yes, but we need proof.'

'Of course.'

'Mike, George, do some digging into Hunter's past, see what it turns up.'

'Yes, Ma'am.'

'Katie, Greg, get eyes on Hunter's property. We need to make sure he is in, and if he leaves, make sure you follow. Lee, I want you to unpick Hunter's social media. Any questions?' Mercer asked, and when no one spoke, she added, 'Right, I'll apply to the courts for a warrant on Hunter's place. Just find me something to justify it.'

As we left the office, Mike and I headed for our desks.

'Mercer's doing some leg work?' Mike said.

'It's Henry Mantel.'

'Yeah, but still.'

'By the way, Mike, thanks for messaging me.'

'I almost didn't but I didn't want you finding this out when you're back on shift. I'm assuming Clara is okay with you leaving?'

'Yeah, with the results being as they were, it was fine.'

'Good, I'd not want to be on the wrong side of Clara.'

'Yeah, me neither.' I smiled.

'I'm glad Tabatha's getting better, mate,'

'Thanks.' I sat at my desk, keen to change the subject. 'What do you think he's up to, then?'

'As I said, it won't be anything good.'

'I want to get inside that flat before that bag disappears somewhere,' I said, my resolve toughening, the idea solidifying again. Stop Mantel and everything would work out. 'I want to get that bag, and arrest Henry fucking Mantel.'

CHAPTER EIGHT

Clara

After my call with the hospital in Philadelphia, I sat watching my daughter resting, the stem cell extraction ongoing, for over an hour, wondering if what I just discussed with Clarke was even possible. The conversation had gone so fast and I struggled to process the finer details. But after sitting by Tabatha's side for a while and trying to catch up with my thoughts, thinking about the 50-50 prognosis she had been given, I knew I needed to talk to someone about it all. Despite wishing that someone could be – and should be – George, I knew it wasn't going to be, so, I rang Mum and told her what the doctor had said. I needed my mum. I needed my mum more than I could remember. As I waited by my daughter's side, I fought to process everything I had been told, and what it all meant for our family. I needed someone to see the glimmer of the hope I saw when thinking about Floxiline.

Mum rushed into the room. 'Clara, darling. What's happening?' As she took me in her arms and held me I sank into her, the tears flowing and turning into long deep sobs that I couldn't stop. I cried until I felt numb. Mum kept calm, despite the tears forming in her own eyes. I forced myself to be positive about the treatment options, and she echoed this, reassuring me that they 'do such wonderful things now.' I agreed, of course, but between each breath, there was a silence that felt heavy.

50-50 odds.

Mum didn't ask where George was, and I didn't offer any explanation. Although I'd agreed he should go to work, I was still pissed off at him for leaving. It always felt like we came last these days, that I came last. I needed his support more than ever, to feel like we were a team facing this together. But instead, I felt overwhelmed and alone.

'It's not fair, Mum.'

'I know, love.'

'It's not fucking fair.' I wobbled, with fresh tears threatening to form.

'Clara, look at me. It will be okay.' She had a look of fierce determination.

'Mum, she only has a fifty per cent chance. Those odds aren't good enough.'

'I understand, and no, they're not.'

'I need to talk to you about something I've found.'

'Oh?' she said.

'My friend told me about it, and I've already spoken with them on the phone and . . .'

'Clara?'

'There's this drug called Floxiline, which is having amazing results,' I started, acknowledging I had said the same thing several times, no doubt to reassure myself. 'They are doing a trial in America. I called them after our appointment, told them about Tabatha, and . . . they can make a space in the next trial window which begins soon, if she needs it, if we can afford it. I know it's probably impossible, but I just can't go on feeling hopeless like this. I need to feel like we're doing everything we can to give her the best chance of her getting well again,' I said, directing the last statement towards my baby. 'I know it's crazy but—'

'When is the trial?' Mum asked, cutting me off.

'The next one starts in fifteen days.'

'And they confirmed you could have a place on it?'

'Yes, well maybe. They told me a space had become available. But all applications have to go to a panel, medical records need to be accessed, conversations with our doctor here would need to be had to make sure she's well enough to travel.'

'It's amazing they have space.'

'For us, yes.'

Clarke hadn't needed to tell me that space had only become available because it was too late for someone else's child.

'When is the next trial, after this one?'

'In six months' time.'

'I see,' Mum nodded thoughtfully. I waited for her to speak. I needed her guidance more than ever. But she stayed silent.

'It's such a long shot,' I said, when I couldn't bear the silence any longer.

'Why?' she asked.

'Because of how much it costs.'

'How much?'

'With the chartered flight to get her there safely, hotels and hospital fees, it's two hundred and thirty grand.'

'It's a lot.'

'It's so much, I doubt even my life insurance is for that much money.'

'Don't even joke, love.'

'Sorry. It's just it's so much and we might not even need it. God knows I hope we don't. What if . . .'

'Yeah, what if. How long do we have? To tell them?'

'That we wish to be considered? Two days.'

'And what happens if you confirm and then you don't need to do it?' Mum asked.

'If we passed panel and then pulled out, we would still be liable for ten per cent.'

'I'm guessing to apply you need to show proof that you have that deposit?'

'Yep.' I realized how stupid I was for thinking it might be doable. 'And even then, even if I somehow miraculously had that kind of money, there is still no guarantee we'd get a place. I've not even really researched it properly, I plan to now, I just needed to know if it was even an option before I got my hopes up.'

'Did you speak with Dr Bhari about it?' Mum asked.

'Yes, he said he knows of the treatment, and it's getting great results, but it won't be here in the UK for a long time.'

'So, it's something that does help children?'

'Yes, I mean, from what I have seen, what I've been told, yes, Floxiline works.'

Mum nodded, and her vision drifted as she sat there think-ing. Again, the silence was too much to bear. 'Mum? What would you do? If this was me?'

'I think you know exactly what I would do.'

'But what if we say yes and then we don't need it? We'll lose a lot of money.'

'True, true, but Clara, it's only money. You are worried about her, I am too, and George, we all want to see her well in any way we can. I think you need to explore this.'

'Where do I even start?'

'By saying you want that space, that you want to be considered, by getting the ball rolling.'

'But the money? They'll want to see we have the deposit.'

'Yes, they will,' she said. 'How much have you got in your savings?'

'Only a couple of grand at most.'

'I've got about five, so that's seven in total. How much is the deposit?

'The treatment is a hundred and ninety. The other forty we'd need would be for everything else.'

'So, nineteen would cover the deposit. I'll go to the bank.'

'What? No, Mum.'

'Love, it's okay. The bookshop is a good asset, the bank is always trying to offer loans, I'll take one out.'

'Mum, you can't do that for me.'

'It's not for you,' she said smiling gently at me, and I began to cry once more. 'So, that will be the ten per cent sorted, if they accept her onto the programme.'

'Mum, what if they don't? You've just put yourself twelve grand in debt, lost all of your savings.'

'Clara, it's fine. Honestly, I can repay it, the shop is ticking over. We'll manage. Besides, some things are much more important.'

There was no way I could deny that. Tabatha's survival was worth more than all the money in the world. 'Thank you, Mum. But how the hell are we gonna raise over two hundred grand more?'

'We'll find a way,' Mum took her phone out and began tapping on it. She was focused intently on something, and excused herself. After maybe half an hour, she was back.

'That's that sorted.'

'What, already?'

'Benefit of having a business and good credit. It's all automated these days, I just applied and was accepted though my banking app.'

'Mum, we should have talked about it more. I've not even told George.'

'It's going to take a few days for the panel to decide, right?'

'Yes.'

'So you have a few days to talk to him. And one of two things will happen. Either they will say she doesn't have a place and no harm is done, or they say she can have a place. And that gives you time to get George onside.'

I nodded, but I was struggling to keep up. I'd been so sure we would get good news today, yet now Tabatha was really poorly, Mum had put herself in debt and we were discussing sending Tabby to the US in two weeks' time.

'Love, give me that number. I'll ring them now, tell them we want to be considered. Go for a walk, get some air, I'll sort the deposit, and then you and I can get to work on what we do next with clearer heads.'

'Oh Mum,' I got up and gave her a hug. She held me tight and told me that everything was going to be okay.

Mid-embrace, I heard a gentle tap on the door. I turned, wiping my eyes as a nurse came in.

'Mrs Goodwin?'

'Yes,' I said, clearing my throat.

'Hi, I'm Sarah. I just wanted to inform you that someone will be with you in about an hour to finish the stem cell extraction. Can I get you anything?'

'No, it's fine and thank you, we are fine.'

'If you need anything just press that button,' she said, gesturing to a remote attached to the bed via a cable.

'I will, thank you.'

The nurse smiled and backed out of the room.

'Right,' Mum continued. 'Give me all those details, and get out of my hair for ten minutes. Sort yourself out. We have a lot of work to do.'

'Mum, I can't leave.'

'Tabs is fine. You need a minute. You heard the nurse, it's going to be another hour. Go to a shop, get some bits, let me make a start with Philadelphia.'

'I don't want to leave her side.'

'I understand that. But you need to get something to eat so you can be strong for Tabatha. You can't do anything for her if you end up running yourself into the ground.'

'Yes, I suppose you're right,' I sighed.

'Then go clear your head, get yourself together.'

She was right, but even knowing the fresh air was what I needed, that it was what would help me to stay objective for the road ahead, I still felt crushing guilt as I left the room. But I also felt something else, something renewed. Something akin to fresh hope.

CHAPTER NINE

George

Mercer secured the warrant quickly; there was enough in the brief statement from the kid in hospital and the CCTV footage to mean that we could search Hunter's property. She then briefed me and Mike as well as six others who would make up three teams to assist, and we set off. We didn't know if the bag was still in the flat, but we hoped the search would prove fruitful nonetheless.

Mike drove while I messaged Clara to see if the treatment had finished and if my daughter was alright. As I waited for her to reply, I tried to focus on the job at hand, though all I could think about was my girl. We parked up within sight of the door we had seen in the CCTV footage, far enough away to not draw attention, close enough to be able to have a clear view. Over our radio, we could hear the three small teams assigned by Mercer were standing by, waiting for me to green-light an entry. We waited for signs of movement, something to confirm Hunter was present at the property. Mike and I didn't speak. Entering a property was always dangerous; you didn't know what weapons the suspect might have, and given

Hunter was mixed up with Mantel, he could well be dangerous and a volatile character. The operation had come together so quickly, but if there were still drugs on the premises, we had to act fast. I needed to focus. And yet, despite the situation, I couldn't fully focus on what was happening here when my thoughts were with Tabatha and Clara at the hospital.

'George, mate, you sure you should be here?' Mike asked. He had been staring at me, I didn't know how long for.

'Yes, I'm sure.'

'Buddy, you can tal—'

'Mike, it's cool, really. Let's focus on this. We need everything to go to plan.'

'Of course, if you're sure.'

'I really appreciate it but I'm good.'

'I can see people coming,' Mike said suddenly, looking in the wing mirror to the street behind us. I looked in the rear view and watched as a small group of teens approached, then walked past our parked car to Hunter's door. One knocked four times and the door was opened just wide enough for them all to slip into the dark void behind.

'Looks like Hunter is home, then,' Mike said.

I picked up my radio and spoke. 'Stand by. When those teens come out, we go. Team three, take the teens. Team one you're with us towards the front. Two, take the rear in case Hunter makes a run for it.'

Each team radioed back confirmation the instructions had been received and understood. The young people were in the flat for a maximum of five minutes, and as soon as they left and started heading away, I told the units to go. Getting out of the car, Mike and I ran towards the front door. Team one followed quickly behind and shortly after, two relayed they were in position. From somewhere behind us, I heard team three make a grab for the kids. At the front door, team one, carrying the ram to break down the door, positioned themselves and waited for my signal. I took one final deep breath to steady my nerves then gave the all-clear. The door was hit twice and with each pound shards of wood exploded. When it was hanging off its hinges, we stormed in and up a narrow staircase into the flat to find a terrified woman standing in Hunter's living room.

'Get on the ground. Get on the ground now!' I shouted; the woman complied.

'Where is he? Where is Reece Hunter?'

'I don't know. He's not here,' she screamed. As Mike placed her in handcuffs, I searched the living room and kitchen of the two-bedroom flat. There was no sign of Hunter. I made my way towards the rooms at the rear of the property. Team one had already been in and called the all-clear. Over the radio, team three told us that the kids were in custody, with drugs in their possession. But Hunter wasn't in; the intel was wrong. He must have snuck out without being seen.

'Shit!'

Going back into the living room, I stood next to the woman who Mike had picked up off the floor and sat on the sofa.

'Where is he?'

'I swear, I don't know.'

'Don't lie to us!'

'George,' Mike said quietly, trying to calm me down.

'I'm not, I promise you,' she said.

'When was he last here?' I asked.

'An hour ago, two tops. He got a call, then he left.'

'He got a call, what do you mean he got a call? Who from?'

'I don't know.'

'How was he after the call?' Mike asked, calmer than I was able to be.

'Stressed, spooked, he told me he had to go, but he'd be back soon, and he went.'

Mike shot me a look; I could see he was thinking the same as I was. Hunter knew we were coming. The question was, how did he know?

'What's your name?' Mike asked the woman.

'Tanya.'

'Tanya, I'm going to ask you a question and I need you to answer honestly or it will be bad for you. Do you understand what I am saying?'

'Yes.'

'Tanya, is there anything in this flat that shouldn't be?'

She shook her head, but I could see she was lying.

'Tanya,' Mike continued. 'You need to help us here. If Hunter isn't here, that means if there are drugs on this premises, as we think there are, then it's you who has just supplied those teenagers who've been arrested for possession. If we find anything, it's not going to be good for you. You'll be charged with it all. Do you understand?'

'Yes,' she whispered again.

'But we know that the stuff is Hunter's, so if you co-operate fully, it will help you,' Mike told her.

Tanya looked afraid and the colour drained from her face. She didn't say anything, but gestured to the kitchen.

Leaving Mike with her to try and get her to open up, I headed in there and pulling on a pair of surgical gloves,

I began to search. I checked the cupboards, cooker, fridge, oven. Nothing. I got onto the floor and looked at the kick-boards between the cupboards and the linoleum. One panel looked slightly out of place. Crawling towards it, I could see something behind and pulling the panel off, I smiled. I didn't know for sure, but it looked like the bag we had seen on the CCTV. I pulled it out and lifted it onto the table; it was heavy. Unzipping it, I was stunned by what I saw. In the holdall were dozens of clear bags, each containing what looked like cannabis and barbiturates.

I had hoped we'd some evidence of drugs, but this, this was massive.

'DS Goodwin.' A voice called from a back bedroom. Walking back through the living room, I caught Mike's eye, giving him a nod as if to say, 'We got something' before following the sound of the voice that had called me.

'What have you found?'

'Jackpot, George. We flipped the room. At first we thought it was clean, but in the base of the wardrobe, we found a small hatch. Under it we found a bag.'

'He definitely knew we were coming,' I said quietly. 'What have you found?'

'There must be fifteen grand in cash, another ten or so in drugs.'

'Shit,'

'Yeah, shit.'

He showed me the stack of cash. I knew, even without further proof, this had Mantel written all over it.

'Good job, Jonah. Keep going, make sure we get it all.'

'You got it.'

Back in the living room, Tanya was muttering to herself incoherently.

'What's she saying?' I asked Mike.

'I asked if she knew Mantel, and she mumbled something about being a dead woman. I pressed and she started doing that. I've placed her under arrest. She knows her rights.'

I looked at Tanya rocking on the sofa, her hands still cuffed behind her back. She was clearly in shock.

'Found much?' Mike asked. Another officer from team two was now in the room, so I led him towards the kitchen, keeping one eye on Tanya, even though it was clear she wasn't going to try and run. Seeing the table and the open bag, Mike whistled.

'Holy shit.'

'Yep, there must be tens of thousands of pounds' worth in this house, more in cash on top. Jonah found a load in the bedroom, too,' I told him.

'It has to be Mantel's.'

'Oh yes. We just got to find something concrete that links this all back to him now. We need that smoking gun.'

'You know she won't talk?' Mike said, gesturing back to Tanya who was still babbling. 'People are too afraid of Mantel.'

'Let's hope we find something linking all this to him, then.'

'I'll not hold my breath.'

'Still . . .' I smiled. 'Two good things have come from this. And one question.'

'Okay, I'll bite,' Mike said.

'First good thing, all this shit is off the street.'

'And the second?'

'Mantel will know we are getting closer.'

'And the question?'

71

'Mike, don't talk to anyone about this,' I said, looking behind me to make sure no one else could hear. 'Hunter knew we were coming, he hid the drugs and money and got out before we arrived. From Mercer giving the operation the green light, to the first team arriving for surveillance, it was what? Thirty minutes tops.'

'George, what are you saying?'

'Someone tipped off Hunter, and I think it's someone from the force. I mean, how else could he know?'

'Shit.'

'Mantel has someone inside, one of us, and they are telling him everything.'

CHAPTER TEN

Henry Mantel

Hunter's phone kept ringing and ringing, eventually going to voicemail. Mantel tried ringing back, and this time it went to voicemail straight away. Hunter had clearly turned his phone off. The automated voice on the other end told him to leave a message, but he didn't.

Putting the phone down on his desk, he sat back, and breathed deeply. He'd known the police were going to the flat, his man on the inside hadn't let him down. But as Hunter wasn't picking up the phone, he didn't know the outcome of Goodwin's little visit. If Hunter had done as he was told, all would be fine; he was under strict instructions, instructions Mantel himself had delivered in person, and that he'd warned him to abide by. The product was for Hunter to distribute, to sell to his database of users –both recreational and medicinal – and the cash that came with it was to be held until all the drugs were sold, then, both the new money and old would be sent for cleaning through the nail technician shop Mantel owned. Hunter had to hide it all straightaway, and keep his head low. If something happened, he was to clean up, collect everything and leave. If he did as he was told, the police would find nothing. George Goodwin would find nothing.

A phone call would come at some point; all he could do was wait. And he didn't like to be kept waiting.

Behind him, the office door opened and Mantel's wife, Ashlee, who was fifteen years his junior, walked in smiling.

'Are we still going out for dinner?' she asked, already knowing the answer was no as it looked like her husband was still tied up in business.

'I'm sorry, my love, something's come up at work,' he replied, walking over to her and kissing her on the cheek.

'And it can't wait?'

'You know how it is.'

'Yeah.'

'I promise I'll make it up to you. But something's happened, something out of my control, and I'm just in the middle of clearing it all up.'

'Is it bad?'

'No, my love, I'll have it sorted in no time. Why don't you cancel the babysitter, order a takeaway?'

'What do you fancy?' she asked, trying to hide her disappointment.

'I'm not hungry, you and kids choose. If it's pizza, save me a slice for later?'

'Are you sure you're okay?'

Mantel smiled, kissed her again. 'I'm fine, my love.'

She smiled back, although she could tell he wasn't, she'd learned not to ask questions and to leave him when he was like this. Behind them, Mantel's phone began to vibrate on his desk.

'I gotta get that,' he said softly.

74

'Don't work too late?'

'I won't. Kiss the kids goodnight for me. Tell them I love them.'

Ashlee left the room, closing the door behind her and he walked back to his desk and picked up the phone. It was Tony.

'Talk.'

'They raided, just like our guy said they would.'

'So, what's the issue?'

'It's gone, Henry, all of it, I've watched the pigs carry it all out into the back of a van.'

Mantel didn't reply.

'You there?' Tony asked.

'Where the fuck is Hunter?' Mantel hissed. The softness that had been in his voice moments before with his wife was gone.

'We don't know. His woman was arrested, but Hunter wasn't there.'

'Did you speak with him?'

'Yes. Just as you told me. As soon as you called with what the pig had warned you of. I called him, told him he needed to do what he was instructed. I told him to meet me at the unit out of town with it all.'

'Is he there?'

'No, boss, I'm here now, he ain't. Hunter's fucked off.'

'Find him,' Mantel said. 'Find him and bring him to me.'

CHAPTER ELEVEN

Clara

As I looked at the small bakery section near the doors of the Tesco Metro by the hospital, I felt my stomach knot with hunger. Mum was right to insist I get some fresh air and something to eat so I could be there for Tabatha after the stem cell extraction had finished.

I searched for the meal deal section and grabbed a chicken wrap, drink and chocolate bar before making my way towards the tills. I was so caught up in my thoughts about my daughter's health, I didn't see something was terribly wrong at the till. The old me, the me before Tabatha got sick, would have noticed it way before I was that close.

Two men were at the till in front of me, I thought they were loading groceries and paying for their things. But there was nothing on the conveyor belt. I watched as one of them leant into the cashier, whispering something, and the fear on the poor boy's face told me they were robbing him. Stepping back down an aisle I watched, making sure I couldn't be seen. The two men moved like predators pacing before a kill, muscles twitching. I knew even before I saw the knife that they would be armed. Being a copper you instinctively know when someone is carrying a weapon, it's in the way they move, the anticipation of using it. They pulled the knife – it was a large one you would find in a kitchen – and then I heard one of them speak.

'Fucking hurry up. Get it all, put it in the fucking bag or I swear I'll gut you.'

'I will. It's just there's a time release on the money box.'

'Shut up, just get on with it.'

I knew I should have stepped in, intervened, or at the very least assessed the situation and found a solution. But I didn't, I couldn't; I was paralyzed. My once sharp mind was dulled, dulled by sickness and time away from the job, dulled by fear for my daughter and the powerlessness I felt. I wasn't a copper now. I was just a mum, scared and confused and unable to act. Both men were young, angry. I could see they were accustomed to violence, although they both looked nervous. Not in control. That was dangerous. I had come across men like this before, and I had always managed to deal with whatever came my way, but still, now I couldn't move. My mind, my police instinct had failed me.

From behind, another shopper came down the aisle, a man with headphones in, humming to himself. As he drew close, I waved to get his attention and placed my finger to my lips. Confused he pulled out one headphone.

'What?' he said, too loudly, I flashed a look towards the two men; they hadn't heard.

'Keep quiet. There's a robbery going on. Have you got a phone?'

'What? A robbery?'

77

'Yes, have you got a phone?'

'Yes, um, shit. What do we do?'

'Ring 999,' I whispered, wondering why I hadn't done so already.

The two men grew frantic, as another person had now come into the shop, seen them, and run away. They would know the police would be coming soon. The one with the knife was animated, waving it around as his accomplice told him it was taking too much time and they needed to bolt.

'No, I'm not going fucking anywhere without that money.'

I knew that unless I did something, the poor Tesco employee would likely get cut, or worse, just for messing up the plan.

And yet, still I couldn't move.

I turned to the guy behind me, who was now whispering on the phone. He nodded my way, telling me the police were on their way. And I lowered myself to the floor, made myself as small as I could. I was too afraid to do anything else.

'Fucking hurry up,' the one with the knife hissed again. 'If it ain't open in the next ten seconds, you're a dead man.' I knew someone could get killed unless I acted, but still I was frozen. I never used to feel doubt but I realized that fear about Tabatha's illness had made me a shadow of my former self. What if they turned on me, killed me? How would I help my baby then? But the harder I fought to process, understand, act, the more I felt stuck, as though quicksand was sucking me in.

Finally, the timer on the cash holder opened. The clink of the mechanical lock disengaging snapped the knife-wielding man's attention back to the cashier and he turned and pointed his knife dangerously close to his face.

'Bag it all motherfucker!' he shouted. The cashier did as

he was told, his hands shaking as he forced handfuls of £20 notes into a cloth bag. Once it was full, he handed it over. The thieves turned to leave, and as they did, I pulled myself onto my feet. My legs felt hollow. One of the guys, the angrier one, saw me. He stared, and still, I just watched.

As the pair ran off, I slumped to the floor once more, my heart racing. I did nothing, I was powerless. I failed. Again.

'Get up, Clara,' I told myself, and grabbing the shelf of crisps I was next to, I pulled myself upright and staggered out into the main aisle that led to the till. In front of me, the kid behind the till was stood motionless, in shock, and seeing him so vulnerable flicked a switch and snapped me into action. As I approached, I kept my hands up, palms out.

'Hey, it's okay, you're all right. Sit down, the police are coming.'

He stumbled backwards and sat. 'I couldn't stop them, I couldn't.'

'You did the right thing, it's only money. The police will say the same.'

'How do you know; they might say I should have stopped them?'

'They won't.'

'How do you know?'

'I am a police officer.'

'What?' he said, his expression morphing from shock to bewilderment.

'I'm a police officer, you did the right thing.'

'Why didn't you help me?' he asked. 'Why didn't you stop them?'

He waited for an answer, one that didn't come, and when

79

I mumbled a non-response, he lowered his head into his hands and began to cry.

'I'm sorry. I'm so sorry,'

Outside I heard sirens approaching, and knowing some of my old colleagues were coming, the best people I knew, put me at ease. The men wouldn't come back in, they would be long gone.

The guy who'd rung the police for me stepped out of the aisle, his hands on his head.

'Shit, shit that was insane. Is he hurt?'

'No, just shaken up. Can you hang tight? The police will want a statement.'

'Yeah, of course.'

I headed behind the till to try and comfort the cashier, who was just a boy, to make amends for my failing and as I stepped behind the counter, I saw that in his panic, he hadn't managed to bag all of the money. Behind the till, obscured from view of the shop floor, there was a scattering of notes.

The boy was still crying, still with his head buried in his hands and the other man was looking outside to see the approaching blue lights. I glanced up at the mounted camera. The angle of it wasn't on the floor, but pointing out into the shop – the camera couldn't see the money laying there, and no one was watching me. I thought of the conversation Mum and I had about trying to raise such a huge sum of money and I bent over, keeping an eye on the boy just in case, though he was too deep in shock to know what I was doing. I picked up the cash and stuffed it in my pocket just before two officers stepped into the supermarket. One of them recognized me straight away.

'DI Goodwin? What are you doing here? Is everyone all right?'

'Just the wrong place at the wrong time, and yes, no one is hurt,' I told him as I got to my feet, feigning that I'd been crouched down to comfort the cashier. Which made me feel even more terrible, as that's what I should have been doing. I knew I should have handed over the cash, and yet it stayed in my pocket, white hot. 'The poor boy who works here is in shock. And I'm not DI Goodwin, just Clara,' I said, hoping my voice didn't crack.

'Right. So did you get a look at them?'

'Not really. CCTV will have something though.'

As the boy was tended to, I gave a statement. They told me if they needed more they would call but I was free to leave.

After saying goodbye to the officers, I stepped outside into the cool air. I kept my head up and walked away. Only when I was sure no one could see, did I stop.

Leaning against a wall, I realized my hands were trembling. I struggled to catch my breath; it was like someone was sitting on my chest. I could draw air in, just not enough, and it hurt. For a moment I thought I was having a heart attack. I checked my pulse, it was racing too fast.

I understood what was happening to me. I was having a panic attack. I had seen dozens, hundreds in my career, when people had experienced shock, trauma, loss, when they were victims of crime or violence, but this was the first time I had experienced one.

Lowering myself to the floor, my back sliding down the red brick I was leaning against, I tried to convince myself it would pass, that I would be fine, just like I had done all those times before to people who were having an attack in my presence. But as much as I told myself I'd be all right, I just had to keep breathing, as much as I knew it would pass, I couldn't stop myself thinking I was going to pass out – or die.

It took about ten minutes for me to get it under control and start to feel steadier. I stood up and slowly made my way back to my little girl. My hands went to my pockets and I felt the money – money I had just stolen – and a fresh wave of panic flooded over me. Thankfully, this time I was able to control it a little more. But it didn't stop me questioning what it was I had just done. Even though I was only thinking of my daughter, I had just committed a crime.

By the time I got back to Tabatha's room, the panic had subsided. Mum was still in her chair, the glow of the phone screen making her look younger than she was. When she saw me, she smiled.

'How's she doing?'

'She's fine, she's slept throughout. A nurse popped in and said they will be done soon.'

'Good.'

'Is everything all right?' Mum asked, as I sat in the chair opposite her. 'You don't have any food?'

'Yeah, there was an incident in the supermarket. A robbery.'

'Shit, are you okay?'

'Yes,' I lied. Then, 'Mum?' I wanted to tell her about what just happened to me, what I had just done, but I stopped myself. I had broken the law. I was a police officer and I had broken the law.

'Love?'

'Nothing,' I said, suddenly exhausted. The stolen money felt like it was burning a hole in my pocket.

'Are you sure you're all right, Clara?'

'I'll be fine,' I whispered, watching my baby sleep. 'Mum, if something like this had happened to me when I was a baby, what would you have done to help?'

'The same as I would do right now for my granddaughter.'

'Which is?'

Mum lowered her phone and looked at me. 'I would move heaven and earth.'

'Even if you had to do something bad?' I asked.

'Clara, when you were little, tiny, your dad and I . . . we fell on some tough times.'

'Did you?'

'Yes, we lost everything. Our jobs, our first home, the lot.'

'You never told me.'

'I never needed to.'

'What did you do?'

'We survived. We had to because we had you. And although he never talked about it, I knew your dad did things to put food on the table.'

'What things?'

'Whatever it took.'

I nodded, and the money in my pocket didn't feel quite so hot any more.

'So,' Mum continued. 'I've spoken to the hospital, the paperwork is coming. We need to fill it in and scan it back. Then they will get in touch with doctors here and it will go to panel.'

'But Mum, what about the rest of the money?'

'We'll go to the local papers, radio stations, we'll set up a FundMyCause page and a Facebook page. We'll tell the world what's happening and what we are doing, and we go for it. It's important that you have a plan B.'

'A plan B, yeah. Do you really think we can raise that much?'

'Yes, I do.'

Reaching over, I took Tabs' tiny hand in mine and in her sleep she gripped my finger. I hoped I was strong enough to do what I needed to for my daughter, but with my inaction in the supermarket, the panic attack I'd had after, I just didn't know if I was.

21ST JULY 2023

5 days later . . .

CHAPTER TWELVE

Clara

It had been almost a week since we'd received the devastating news that the first round of treatment hadn't worked and despite the constant clawing of dread that tried to climb up my chest from some dark place within me, we were making progress with plan B. Mum and I had thrown ourselves into fundraising. We'd been busy setting up a Facebook community page that would run alongside the FundMyCause page and which we were sharing as far and as wide as we could. We had discovered that people were kind, and as a result we had already managed to raise close to £20,000 on top of our deposit of £19,000. It was still a long way away from the £230,000 we needed, but again, we were making progress. George and I had talked more about the trial being a possibility, and I showed him more detailed research into the Floxiline programme, which only strengthened my resolve to make sure, if we were successful, we could get on a plane as soon as possible. We hadn't heard back from Philadelphia yet, but even Dr Bhari had said that he would support the decision to go if we felt it best.

If we got a place.

If we raised the money in time.

I could see George still didn't like the idea of a programme that wasn't through the NHS. But he didn't say it, and conceded that if we raised the cash, and as long as Dr Bhari signed off on it, we would go – though without being told we had even passed the panel stage, it was a big if. And because of it, I was stuck somewhere between places, a liminal existence. Not where I was, but not where I wanted to be either.

I wanted George to understand and be in my corner, on my side. But the further away we got from that awful day when we first discovered our daughter was sick, the more I was coming to realise that George and I, we weren't the same people any more. The sickness had taken its toll on us, too. Our relationship felt fractured. With each day, the gulf seemed to grow between us, and despite the occasional smile, hug, Post-it note which offered a glimmer of hope, deep down I think we both knew we were likely heading in one direction. The end of us. The fear was confirmed when George came back from work at just after three in the morning. I knew he heard me crying in our bedroom, and he didn't come to comfort me. Instead, he took himself off into the spare room for the third night in a row. And earlier, as I showered, George got up to use the bathroom and I covered myself, embarrassed to be naked in front of my own husband. Not that it mattered, because George didn't look anyway.

Once he would have looked. Once I would have wanted him too.

I was heartbroken at the idea of us drifting apart, our grief too deep to save us, but it wasn't an issue we could fix right now. My focus, our focus, had to stay on keeping Tabs comfortable, and raising as much money as possible. Mum had set up a radio interview to raise the profile of our fundraising page, and I forced myself to think of that, and not my struggling marriage.

With Tabatha lying on my bed, I got ready to leave, and once I was dressed, a little make-up to cover the bags under my eyes, I picked her up and walked across the landing to the third bedroom, which George had retreated back to after using the bathroom. Knocking on the door, I heard movement on the other side before it opened.

'Hey,' George said, his eyes blurry as if he had fallen asleep again. He looked older somehow. Less like the bright and fun man I married. 'What time is it?'

'It's almost nine.'

'Is Tabs okay?'

'Yes, a little grouchy today. I've got to go out, remember? The radio thing.'

'Oh shit, yes, sorry.'

'It's fine,' I said. 'I'm guessing it's busy at work?'

'Since the raid it's been relentless.'

I handed George our daughter and saw that as soon as she was in his arms, he was a different person. Although still tired, his eyes came alive, a smile spread across his face and he looked younger for it. It made me smile too, but it also made me sad.

'See you soon.'

'See you soon,' he replied.

I wanted to say I loved him, but it didn't feel so natural any more. So I kissed Tabs on the forehead and grabbed my bag.

As I left the flat, carrying so much guilt that I was sure I would buckle, I made my way through the bookshop. Mum was behind the counter. I caught her eye and she mouthed 'good luck'.

I didn't know what I was so nervous about. The interview was a lot shorter, and a lot easier, than I imagined. I'd assumed I would be there all morning, waiting for my time on air. But shortly after arriving I was guided to a green room and then a producer brought me into the studio where I took a seat and chatted with the presenter. I think it went well; I made sure I was open about our struggles, about the help we needed. Prompted, I mentioned both the FundMyCause page and the Facebook group. Then I just had to wait and see the impact, if any, the interview had.

I was glad I did it, though. It was nerve-wracking and I wasn't sure it would do any good, but doing something made me feel like I was being useful. The small things mattered, I just had to remember that.

I got back to the bookshop just after eleven, and as I approached the door, I heard sirens drawing closer. I stopped, leaning against a wall outside and waiting to see where they were coming from. When a police car came into sight I assumed it was for me.

'Fuck.'

I was sure they had seen me on CCTV somewhere else in the supermarket, and they were coming to arrest me for stealing that few hundred pounds, for following my impulsive decision in the heat of the moment when making money was all I could think about. I was angry at myself for my recklessness. But instead of pulling to a stop, the police car didn't slow and instead sped past.

I'd got away with it, for now at least.

Composing myself, I headed inside and greeted Mum who was in the café area with Tabatha sleeping in her buggy beside her.

The shop was busy, busier than I expected, most customers here for the coffee shop, showing support after the *Buxton Tribune* printed our story. It was another small thing but one that could help. As I walked over to my daughter, I saw people looking at me, pity in their eyes, which I tried not to notice.

'You were brilliant!' Mum said when she saw me, giving me a tight and much-needed hug.

'You listened?'

'I put the radio on in the café. Everyone agreed, you handled it so well.'

'I hope it makes a difference.'

'It will, it has, so many people have come in to send their best. I reckon there's an extra £50 in the pot following it.'

'That's great.' I sighed with relief. 'Where's George? I thought he would be looking after Tabatha.'

'He had a call from work, something had come up.'

'For God's sake. I'm so sorry, Mum. George shouldn't have left you with her.'

'It's not a problem. Tabs has been asleep, and he looked stressed,' she said, coming to his defence.

'Aren't we all stressed, Mum?' I joked, but I couldn't hide my frustration at George. I felt like I put up with a lot, but for him to leave the one time I'd asked him to look after Tabatha for a few hours made me feel yet again that work always came first.

CHAPTER THIRTEEN

George

When the message came from Mike telling me I needed to get to Cavendish Golf Club as soon as I could, Clara had only been out of the flat for less than thirty minutes. I knew she was going to think I was being selfish, that I wasn't thinking of our daughter, and in some ways that was true. But given what Mike had told me, I also knew I didn't have a choice. Besides, I didn't think I was being any more selfish than she was. We were both doing what we needed to to cope. I was working, Clara was fundraising. Tabatha was safe with Clara's mum, who doted on her.

I still didn't think the fundraising was the right course of action, but I knew better than to voice my concerns. I could see Clara was passionate, determined, and maybe it was best for her to have something else to focus on. As I say, it was her way of coping, just like cracking the Mantel case was mine. I was now completely consumed with the idea that if I did, somehow Tabatha would be all right. I knew it didn't make sense, but I kept living in hope . . . If I did what I could to stop him, somehow my daughter would get better. But whereas I knew we were closing in on Henry Mantel, I didn't think Clara would ever get close to the two hundred and thirty grand she needed. I'd looked at the fundraising page earlier, and although £37,000 was a lot of money, it wasn't even a fraction of what was needed. I had worked out the maths; to hit the target she needed to raise a massive £804 per hour, every hour, right up until the deadline in ten days' time.

It was impossible.

I was sure that Clara would have worked out the numbers too. But even so, she kept her hope alive. My hope rested in the brilliant doctors and nurses we already had at our disposal, my hope rested in stopping Henry Mantel.

Arriving at the golf club, I parked my car beside a patrol vehicle and climbed out. In the distance, I could make out a forensic tent on the far side of the course. It had been erected beside a small feature lake by one of the holes. Living in a small town, a white tent being put up to cover a body was a rare occurrence.

'Hi, George,' Mike said when I was close enough that he didn't need to raise his voice. 'You look like you've not slept.'

'I haven't.'

'Everything good?'

'Fine.'

'George, mate, you've been going through a lot, I know I sound like a broken record but if you ever wanna—'

'This looks like a shitshow,' I said cutting him off. I didn't want to talk about anything right now, especially bringing Tabatha into the realm of Mantel's fucked-up games.

'It's bad, mate.'

'Anyone we know?'

'Take one guess.' From the way Mike looked at me, I knew exactly whose body I was about to see. 'Looks like Mantel found him first.'

'Right,' I said, forcing myself to stay calm. 'Shall we have a look?'

After donning white overalls and blue surgical gloves, as well as face masks, to protect the crime scene from DNA contamination, we made our way to the tent. Mike lifted the entrance flap and we both ducked inside. A forensic photographer was taking pictures for evidence. They said hello and continued working, and Mike and I waited while they finished. Once they had, they backed away, allowing me to see the victim who had been dumped in a sand bunker.

'Jesus, what a mess.'

'Yeah. I said something similar.'

The body of Reece Hunter lay face up, his eyes swollen shut, blood matting his hair. His shirt buttons were torn open exposing some of his tattooed chest. The bright sunlight streaming through the thin forensic tent illuminated every mark and tear and dent and bruise on his skin. His hands were bound behind his back. He was beaten so badly he was almost unrecognisable but for the tattoos on his chest, face and neck.

'He took one hell of a beating,' I said.

The forensic photographer informed us that they were finished and left the tent which allowed us some space to take a closer look.

'Can you see that boot mark?' I asked, noticing a footprint on Hunter's sternum.

'Yeah, there's another clear one on the side of his head, too.'

'I want to know whose boot that is.'

'George, what do you think happened here?'

'Hunter fucked up. He was sloppy.' I looked over Mike's shoulder, to make sure no one else was nearby before I continued. 'I still think he was tipped off somehow.'

'Me too.'

'So Hunter was tipped off by one of us. He panicked, ran, but did nothing to safeguard the drugs and money he was holding and distributing.'

'He probably hoped we wouldn't find it.'

'It was a costly mistake,' I said, looking down at the twisted corpse staring up at nothing. 'Mantel is pissed off, and angry people make mistakes. Let's hope he has, and we can nail this on him. I want to get his phone records over the past week. And let's tap his phone.'

'George, we don't have a warrant.'

I looked down at the lifeless corpse of Reece Hunter. His broken and battered body. His final few moments must have been excruciatingly painful.

'I think we might be able to get one now. Mantel will find out we have discovered Hunter's body. He is going to be tense, maybe even panic. I want to hear who he speaks to over the next twenty-four hours.'

I stepped out of the tent and looked out across the golf course.

'What next?' Mike asked, joining me.

'He must be talking to someone. We need to ask DCI Mercer to get that warrant. We need to get some ears on him. I want to know who he is talking to, and what they are saying.'

'Think we might find out who tipped him off about the Hunter raid?'

'I hope so. Because if we don't, Mantel will always be one step ahead of us, and we will never catch up. And more people are gonna get hurt.'

CHAPTER FOURTEEN

Henry Mantel

Hanging up, Mantel walked over from his desk and looked down at the staff on the workshop floor. The call from Tony was troubling. It was brief, and only two things were discussed. The first he knew was coming; the police had found Hunter's body. And although he knew Goodwin would automatically realise it had something to do with him, Mantel also knew he would not be able to prove it.

The second thing was the kid, Connor. He had been discharged from hospital and hadn't returned home. The little shit was gone, which told Mantel he must have spoken to George Goodwin after all. That was why Hunter's place had been raided. That was why Mantel now had the extra pressure of owing further up the chain. As much as he wanted to control his rage, the insult, the betrayal coursed through his veins. He grabbed his mobile and threw it against the wall, making a hole in the plasterboard and smashing the phone's screen in the process.

Mantel paced. He wanted to scream, to trash his entire office, but people would be watching, customers in the workshop, staff, subordinates, and if he lost control of himself, he would lose them too. He was under no illusion people would learn of Connor's brazen actions, but Reece Hunter acted as a counter-balance. The kid had crossed the line that was clearly drawn in the sand by speaking to the police and now he was on borrowed time. Hunter's death was a message, you didn't fuck with Henry Mantel. But Connor was the least of his immediate concerns; he had bigger things to worry about. Namely a large sum of money and drugs that he had to account for.

Taking some deep, measured breaths, Mantel sat back behind his desk and ran his fingers through his greying hair. He opened his laptop, unlocked it and logging into a portal, he punched in his password which opened an encrypted folder. Opening a spreadsheet, he looked at the numbers. Mantel had discovered early on in his career that making money wasn't an issue; it was something that came naturally to him. He had several streams of legitimate income – his garage, café, night-club, as well as several nail technician shops and stalls dotted around. He also had illegitimate streams, mostly through the drug trade. His turnover was constant. The legitimate businesses were easy to account for; all the money earned was clean, genuine, untouchable. He paid his taxes, invested in pension schemes and property. Gave to charitable causes. However, processing money earned the other way without causing suspicion was much more difficult. Every pound earned that wasn't on the books through one of his businesses needed to be cleaned and processed, though owning cash-heavy businesses ensured that could happen. Money earned through the sale and distribution of drugs would be funnelled into his nail technician stall in Bolton, or his hairdressers in Buxton, or the nightclub in Stockport, marked as cash income through the sale of the services, and then accounted for. Turning dirty money into clean money. Mantel paid his taxes, kept it all above board. As far as the Inland Revenue was concerned, Henry Mantel was as good as they come, and that was exactly how things needed to stay, with him as a symbol of propriety and caring for the community. He had worked hard to build this image and to protect it. It meant the cleaning and processing of dirty money took time. Mantel knew that if he dumped a large amount of cash into any business at this point, it would raise another eyebrow of suspicion. It was how Goodwin first became aware of him. So all the money made had to be stashed somewhere secure and trickled in, pound by pound. The seizing of a substantial amount of cash and drugs that would have generated a sizable profit posed a problem. Mantel owed his cut. He looked at what money he had in his business right now and money waiting to be cleaned and totalled it up. It was enough to pay for Hunter's mistake, more than enough, but with Goodwin watching, getting to that money to move it, clean it and deposit it where he needed to would pose a challenge. Mantel needed time.

From the floor, where his phone had landed after his outburst, the smashed screen lit up. He couldn't properly see who it was on the caller ID. Regardless, he picked it up and answered.

'Yes?'

'It seems we have a problem,' came a voice on the other end.

'Nothing I can't fix,' Mantel said, hoping he sounded calmer than he felt.

'We expect it to come to us in the same manner as agreed.'

'Don't worry, it will.'

'When?'

'Give me twenty-four hours to finalise the plan to resolve this blip, and then call me back. I'll give you an answer then.'

'You've got twenty-four hours, and then we want to know exactly how you intend to pay us what you owe. Twenty-four hours, not a second more,' the voice replied, and the line went dead.

22ND JULY 2023

9 days until the deadline . . .

Help for Tabatha
We are raising money to send our daughter, Tabatha, to the US for treatment to help her overcome neuroblastoma.

20%

£46,819
raised of £230,000 target

Donate Now

9 days remaining to reach required target

In April 2023 Tabatha was taken to A&E at the Royal Manchester Children's Hospital after presenting as being lethargic and with no appetite. At first we thought it was a viral infection, something all babies have, however, a scan during this process showed evidence of a mass above her adrenal gland. Tabatha was diagnosed with neuroblastoma, and our beautiful baby has a 50 per cent chance of survival.

Tabatha has now begun aggressive treatment here in the UK, but we have discovered a potentially lifesaving treatment in the United States. It is a revolutionary drug called Floxiline, but it is very expensive, and to get her there and treated is likely to be £230,000. The deadline for this is in just nine days; the next programme isn't for six months, which might be too late.

We aren't people who ever ask for help, but we are desperate, and with your generosity, we can get Tabatha onto this programme and save her life.

Please know, if the treatment works here, then any donations will be returned, but we need to ensure that if Tabatha needs this, we can do it.

We want to thank everyone who has donated so far. It is making a difference and giving us hope.

Clara, George and Tabatha x

Supporters

J Marr
£100

Peter Jackson
£10

John & Jo Highton
£30

R. Kort
£30

Mrs Jones
£15

S. Hussain
£50

Katie. S
£20

Mum
£50

CHAPTER FIFTEEN

Clara

A new day, one closer to Philadelphia if we got our place confirmed and could raise the money. They had originally stated our application would go to panel in two days, but six days had now passed and there was still no news. I tried not to worry about what that could mean.

I lifted Tabs from her cot, hoping George was still at home. But as I wandered around the flat, I could tell he was long gone. He'd told me that following an incident at work, he was going to take a double shift. We used to work on these types of things together. Even when I went on maternity leave, he would still share stuff over dinner. Now, they were just 'work incidents' and nothing more. What would be left of us after this?

One day I would have time to reflect on us, but now was not that time. Tabs had woken in a grizzly mood due to another awful night's sleep. Soothing her and making her comfortable took priority. I spent the morning doing whatever I could to try make her happier, but it was an uphill battle. Some days were just like that. The boost that was keeping me going was that after the radio interview we'd had a spike and received a further £10,000 in donations. Ten thousand pounds, thanks to the kindness of strangers. It was so much, a huge amount of money, a big and hopeful step in the right direction.

I wanted nothing more than to stay in my pjs and spend the day in front of the TV, watching *Mr Tumble* and *In the Night Garden*, which were two of Tabatha's favourites and try to make her smile. However, sticking to our routine was important to give us a sense of normality, so I started to get ready for the group meeting that was happening later this morning. The group usually met on a Sunday, however, it had been re-scheduled. I didn't mind, I was grateful that it gave me something to do, and I knew the fresh air on the walk over there would do Tabatha the world of good and seeing Gary and Sadie, with their unwavering understanding and positivity, would lift my mood too. Tabs was clingy and irritable, so I gave up on the idea of a hot shower and tied my hair up as best I could and threw on a clean black top and jeans. Outside on the high street, Tabs comfortable in her buggy, I was glad that I'd made myself leave the flat.

As we walked up the path towards the entrance to the church hall, and opened the door to go inside, Gary saw me struggling up with the buggy and came to our aid.

'Thank you, Gary. I'm sorry we're a few minutes late.'

'No, don't be, you're absolutely fine. Come in.'

As I followed Gary into the hall some parents looked up, most didn't. I scanned the room for Sadie, but to my disappointment, she wasn't there. Getting Tabatha out of the buggy, we sat in the circle. Without Sadie there, the energy of the room felt different. Sadie was a ray of sunshine with her optimism and today the group had clouded over. The circle was the same, the room was the same, everyone seemed resigned to the way things were in the same way. Gary spoke of the same things, and yet everyone was deep in their own thoughts as they listened. Gary tried, really tried, to have the same upbeat positivity as he usually did, but he was running flat. And although he was still in charge, today he had the energy of a grieving parent, just like the rest of us.

Tabatha was tired and becoming fidgety so I put her back in her buggy to sleep. Part of me wanted to leave. I had only come to see Sadie; it was our regular meet-up and one neither of us had missed before. I couldn't help but worry about her so took out my phone to send her a message.

Hey, it's me, is everything ok?

I hit send and kept my phone in my hand. Despite a feeling of dread I couldn't shake, I tried to reason that I was overthinking and there was probably a simple explanation for Sadie's absence. Perhaps Sophie had a bad night or Sadie had family visiting and had forgotten to mention she couldn't make today. Sophie was doing well, responding brilliantly – that's what Sadie told me last week. So there had to be another reason for her absence. Maybe there had been some good news. Maybe Sophie had rung that bell. Sadie would message soon, and I held on to the idea that she would text back to tell me her baby had won. Then Tabatha would be next, following in Sophie's footsteps.

Gary went to make coffee and I followed him to the kitchen.

'Hi, um, Gary. I was wondering, have you heard anything from Sadie? I was supposed to meet her today,' I said softly.

'Sadie, yes,' Gary said, putting his cup down and looking me dead in the eye. 'Sophie, she took a turn . . .'

'Took a turn?'

'They've been transferred to Great Ormond Street.'

'Oh, God.'

'I spoke with Sadie briefly last night; Sophie is really ill.'

'How ill?'

'She didn't say any more than that,' he replied. 'We have to hope. That's all we can do.'

'But she was getting better . . .' I managed to say shakily.

'She's in the best hands,' was all Gary said back.

I felt my hands begin to tremble as I looked over at Tabatha. Sophie and Tabatha had the same type of cancer. Sophie had been doing better than Tabs but had still taken a turn for the worse. As the thoughts whirred through my head, my breathing became more rapid and shallow, as if I was gasping for air. It felt just like after I left the Tesco the night of the robbery, and worrying that I was about to have another panic attack, I wanted to leave straight away.

'Sorry, Gary, I've got to go,' I managed to splutter. I didn't care if I looked rude. I took my daughter, and I left. As I walked home, still struggling to catch my breath, I looked at my phone. Sadie hadn't opened my message and I didn't know what that meant. My hands began to tingle, I wasn't getting enough oxygen in my body. Stepping off the main path into the entrance to park, I sat on a bench, and even though I knew it wouldn't help and someone might see me, I covered my face with my hands and cried. Sophie was beating it, Sophie was winning, and still the cancer wanted to take her. I felt so sorry for her, she was too young. Sadie had been a tower of strength for both of us and I wondered how she was coping now.

I didn't want to be alone. I went to call George, but my fingers hovered over the call button. He wouldn't pick up and was probably out following up the latest lead in this case that had taken over his life. I needed my mum, so I got up and headed home as quickly as I could, forcing myself to try and keep it together. Poor Sadie, I couldn't imagine what she was going through.

Walking into the bookshop, grateful that it was quiet, I caught Mum's eye and she came straight over to me.

'Clara?'

I tried to speak, but the words snagged in my throat.

'Clara, is Tabatha okay?'

'Mum,' I said quietly.

'Is she okay?'

'Yes, she's fine. Mum, will you come and stay with me tonight? I don't want to be alone.'

'Of course, love. Of course.'

'Has there been anything from Philadelphia yet?'

'Nothing so far'

'It's been six days, what does that mean?'

'Try not to overthink it,' was all Mum could say by way of comfort.

'Mum, I need Tabatha in that trial.'

'I know.'

'No, I don't want this as a plan B. I need her on that plane, I need her to be in Philadelphia. Even if she starts to respond to treatment here, I need her on that Floxiline programme.'

'Clara, are you all right? What's happened?'

'It's Sadie. From the support group. Her daughter has the same cancer as Tabs. She was doing so well, Sadie was so sure she was beating it. She looked like she was doing better, too. But they had to transfer her to Great Ormond Street.'

'Oh love.' Mum said, taking my hand. 'They have some of the best doctors in the world there, I'm sure they are doing everything they can.'

'I know,' I said, wiping away a tear. 'But I'm not letting that happen to my girl. We both know the drug seems to be working, I need my daughter to have it. Whatever the cost.'

'And I'm with you, every step,' Mum said, giving my hand another reassuring squeeze. 'Do you want me to make you a coffee?'

'No thanks. I'm going to go up to the flat. I don't really want to talk to anyone at the moment.'

'I understand. I'll come up as soon as I lock up.'

'Thanks, Mum.'

After what had happened to Sadie and Sophie, I was realising that this fight was not just against the disease that was taking over Tabatha's body, but against time. Poor Sophie had proved that now. The fundraising target on our FundMyCause page was creeping up and we were at just under fifty grand now. It was a lot, but still less than a quarter of what we needed. Still so short. We only had nine days until we missed our window and the next trial wasn't for another six months. Time was the enemy, and it was now a race against the enemy to raise the rest of the money and get Tabatha on the trial that could potentially save her life.

CHAPTER SIXTEEN

George

Sat at my desk, I reviewed the reports and looked at the photos taken at the crime scene. I could almost see the attack play out in my mind. A story told by the marks, cuts, bruises and breaks on the dead man's body. Reece Hunter was a bad man, sure, but he didn't deserve to die, especially in such a violent attack. It fuelled my anger at what Mantel had been allowed to get away with it but strengthened my resolve to bring him to justice at last. Even though I knew Mercer wouldn't be happy with it, I decided I would go and pay Mantel a visit. I wanted him to know I was watching. I wanted him to crack. I'd show up not as a police officer, but as a customer wanting to book my car into his garage. Mantel would be aware that I knew the truth about Reece Hunter and that we were onto him. I wouldn't need to say it, of course, but I wanted him to understand I was going to stay close and would be ready when the time came. Just as I was about to leave, Mercer popped her head out of her office.

'Mike, George. Warrant approved. We can listen to Mantel's calls. A team is going into place right now,' she said.

'Great, thanks Ma'am.'

'George?'

'Yes Ma'am?'

'You are going home, I hope?'

'Ma'am?'

'You look exhausted. Go home, be with your family.'

'I'm all right.'

'George, you're pulling some serious shifts, and I understand why, I do. But please, go home, be with your family, even if it's for a few hours. Freshen up. You won't be docked any overtime. We'll call if there are any significant developments.'

'Thank you, Ma'am, I'll head home for an hour or so,' I said, leaving out the fact that I was going via Mantel's garage. It was my excuse to leave the office and I was grateful for the good fortune. Feeling like we had taken another step closer to finally being able to arrest Mantel, I headed into town.

Parking the car on the road outside the garage I locked it and approached Mantel's place of business. As I opened the door to the reception of the garage, I saw a kid I knew called Ethan and smiled. Ethan didn't smile back.

I looked into the workshop, my eye scanning the staff before turning my attention to the upstairs office. I could make out someone up there, it had to be him.

'DS Goodwin?'

'Hello, Ethan.'

'I ain't done nothing.'

'Well, that's not at all guilty, is it?'

'I'm telling you, whatever it is, I'm not involved.'

'Ethan, calm down. I'm not on duty, I just want to book my car in.'

'Oh.'

'I swear.'

'You had me worried.' He laughed nervously. 'I promise I ain't done nothing since I got caught.'

'Ethan, that was two years ago now. It's okay to leave it behind.'

'Yeah, well, my mum hasn't; she's still on at me now.'

'You shouldn't have shoplifted.'

'Yeah, I know.' He shrugged, resigned to his mistake.

'I'm glad you're doing well now, Ethan,' I said, meaning it. Not many kids turned things around for themselves. Ethan had, and despite him working here, I knew he wasn't involved in any of Mantel's dodgy dealings. Mantel was a dangerous man, but Ethan's mother was something else. I watched as Ethan looked at the computer screen in front of him.

'What are you booking your car in for?' he asked.

'I need new tyres, and think I'll need my brakes checking, too.'

'We can slot you in on Friday. Can you drop it off around nine, leave it with us for the day?'

'Sounds great. Hey, listen, it's cheeky, I know, but do you guys offer discount for the services. Like blue light discount, or key worker discount or something?'

'No, I don't think we do.'

'Could you check?'

'I really don't think—'

'Could you ask the boss? You never know.'

Ethan made no attempt to hide his annoyance that I was sending him on a fool's errand as he got up and marched through the workshop toward the stairs. I waited until he was out of range, before opening the adjoining door from the reception to the workshop floor, to watch what happened. Ethan got to the top of the stairs and knocked. I saw Mantel stand up, coming into view though the glass. Why was he sitting on the floor? He waved Ethan in. I watched as the kid went inside gingerly. I couldn't hear what he asked, of course, but I could hear Mantel's reply, everyone could.

'I'm trying to run a fucking business. No, no one gets a discount. I don't give a shit who he is.'

Ethan scurried out of the office and back down the stairs, and as he walked back to the reception, I stepped away from the door. I watched through the glass as the other mechanics gave the kid a knowing smile and could almost hear them say, 'We've all been there. Don't take it to heart.' When he came back into the reception area, his cheeks were flushed.

'Unfortunately, the owner said we don't offer any discounts.'

'No worries, thank you for asking. And if I see your mum, I promise not to mention we've spoken.'

'Thanks, she'd only assume the worst.'

'Keep your head down, yeah?'

I smiled at him and left. As I opened the car door, I glanced upward towards the office again. It didn't take long for Mantel to show his face. He stepped out onto the metal platform outside his office, and our eyes met. Mantel didn't move. He stood there staring, then pulled his phone out of his pocket, answered it, and went back inside. He closed the door, but not before giving me one final menacing glare through the glass before disappearing back to his desk.

'Yes, motherfucker, I'm watching,' I muttered under my breath. 'And pretty soon, I'll be listening, too.'

CHAPTER SEVENTEEN

Clara

Even though I was exhausted, both physically and emotionally, I couldn't sit still, so as Tabs napped, I tidied the flat, put on a load of washing, dusted the furniture and mopped the floor in a vain attempt to stop myself thinking. Always thinking. If exhaustion didn't floor me, thinking would. And despite trying to stop myself, I couldn't shift the image of what Sadie must be going through. For Sophie to be transferred to Great Ormond Street, it was impossible not to fear the worst. I sent her another message, letting her know I was thinking of her and that I was here if she needed to talk. Again, the message remained unread.

Just as I felt myself begin to close my eyes and drift off, I heard the front door open.

'Mum?' I called out confused; she'd mentioned she wouldn't be finished at the shop until later.

'No, it's me.'

Hearing George's voice, I got up, and met in him the hallway.

'I wasn't expecting you home?'

'Mercer told me to, said I look tired.'

'You do look tired,' I said. 'What about the overtime though?

'She isn't going to dock me.'

'That's good.'

'How are you?' he asked, and I shook my head.

'You know Sadie, my friend from the support group?'

'Yeah?'

'Her baby is sick, really sick.'

'Oh,' he said, offering no more.

'Her daughter, she has the same cancer as Tabs and I . . .'
I trailed off as I started to cry.

'Oh, Clara, love,' George said, stepping towards me and wrapping me in his arms. 'I'm sorry. I can't imagine how horrible this feels. But don't think that because it's the same cancer, it will have the same outcome. This is why I have been worried about you going to the group so often. You have so much on your plate without worrying for other families.'

'George!' I said, pulling away from him.

'We know how the world works, we've seen it in our jobs. Life is sometimes cruel. But that doesn't mean because one family is having a tough time, we will too. It's not the same. I'm really sorry for what is happening to your friend, but your friend isn't us, her baby isn't Tabatha.'

'It's just hard not to think the worst.'

'It's so hard. But you can't.'

'I know.'

'Do you want a cuppa?' he asked, his voice soft and caring.

'Please.'

'Go sit down, and as impossible as it is, try not to think about it too much.'

'I'll try.'

I went into the living room and wiped my tears, listening to my husband in the kitchen taking cups from the cupboard and filling up the kettle; for the first time in a long time, I felt something akin to closeness with him. This felt almost normal, and I wanted to hold onto it, so instead of sitting, I checked on Tabs before heading to the kitchen to be with George. As I opened the door, I saw him leaning against the side, his back to me. He looked tired and defeated. I wanted to return the hug he had just gifted, hopefully lift him as he had just lifted me, but his phone pinged and he pulled it from his pocket.

I expected him to read a message, but instead Mike's voice came through on a voice note.

'Hey, buddy. So, we got a hit. You've got a copy of it in your inbox. See what you make of it, because if I'm honest, I don't have a clue.'

George logged into his emails, still unaware of my presence in the doorway, and played a conversation between two people. The sound quality wasn't great, but I could hear well enough.

'It's been 24 hours.'

'No, it hasn't.'

'It's been long enough. And we don't like to be kept waiting. So what are you going to do about it?'

'As I said to you, nothing will be traceable to you.'

'How long until you repay your debt?'

'One week and it will all be back with you, untraceable as promised.'

'You wouldn't be lying to us now, would you?'

'*I have a reserve, it will come, it just needs to be processed, nothing more.*'

'*You have a week. Or we will find our own way to reclaim what is ours.*'

George played the recording a second time, but sensing my presence there, hastily paused it.

'Shit, you made me jump,' he said.

'Sorry. What was that?'

'It doesn't matter. Just work stuff.'

'Play it again.'

'No, I shouldn't be bringing it home with—'

I cut him off. 'Please, I want to hear it.'

'Why?'

'I don't know, for something normal,' I answered, unsure how else to explain that I needed something to remind me of a time when life wasn't so hard. When this would have been the biggest thing we had to deal with. A time when I was in control of my life. Thankfully, I didn't need to try and explain any more as George looked at me for a moment, weighing up whether it was a good idea, then he pressed play.

I stepped closer to him, our shoulders touching as I looked at the phone and focused on what was being said.

'So that's Mantel's phone?' I asked once it had finished.

'Yep.'

'And the other person?'

'No idea.'

'He's struggling right now,' I said.

'Mantel?'

'Uh-huh.'

'Struggling, what do you mean?' George asked.

'The need to clarify he had more time, the reiterating it won't be traceable, the fact he didn't hang up first. Whoever that person is, Mantel is not their boss, and I think he's afraid.'

'You think so?'

'Yeah, I do. At that raid, how much did you seize?'

'Tens of thousands. Drugs too.'

'That's a lot to owe.'

'Henry Mantel has a lot of money.'

'He does, but he said he needs time to process it, and none of it will be able to be traced back. The money he has needs to go back clean. That takes time, even more because you have him under surveillance. Mantel can't just hand over a ton of cash. It has to be accounted for; it has to be legitimate or it incriminates him and whoever that other person is.'

'Clara, why are you doing this?'

'What?'

'Profiling him. You get so upset when I think about work.'

'I just want to feel like me, I guess. You might not get it—'

'No, I do, it makes total sense,' George reassured me. 'So, you think Mantel has cash?'

'He said so himself. My take on Mantel is he is a man who is used to things going his way. Now you've interrupted that the pressure will get to him, he'll make a mistake.'

'You seem certain about this.'

'I can't be, of course, but that's what my gut tells me.'

'So, I should stay close?'

'But not too close. Just close enough for him to feel the pressure. In the call, they told him that he had a week. It will be interesting to see what happens after that.'

'They might kill him?'

'I think he'll make a mistake before the week is up.'

'Thanks, love. I needed this,' George said.

'I kinda needed it too.'

'Feels like old times, doesn't it?'

'Yeah, it does,' I replied, feeling that there might be hope for me and George after all. Work used to bring us together so maybe, if I helped a little, it would keep us together. And it would be good for me to have something to think about other than hospital appointments and drug trials.

'Clara, I'm going to go back soon, unless I should stay?'

'No, its fine, I wasn't expecting you back at all. I'm glad you did come though, I'm glad I saw you.'

'Me too,' he said.

George made my tea, as promised, and walked past me towards our bedroom where Tabatha lay asleep. I hung back and watched as he gave Tabatha a gentle kiss on her forehead.

'I love you, my baby. Daddy will be home later.'

He stood and watched her for a full minute before wiping his eyes and turning to look at me.

'I don't like leaving you alone.'

'No?'

'Never have. I just—'

'It's fine, Mum is coming up to join me after work. She's going to stay the night. Hopefully I'll be able to get a little sleep.'

'Great.'

George walked towards me and hugged me again.

'I do love you, Clara,' he said, and before I could reply,

he stepped outside, closing the door behind him, and was gone.

I smiled because of what he just said, but then I wondered, had he told me he loved me because it felt right, or because he felt he had to? And was it the love we once had, or had it evolved into something else? I couldn't tell.

23RD JULY 2023

8 days until the deadline . . .

FundMyCause™   Menu   Log In   Sign Up   Search 🔍

Help for Tabatha

We are raising money to send our daughter, Tabatha, to the US for treatment to help her overcome neuroblastoma.

29%

£67,219
raised of £230,000 target

Donate Now

---

8 days remaining to reach required target

In April 2023 Tabatha was taken to A&E at the Royal Manchester Children's Hospital after presenting as being lethargic and with no appetite. At first we thought it was a viral infection, something all babies have, however, a scan during this process showed evidence of a mass above her adrenal gland. Tabatha was diagnosed with neuroblastoma, and our beautiful baby has a 50 per cent chance of survival.

Tabatha has now begun aggressive treatment here in the UK, but we have discovered a potentially lifesaving treatment in the United States. It is a revolutionary drug called Floxiline, but it is very expensive, and to get her there and treated is likely to be £230,000. The deadline for this is in just nine days; the next programme isn't for six months, which might be too late.

We aren't people who ever ask for help, but we are desperate, and with your generosity, we can get Tabatha onto this programme and save her life.

Please know, if the treatment works here, then any donations will be returned, but we need to ensure that if Tabatha needs this, we can do it.

We want to thank everyone who has donated so far. It is making a difference and giving us hope.

Clara, George and Tabatha x

Supporters

Peter Mullis
£100

J. Reymund
£25

Katie Frances
£30

Sue B
£30

Mrs Jones
£15

J. Kelly
£50

Jenny Bonass
£20

Mum
£150

CHAPTER EIGHTEEN

Henry Mantel

When Mantel received the call about his café being robbed, it was a little after six in the morning. The call was short and straight to the point. Even with his mind slow with sleep, he understood exactly what had happened, and why. He arrived at the café an hour later, a solitary police car was parked outside, and talking to a police officer just inside was Janice, the café manager. He surveyed the place as he walked in. Everything seemed to be where it should be and there was nothing that looked out of the ordinary. He smiled, trying to appear cool.

'Hi Janice. Is anything missing?' Mantel asked, not caring if he was interrupting.

'Hi Henry, I was just explaining to DS, sorry I can't remember your name?'

'Mike Cole'

'I was just explaining to DS Cole that they got into the till.'

'How much was in there?'

'Just the fifty pound float, as always.'

'A fifty pound float?' Mike asked.

'Yes, at the end of each day I put the daily takings in the

safe, except a fifty pound float in coins and some notes, for the following day,' Janice said.

'I see.'

'Show me where they broke in.' Mantel interrupted.

'Yes, of course.'

Janice lead Mantel to the rear and the smashed glass pane. He looked at the gap, tried to visualise someone crawling into his café. Janice was saying something about how awful it was and the copper was asking questions, but he didn't listen. This break-in looked like it was just a botched robbery attempt, and he knew that besides a crime reference number, the police would do very little. He knew, or at least suspected, what had really happened and who was responsible. As he walked away towards his stockroom, he heard the copper ask a pertinent question.

'Mrs Murray, do you happen to have CCTV?'

'Yes.'

'Could I take a look?'

'It saves directly to Mr Mantel's hard drive. I didn't see him with his laptop just now, but I can ask him to send it over.'

'That'll be great.'

Making sure he could be seen by Mike, who he knew was Goodwin's partner, Mantel opened the safe and looked inside. The café's takings were still there, bagged up and ready to be deposited. He expected as much.

'Is everything okay, Mr Mantel?' Mike asked, looking through to him.

'Fine.'

He watched the copper nod and return to talking to Janice. But despite everyone assuming now that the break-in was small, causing minimal damage and with only £50 taken, Mantel needed to be sure. Which meant he had to wait for the police to fuck off. Each minute that passed, Mantel felt increasingly agitated until half an hour later, Mike left, with Janice once again saying she would send over the CCTV footage. Once Mike was gone, Mantel turned to her as she looked around, still in shock and seemingly lost as to what to do.

'Janice, you should go home, you've had quite the shock,' he said gently.

'What? No, Mr Mantel, I can stay.'

'Until the back door can be fixed, we can't reopen.'

'I want to help.'

'Why don't you go online, post on our Facebook page to say what's happened and that we will be open for business again as soon as we can.'

'Are you sure?'

'Yes. This is awful, but it isn't your fault, and I can only imagine how upset you're feeling.'

'The police want to see the CCTV. I could—'

'I'll sort it,' he snapped, startling her. 'I'm sorry, it's been a tough morning. Thank you, Janice. You've done enough,' he said, smiling.

Mantel helped Janice collect her things and saw her on her way, leaving him alone in the café. Ensuring no one was looking in, he moved behind the counter. The till was on the floor, smashed open, but he wasn't there to see the damage. He wanted to see behind the till where a small nook was cut into the back of the counter. It was just big enough to squeeze his hand into. He reached inside and should have felt a bag, the rectangular shape of a small bundle of bank notes waiting to be cleaned through the café over the next few bank runs. But instead he found nothing. He dug further, his entire forearm inside the tunnel now, but still came out empty-handed.

'Fuck!' he screamed, grabbing the nearest thing to him, a coffee mug, and hurling it against the wall. The cup exploded on impact, and yet it didn't dim his rage. Mantel grabbed another cup and threw it across the café where it shattered on the floor. Then bounding from behind the counter he flipped over a chair in his way, cursing as he did.

Seething, he pulled out his phone and logged into his remote CCTV cloud. He scrolled back to look at the night's footage. Mantel had three cameras at the café; one outside the rear, covering the garden and back door, one in the stockroom and one inside the café, looking down at the till.

He tapped the icon for the camera that sat outside. The time stamp said it was 2.56 a.m.

For a while, nothing happened then Mantel saw a man dressed in dark clothes, his face covered with a mask, climb over the café's rear wall. He kept close to the wall, knowing it would make him difficult to see. He became a smudge on a grainy image, his features hidden in shadow, but not completely, but still Mantel watched as he moved his way towards the back door, temporarily startled when the security light lit up.

'Who the fuck are you?' Mantel muttered, desperate to see more of the man's features.

He watched as the man slid his right arm out of a rucksack he was carrying and swung it in front of him to pull out a hammer and a towel. Covering the bottom corner of the glass in the rear door with the towel, he paused. He swung the hammer, hitting the towel in the middle, breaking the glass behind it. It didn't completely dull the sound, as Mantel could hear it on the footage, but it helped. Moving quickly, he cleared some of the glass, collecting it before it fell out of the frame and made more noise, and then with the gap big enough, he slipped inside.

'You know exactly what you are doing, don't you?' Mantel whispered, as his phone rang, interrupting the footage. Tony's caller ID flashed on the screen.

'Tony.'

'Boss, is it what you think?'

'Maybe, I'm watching the CCTV now, call me back in five.'

Hanging up, he continued watching as the man moved quickly through the café quickly finding the hiding hole behind the till. As he watched, Mantel grew more and more convinced he was being robbed by those he owed. He had stated he needed twenty-four hours to find a solution, and they weren't prepared to wait. Then in the last call he stated he needed a week to get the money to them, and again, it was clear, they weren't prepared to wait.

As the thief pulled out the cash, Mantel saw him check his watch. He knew a silent alarm would have sounded, and the police would be on their way; he was clearly a professional. The time stamp said 2.59 a.m.

'I'm going to fucking kill you, whoever you are,' Mantel growled, seething at the CCTV recording.

The thief then put the money into the rucksack before zipping it up and leaving.

Mantel saved a copy of the footage, sending it to his email address, then he deleted the file. When the police asked, he would say he didn't catch anything. This man wasn't for them to find. They were for him, and him alone.

Tony rang back, as instructed.

'Boss?'

'Those fuckers haven't given me the week, as they promised.'

'What do you mean?'

'They've robbed the Bean Hut; they found the money.'

'Shit. How much?'

'Six and a half.'

'I don't get it, I thought we had time.'

'They are trying to fuck with me, to send me a message. Tony, I need you to find out exactly who they are, I want names, and I want to know how I find them.'

'Henry, don't do anything stupid.'

'They assured me I could fix the mistake made by Hunter, and they've not let me. If they are going to try and ruin me, I'm coming out swinging. Start digging, I'll send you the CCTV, find out who robbed me.'

'Henry, these people, they are powerful.'

'I don't care, they need to understand you don't fuck with me. Start looking. Find that man.'

'Got it.'

CHAPTER NINETEEN

Clara

I'd been unable to get to sleep and I knew I needed to do something. I recorded and then uploaded a video onto my small and limited social media feeds asking for help, asking people to be generous and give to my daughter. I asked people to share my message. I needed it to reach far and wide. I was still in shock at what had happened to Sadie and Sophie and wanted to do absolutely everything I could for Tabatha. I knew George would be angry when he saw it, that he'd think it was begging and desperate, but I didn't care. I was worried time was running out.

Afterwards, I drifted off on the sofa, but it couldn't have been for long. I had a dream about Tabatha and when I woke, I panicked that something really was wrong and it wasn't a dream at all. I got up, unsteady on my legs and as my head swam into wakefulness, I stumbled from the sofa, as I'd insisted mum stay in my bed – the spare room felt too much like George's personal space to offer it out – through to Tabatha's room. I need not have worried, though. George was home and playing with Tabs.

'Morning,' he said.

'Morning,' I replied, shocked that he was there. 'I didn't hear you come in.'

'You were dead to the world.'

'How long have you been home?'

'About an hour.'

'I didn't hear Tabs wake.'

'I was already in her room when she stirred. Don't worry, Clara, she's okay. I was about to come and wake you.'

I looked at the time, and saw it was nearly eight.

'Where's Mum?'

'Downstairs. Getting ready to open the shop.'

'God, I really was dead to the world,' I sighed.

'You must have needed it,' George said, his attention back on Tabs. He was right, I did. Mum and I had stayed up until almost midnight and I didn't fall asleep until the sun was breaking along the horizon. I ached; my muscles felt overworked, like I'd been in a gym after years of not exercising.

'Coffee?' I asked.

'Please,' George replied, getting up and going into the living room with Tabs in his arms. Walking into the kitchen to make the coffee, I wondered how and why I'd managed to sleep so soundly. Guilt riddled my body from what I had done in the past week. Guilt because I had stolen that money from Tesco, guilt because I needed the help of strangers to make my daughter well, guilt because as awful as it was, as much as my heart ached for her, as much as even thinking it made me a bad person, I was thankful that what was happening to Sadie, wasn't happening to me.

Making two coffees and trying to pull myself together, I checked my emails, hoping to have good news from the hospital in Philadelphia.

Still nothing.

Every day that we waited to hear back from them, the ball of dread grew in my stomach. I'd always believed that she'd get a place but what if she didn't? What would we do then? Pushing the question down, I went back into the living room and put George's coffee down beside him.

'Thanks,' he said, a lightness in his voice. I sat beside him on the sofa and stroked Tabs' head. George placed his free hand on my knee. 'I saw your video.'

'I hope you don't mind, I know what it looks like.'

He shook his head. 'No, it was good, you did well, I hope people get behind it.'

'Thanks, George.'

'How are you feeling about today?'

'Not great,' I said honestly. 'I hate treatment days; it messes her up.'

'It's for her own good.'

'I know, doesn't make it any easier, does it?'

'No. It doesn't. I'm dreading it, too.'

I was grateful he was being honest. 'How was work?' I asked, I didn't want to dwell on the chemo round later, the sickness, the shaking, the tears.

'It's work. I've had a lot of messages of support because of the video.'

'Did people not know?' I asked.

'Everyone knows she's ill, I just, well I've not really told anyone what we learnt at the appointment last week.'

'Why?'

'Fear, I guess. Anyway, they know now.'

'George, I just assumed—'

'It's okay, I should have just been honest that our news wasn't great,' he said, looking down at Tabatha. We fell into a silence. It was brief, but it felt heavy. And I knew why now. Tabatha being really poorly was normal. The shock was gone, as we both were able to talk out loud about it, and that was frightening.

'There was a break-in at the Bean Hut,' George continued, changing the subject.

'Sorry? A break-in?'

'Yeah. Someone put in the back window, robbed from the till,' he said, and I could see that he was relieved I had shown an interest, if for no other reason than to stop us talking about cancer.

'Oh, anyone arrested for it?'

'Not yet.'

'Wait, doesn't the bean hut belong to—'

'Yep, Henry Mantel.'

'Shit. Surely no one is stupid enough to rob him? Surely everyone knows who owns the place?'

'I think that's the point though. Mike told me Mantel was twitchy when he arrived this morning.'

'Twitchy?'

'Yeah, like he was worried about something.'

'Doesn't sound like Mantel.'

'I agree. I think, whoever he owes money to from that call we both heard, they are trying to get it back.'

'Jesus, George, this is getting messy. He must be in deep with the people above him.'

'Yep,' he said, nodding. I could see him taking in that in the space of just a few days there had been a drug bust, a murder, and now a revenge robbery. It was getting out of control.

'You gonna manage all this, love?' I asked.

'I have to. But, today it's about her,' he said, looking down at our daughter. I knew he meant it, too, that today was about her, but still I wondered if he would need to leave us again for work. It was like he read my mind.

'Clara, I've spoken with Mercer, she knows Tabatha is going in for more treatment. I've told her I need to be with my family.'

'Promise you won't leave?'

'I promise, and I know I have before and then—'

'George,' I cut him off. 'I believe you. Thanks for being there for us, we need you. Both me and Tabatha.'

CHAPTER TWENTY

Clara

'She was really brave today,' George said quietly, so as to not disturb the other children and families on the ward. All of whom, like us, were either young and sick, or desperate parents. He didn't look at me as he spoke. His eyes focused on Tabs who lay sleeping in her hospital bed after her round of treatment.

'Yes, she was,' I replied, looking at our daughter too.

'Clara, I'm worried about you. You look so tired.'

'I am tired, but you don't need to worry about me. We're worrying enough about Tabatha as it is.'

'I am worried about her, of course I am, but I worry about you, too. We're dealing with a lot.'

'George, I'm fine. We've just got to keep going.'

'Yeah,' he agreed. 'We do.'

Neither of us knew what else to say so we just sat there, exhausted.

I gazed out of the hospital window, over to a green area close by where the trees were swaying in the gentle summer breeze. Out on the field, a family sat having a picnic. The mum and dad lay either side of the hamper, two children, aged five or six, possibly twins, were running and playing. They were too far away from me to see properly or hear, but they all looked happy. It seemed cruel that the future I'd longed for with my own family now seemed so far away, and yet I was watching someone else's out of a window.

'How much have we raised?' George asked, bringing my attention back to the ward.

'Hmm?'

'How much, on the FundMyCause page?'

'I thought that you didn't agree with the fundraising?'

'Clara, I truly believe that what we are doing right now is the best way to help our daughter. But, I'm trying . . .' he said, before looking down at Tabs again.

Taking my phone out of my bag, I opened the app, and when I saw the total, I couldn't believe it. I must have gasped because George looked at me with concern.

'Clara?'

'It's at almost eighty-five grand.'

'How much?

'Eighty-five.'

'That's a lot,' he said, clearly shocked. 'It must have been your video.'

'Yeah, it must have—'

George cut me off. 'So, what's next?'

'Do you really want to know or are you just humouring me?'

'Hey, be fair. I'm trying, I am.'

'Sorry.'

I told him I didn't know what the next step was. The local papers and magazines were all involved. As was the radio.

Mum had managed to get the BBC to speak to us about what we were trying to do, and as much as it was great publicity, in the back of my mind, I wasn't confident that even that would be enough.

'We should do another video.'

'We?'

'I've been thinking, Clara, a lot. You're right, we need to be ready for whatever comes, including the possibility of getting our baby to Philadelphia. Those kids on this wing, your friend Sadie, I can't let . . .' He trailed off, unable to finish his sentence, but I needed him to.

'George?'

He took a deep breath and turned to me. A tear was on the brink of escaping, but it didn't. He wouldn't let it. 'I can't let that happen to our daughter.'

'That's how I feel, how I've always felt. George, I want our daughter in that programme.'

He nodded 'All right.'

'All right?'

'I only want what's best for our daughter. If you think the US thing is it—'

'It is George, I'm convinced it's the right thing to do.'

'Then we do it. That video you posted last night, it's raised so much. If we both do one, maybe more people will help.'

'They will,' I said.

'I'm sorry it's taken a little while for me to get there.'

'I'm glad you're here now.'

George smiled at me from the other side of our sleeping daughter and I reached out my hand. He took it in his and we both turned our attention back to Tabatha. Joined together, our baby between us. As it should have always been.

'We can do one every day if we need to, just to make sure people hear us. What have we got to lose?' he said quietly.

'It doesn't bear thinking about.'

George let go of my hand again as he sat back in his chair, closing his eyes. It was just for a moment, but long enough for me to see how much he was hurting too.

'Come on then, let's do it,' I said, grabbing my phone.

'Now?'

'Yes, right now.'

As I joined him our thighs touched and I felt a warmth that had been absent for too long. Holding the phone in front of us, I hit record.

'My name is Clara Goodwin.'

'And I am George Goodwin.'

'We are the parents of Tabatha and our daughter is battling cancer. We want to thank everyone who has helped us so far, but we need more, we need you to help save our little girl . . .'

We spoke for only a minute or so, about Tabatha, her condition, the fact that we needed her in the US in a week's time to have treatment to save her. I talked about how much we had raised, and how far we still had to go. We needed hope, and both George and I spoke of how our hope rested in the US, and in the kindness of strangers. Our unscripted conversation was easy, and I felt closer to George in that moment than I had in the months before.

CHAPTER TWENTY-ONE

Clara

With our new, unfiltered video posted, I tried to forget about the fundraising and just look after Tabatha as she recovered from her latest round of chemo. George offered to get some food and a coffee and realising I'd barely eaten all day, I salivated at the idea. Before he went, he gave me a kiss on the cheek, and there it stayed, long after he left.

Tabatha was asleep, but her little body twitched, her face contorted like she was having vivid dreams. I wondered what a baby dreamt of; was it like what an adult would dream, with stories and meaning, however obscure, or were they more visceral, shapes and colours and sounds? She didn't wake, so I didn't wake her – she needed her rest. George was gone for only half an hour, and when he returned, food and coffee in his hands, I could see he had been crying. I wanted to console him, say something, offer comfort but knew better than that. 'I thought you got lost.'

'Sorry.'

'Don't be.'

'As I was going to get food, I walked passed the chapel,

figured I'd pop in,' he said, and although I knew George wasn't a religious man, I wondered if he found something in it that would help. He sat opposite me, our daughter in the bed between us, and we both watched her sleeping. We didn't speak, not really, we simply sat, reacted to our daughter's needs, battling our own tiredness as it had been another exhausting day. My phone was on silent, and every now and then it vibrated. I tried to ignore it, but it didn't relent. Wondering if it was perhaps Mum trying to reach me, I dug in my bag for it. Our message – raw and unedited – had resonated, and the post was being shared over and over. I went to the FundMyCause page, and saw the total was climbing.

By that evening, another £15,878 had been added. We had surpassed the £100,000 mark. When George saw, his mouth dropped open.

'Almost half of this money is from just five people!'

He couldn't believe it. He was elated, but I held back. A little over a week was all that remained for this wave of the trial. That was all. We might get offered a place for the next wave, but I knew in my soul, if we didn't have it all by then, we might be too late. I opened my calculator and did the maths. George saw what I was doing, and he stopped smiling.

£100,567 had been raised, which meant we had £129,433 to go.

'£18,490 a day.' I said. '£770 an hour, every hour for a whole week.'

George looked afraid but somehow determined and I took comfort that he was on my side, at least in part, and I didn't want to lose that. So instead I smiled when he smiled, nodded as he spoke of hope, and counted one hour. I looked at the total on the page. In that hour, we added £540. It was a lot of money raised in a short time, but the rate was slowing, and would eventually stop. Even if by some miracle it didn't, and it stayed at £540 an hour up until we got on that plane, we would still be forty thousand short.

It was a bitter pill to swallow.

Although the money we were trying to raise was a significant hurdle to overcome in the present, the distant future was still so clear in my mind. Despite the pressure and the uncertainty, I could still see my daughter going to school, sitting exams, wearing her school tie in a ridiculous manner because it was what everyone else was doing. I saw her falling in love, landing a job, getting her own home. Having children of her own one day. I saw all of that, and yet at the same time, I couldn't see past the next few weeks.

'You ever think of what she'll be like when she grows up?' I asked George, wanting him to be involved in my distant dreams because of the warmth they made me feel.

'I can't imagine it,' he said. I waited for him to try, but his eyes went from me, back to our sleeping daughter.

'It helps. Picture her fifth birthday.'

He closed his eyes for a long moment and then opened them again.

'I can't,' he whispered, and the hope I felt flickered.

I had expected, as before, that we would be in hospital for the rest of the night, and into the next day, but as the nurses did their evening rounds, we were told we could go home early.

As we made our way to the car, I noted that in the hour we had waited for a doctor to discharge us, another £215 had come in to the fund – £215 when we needed a minimum of £770. By the time we got home, another hour had passed and in that hour, £140 had been added.

We needed a miracle.

24TH JULY 2023.

7 days until the deadline . . .

FundMyCause™   Menu   Log In   Sign Up   Search 🔍

Help for Tabatha
We are raising money to send our daughter, Tabatha, to the US for treatment to help her overcome neuroblastoma.

45%

Donate Now

£104,365
raised of £230,000 target

---

7 days remaining to reach required target

It has been just over a week since we posted about our daughter Tabatha, and the help she needs. And in that time, so many people have reached out, donated, and said kind words.

For this, we are so thankful. But we need continuing support.

In April 2023 Tabatha was diagnosed with Neuroblastoma. And at first, she had a 95% chance of getting well. Recently we were told the treatment wasn't working, and our beautiful baby Tabatha has now only a 50% chance of survival.

Tabatha has begun aggressive treatment here in the UK, but we have discovered a potentially lifesaving treatment in the United States. It is a revolutionary drug called Floxiline, but it is very expensive, and the likely to cost to get her there and treated is £230,000. And we are trying to raise enough to get her there. Her case is on their panel, and we should hear back soon if the place is confirmed. Please know, if the treatment works here, or we do not have the option to go, then any donations will be returned.

We want to thank everyone who has donated so far, for making a difference, and giving us hope.

Clara, George and Tabatha x

Supporters

 S. Tuttle
£500

H. Murphy
£50

H Chilvers
£20

Mrs B Carol
£50

Mr Walsh
£20

K. Sharpe
£20

W. Harold
£20

Jake
£15

CHAPTER TWENTY-TWO

Clara

I lay awake watching my phone screen, hoping for an email, and also dreading receiving it. And then it came, just before one in the morning.

Philadelphia.

The subject simply read: Information regarding your recent application.

Not knowing what the email said, I wanted to wake George, to have him with me when I found out the fate of our daughter. With my phone in my hand, I checked Tabatha was resting comfortably. Her little arms were sprawled above her head, her breathing deep and for now, at least, calm, and walked over to the room where he slept and opened the door. I hoped after the day we had, the closeness we felt, George would share our bed, but it seemed we were a great couple in public, and a completely different one behind closed doors.

As light from the hallway crept into the spare bedroom I could see George was in a deep sleep and even though I needed him, I decided not to wake him. One of us needed to be able to rest, to keep our energy up. I began to close the door and as I did, his phone lit up. He didn't stir so I picked it up and took it into the kitchen. I looked back at my own phone, the email waiting to be read, but I still couldn't open it. The words were too big, too frightening.

'Fucking hell Clara, just open it,' I told myself, and even though I felt I was going to be sick, even though my hands began to tingle, foreshadowing that I might have a panic attack, I tapped the button, and the email opened.

I didn't read the introduction, nor most of its contents; my eyes were drawn to six words in the second paragraph. Six words that would hopefully change my daughter's life.

. . . we are delighted to accept Tabatha . . .

She was in, my baby had a place in Philadelphia. My baby was going into the life-saving trial.

I read the email again, just to make sure I hadn't projected what I wanted instead of reading the truth. But the text remained unchanged. *We are delighted to accept . . .* I dropped my phone on the table and a wave of relief and hope washed over me, those six words looping in my mind. *We are delighted to accept.* I covered my mouth with my hand as a small laugh-cry escaped. Tears pricked and then fell as I let myself be overwhelmed with the victory. I wanted to shout, to scream and jump up and down, but I stopped myself. We had hope, fresh and tangible hope. I wanted to run to George, wake him up and tell him. I wanted to ring Mum and tell her, too. But I knew I shouldn't. The victory, the hope, was delicate, they would have questions about the funds, of how close we were, of what we needed to do to get there, and I didn't have the answers. So instead I stayed where I was and allowed myself to feel warmed by the win, and I thought of the future, of my daughter well and happy. I thought of her fifth birthday, the image so clear, so bright I could almost touch it. I didn't feel guilty any more for taking that money from Tesco, I didn't feel ashamed that I was begging for the help of strangers. None of that mattered. She had a place, she was going to America. One way or another, she was getting on that plane.

CHAPTER TWENTY-THREE

George

'George! Wake up!' Clara shouted, shaking me into consciousness.

'What is it?' I mumbled, sounding more irritated than I was.

'Your phone, it keeps ringing.'

'What?' I asked, feeling for it on the table next to me. It wasn't where I'd left it but instead I looked up to see Clara holding it.

'I moved it, before. I wanted you to sleep properly.'

'What time is it?'

'Just gone four.'

Sitting up, I took the phone from Clara's hand and looked at it. As my eyes blurred into focus, I saw I had two messages, both from Mike, as well as three missed calls.

I opened the messages and read the first, which was sent at 3.20 a.m.

Hey buddy, I know it's late, but thought you'd want to know. There's been a development. Another one of Mantel's businesses has been hit tonight

The second came ten minutes later.

When you get these, a DS Nowak from our friends in Stockport is at the scene. The address is . . .

I knew I had to go, despite the time. This case was the biggest of my career, and I knew that to crack this open, to link the current crimes back to Mantel – as well as linking Mantel to the murder of Reece Hunter – I needed to try and get inside the head of everyone involved. I needed to see how it all connected.

'What happened?' Clara asked.

'Another of Mantel's businesses has been hit. I have to go.'

'George, wait. Before you go, we've had some news. Tabatha got accepted onto the Philadelphia trial.'

'She got a place?' I asked, wanting to make sure I'd heard her right.

'Yes.' Clara said, a beaming smile on her face for the first time in months.

'She's in, because of you,' I gave her a hug, enjoying the rare moment of joy we were sharing after such a difficult few months.

After our embrace I quickly got dressed, and before heading out, I told my wife that if anyone could raise the funds it was her, and I truly believed it, too. Clara was tenacious, pragmatic, determined; it was why I loved her.

Climbing into the car, I thought about the wonderful news Clara had just given me. She had truly believed it was possible, and look what had happened as a result. And maybe the same would be said of the Mantel case. Even though it was dawn, and I was tired, I couldn't help but feel that it was going to be a really good day.

I wondered if Mantel knew yet that another of his businesses had been targeted. I suspected he did. Everyone who worked for him must be aware of what had been going on and given he was a volatile man, I reckoned everyone would be giving him as wide a berth as possible. It must have been a difficult call for the manager of the club. As I drove, I contacted Staffordshire police, telling them I was on my way and arranging to meet DS Nowak. I hoped he would be able to give me something I could follow up on. In the aftermath of the café robbery, Mike had been told by the manager that the CCTV cameras were not working on the night the Bean Hut was robbed. It was either the worst stroke of luck or, more likely, Mantel didn't want us to see the footage. It furthered my suspicions that the robbery was connected to the lost money and drugs from the raid. I hoped by attending the club I would find something more than was found at the café, or at least something that linked the two scenes beyond my own hunch.

The drive took the best part of an hour, roadworks on the A6 making it slow and frustrating. My eyes struggled to stay open and the lights from the cars in front streaked red across my vision. I had to keep all the windows down, the cool air drifting in to help me focus.

Arriving later than I hoped, I hastily parked nearby and dashed over to the waiting police officer by the entrance. 'Sorry for the delay, I'm George.'

'Pavel,' he replied, taking my hand and shaking it firmly. He was stood next to another man, the manager of the club probably. 'Excuse us for a minute,' Pavel said to the man, who muttered a 'no problem' and walked away into the club.

'Thank you for agreeing to meet me,' I said once the

man was out of earshot. 'I promise I'll not take up much of your time.'

'No rush.'

Pavel led me inside and it took a moment for my eyes to adjust in the gloom. Nightclubs had never been on the list of my favourite places; they always felt like they were trying too hard. In the cold light cast by overheard florescent tubes, and devoid of music, drunk young people who were also trying too hard, the building was tired, beaten, sad. A lonely vacuum that sucked the energy from the walls.

As we walked across the dance floor, I could see the stains, dents, cracks that would be hidden under a hundred shoes and as many flashing lights. Some clubs might look fresh and young when empty, but this one didn't; it was old and breaking down.

'Feels different when it's empty,' I offered.

'Yes, it's great when its bouncing,' Pavel said, smiling at me. I'd have to take his word for it.

'This way,' he continued before disappearing around the side of the bar. We came to a door, the glass in the windowpane smashed, shards all over the floor.

'They came in here.'

'Any prints?'

'None, and nothing was touched at all besides in the owner's office.'

'Henry Mantel's office?'

'Yes.'

'May I take a look?'

'DS Goodwin, we have searched the office, we found no prints, no anything.'

'Humour me.'

Pavel led on and I followed as we made our way further behind the bar and up a flight of stairs. The manager looked my way, but offered nothing. Pavel led me into a small room with a window that overlooked the dance floor. Taking a moment, I studied the room. Files were pulled out over the floor, chairs upended . . . whoever was in here had been looking for something specific. I put on some gloves and grabbing my torch, I slowly began to search the room myself, keeping an eye out for anything that seemed out of place. At the Bean Hut, the till had been smashed. I thought back to what Mike had said, that Mantel hadn't been too bothered by that, but had seemed distracted and keen for the police to wrap things up and get off the premises. There must have been something he was trying to keep from us, something he wasn't being upfront about, so I searched extra thoroughly.

'Pavel, when you searched the place, did you find any employment records?'

'Yes, we found a ledger.'

'A ledger?'

'Yes, the owner prefers to have a book, rather than anything on a computer system.'

'I bet he does. Do you still have the ledger?'

'We have images of it, I can forward them to you.'

'Thank you.'

'May I ask why you've come here this morning? Nothing much was stolen.'

'Yes, about that, are you sure?'

'Completely. The safe has marks on it, like someone tried and failed to get in. The tills have been smashed open but only a small float was in there. That's why I'm confused you've come all the way out here, even though this is Mantel's club, it's a simple break in. The alarms were triggered, automatically alerting the police, and when we arrived the manager was already here. He checked but insisted nothing had been taken.'

'What about the owner?'

'He's not been in yet.'

'So whoever broke in caused all this mess?'

'Yep.'

'They were definitely looking for something.'

'Seems so,' Pavel agreed. 'But again, the manager said nothing was taken.'

'Do you believe him?'

'Yes, I do.'

'Can I have a copy of that ledger when you get a sec?'

I gave Pavel my email address, and he saved it.

'I hope you don't mind me saying, but we could have done all this over the phone.'

'I know, I just wanted to get a look at the place, can I have a few more minutes?'

'Take as long as you need.'

'Thank you.'

I waited for DS Nowak to leave and then turned my attention back to the room. There had to be something out of place. Why would they break in here? Why focus on this office?

Using my torch, I crouched and lit under the desk. Nothing seemed disturbed. I kept low and looked around for any imperfections in the skirting boards or floor. I felt sure I would find something, a hidden compartment under a floorboard, a secret hiding place to keep his money while he waited to clean it. But, as much as I looked, I found nothing.

Getting up, I scanned the walls, pausing at a bookcase. I stood there for a moment, trying to work out what was different about it. Then I realised that on the top shelf, three of the books had no gap between them. They were, in fact, one unit made to look like individual spines. Hiding in plain sight. I lifted it down and noticed that on the back, where a lock sat, there were dents around it, as though it had been forced open. It was empty. I expected it would be. Something had been inside though, and now it was gone.

'DS Nowak,' I called, and he came back into the room.

'Found something?' he asked, looking at the container in my hands.

'Whatever they broke in for, it was inside this,' I said. 'You might wanna get forensics in here.'

I had seen enough, and as DS Nowak took over the scene once more and examined my finding, I headed to the car.

Mantel had been hit again, and again nothing much seemed to be missing. I'd had my suspicions after the café robbery that it was connected to the drugs raid, and now I was sure. Clara had made me realise that Mantel had money he needed to clean. Clearly whoever he owed wasn't prepared to wait to collect it. But I still didn't know who that was. What I did know for sure was that if we didn't crack this, if we didn't find out who it was robbing Mantel and bring him to justice alongside Mantel himself for all he had done, someone else was going to get hurt. Or like Reece Hunter, someone else was going to end up dead.

CHAPTER TWENTY-FOUR

Henry Mantel

Mantel answered his phone.

'Boss, there's been an incident.'

'What do you mean there's been an incident, Jamie?' Mantel asked, his knuckles turning white as he gripped the phone tighter in his hand. 'When?'

'In the night.'

'In the night? Why the fuck didn't you call me in the night?'

'I'm sorry, I didn't want to wake you.'

'Don't let the police anywhere inside. You understand?'

'The police have already been.'

Mantel paused, took a deep breath. 'Who?'

'Someone called Nowak. And then a second one joined him.'

'What was the second officer's name?'

'I didn't catch it, I'm sorry boss,' Jamie replied.

'Describe him.'

'Black, about six foot, dark hair. Clean-shaven.'

Mantel sighed. Goodwin. Of course it would be George Goodwin. 'Have the police gone?'

'Forensics are still here.'

'Okay, give me a second,' Mantel said. He thought about Goodwin turning up at the club. He knew what was happening to him. He must, or else why would he be there?

'Boss, I've checked the place. Nothing was taken. Just some stupid fucking kids I reckon. They only got £50 from the till, I'll replace that from my own—'

'No, no need. But Jamie, go check my office. Make sure you're not watched.

'Of course, um, what am I looking for?'

'Go to the book case, make sure nothing looks out of place, and report back.'

'Of course, Mr Ma—'

Mantel hung up before Jamie could finish his sentence. He was reeling, struggling to process what was happening. In his line of work there were always ups and downs, but nothing like this. Two of his businesses had been hit in two consecutive days. Only days after the raid at Hunter's. It was now crystal clear that the people he owed, the people who had told him he had a week, weren't honouring their side of the agreement. No one had ever dared to be so brazen before. He was being laughed at, publicly mocked, and he knew unless he took swift and decisive action, his reputation would be in tatters. He'd be like a lame old lion that was once head of a pride.

The hyenas would come for him.

Pinching the bridge of his nose, Mantel forced away the migraine that was threatening. And in the silence, he tried to formulate a plan in case the call came back not in his favour.

He didn't have to wait long, as his phone began vibrating. He watched it ringing but didn't pick it up straight away.

'Fuck's sake, Henry,' he said to himself and snatched it up. 'Well?'

'The top shelf has been disturbed, books thrown on the floor. Some of the books are missing, I think.'

Mantel hung up. He'd heard enough. He dialled Tony.

'You all right boss?'

'The club's been hit.'

'What?'

'Tony. Whoever it is, they must know where we keep our profits.'

'What are you saying?'

'I think it's someone who works for us.'

'How can you be sure?'

'They've found more.'

'A lot?'

'Yeah, a lot, but that's not the point though. Someone is stealing from me and I want to know who it is.'

'Do you want me to drive to the club now?' Tony asked.

'No, the police are there.'

'Police as in . . .'

'I think so.'

'That fucking copper.'

'Goodwin is a prick,' Mantel said. 'But he's doing his job. He's supposed to try and stop me. Can't blame him. But Tony, I was promised time to make amends for Hunter's fuck-up, and they aren't giving me it. And Tony, I'm thinking whoever this thief is, how do they know I have money stashed? How could they?'

'Good question. I don't know.'

'There is only one answer I can think of. They are using

one of my staff to do it. Someone who isn't customer facing,' Mantel said, not needing to say anymore, those who weren't customer facing were making money illegally for him.

'But how can you—'

'I just know, Tony, don't question me. Someone is fucking with me, and I want to know who.'

'How'd you wanna do it?'

'Get a list of everyone who's worked for me over the past decade.'

'On it.'

'And find me someone who can sniff out a liar.'

'Leave it with me.'

Once Tony had hung up, Mantel logged into the CCTV cloud for the nightclub. As he thought, a little after 3 a.m., the same man who'd targeted his café could be seen in the club. He watched him go into the office, and after much searching, take the box down from the top shelf of his bookcase.

'Who the fuck are you?' he said, closing the app; he had seen enough. Someone close to him was doing this, it had to be, and he wondered if it was someone in his garage.

Making sure no one was on their way up to see him, Mantel lowered himself to the floor. Pulling back a square of carpet, he opened a small hatch underneath and pulled out the contents that were stashed in the confined space. He had enough money here to pay back what he owed – and some – and the intention was to honour his word by cleaning it, processing it, and repaying what was lost. But if he did so now, he would appear weak. His career over. Instead he would pay someone to help find the disloyal employee, and he would find out who was behind the break-ins. And he would show them he wasn't done yet. That the lion was still head of his pride.

Putting the money away, Mantel replaced the carpet square and walked out onto the gangway that overlooked the workshop. Staff were aware he was watching, he could sense them tense up. They all knew something was going on.

Normally, he'd dip back into his office, but today he needed to walk around his patch, and see his subordinates. Show them who was boss. Everyone would know he had been robbed, and he wanted them to see him out there smiling, without a care in the world. Like everything was in hand.

As he headed down the stairs, his staff continued to work, and down on the floor, they greeted him as he walked by.

'Henry.'

'Morning boss.'

'Hello, Mr Mantel.'

He nodded, smiled, patted shoulders and moved like it was any other day. But as he smiled, he was trying to see if any of his staff looked guilty. As he continued through to the reception, he spotted young Ethan.

'Hello kid.'

'Mr Mantel. Everything all right?'

'Yeah, just checking up on you. How are you liking it?'

'It's great, people are nice.'

'Glad to hear it.'

Mantel looked around the space. Ethan kept it tidy, in order. The magazines and papers were neatly stacked. He liked that. The local rag was on top. There was a woman on the front cover, one Mantel thought looked familiar. Picking it up he read the headline.

'Local mother needs your help.'

He read on, and it didn't take long to understand where he knew the face from. It was Goodwin's wife, who was talking about their struggle with their daughter. She was a copper too but her daughter's illness would keep her off the force.

Pity.

He was about to discard the paper but then something caught his eye, something that might be helpful. To him, she was just the copper wife of George Goodwin, but it seemed Clara Goodwin had been a whole lot more when she worked for the Met. The article mentioned her stint in London, how she was a detective specialising in profiling criminals.

And it gave Mantel an idea.

CHAPTER TWENTY-FIVE

Clara

After another bad night, I wondered how long a person could survive without sleep. How long would it be before I would lose my mind and then die? I looked it up. The longest someone had stayed awake for was eleven days. It had only been a few for me and I was struggling. Everyday tasks were difficult to perform. Things I usually took in my stride. Feeding Tabatha, changing her, playing with her. It was tough going, my mind was foggy, my arms and legs ached. But then Tabatha was still smiling. She was still engaging. Even given how tired she must be as she recovered from her latest round of chemo. She still made the effort. She giggled as I sang to her and I couldn't help but think she was only giggling for my benefit. Giggling because she couldn't say to me, 'It will be all right, Mummy. Everything will be all right. Just keep going.'

She couldn't say it, but I heard her nonetheless.

Mum joined us, coming from the shop shortly after I finished with Tabatha's breakfast. She took one look at me and frowned. She could see I hadn't slept.

'We got accepted, Mum, The email came from Philadelphia.'

'We have?' she said, and I could only nod in reply as more tears fell. Mum squealed and grabbed me, and we both laughed and cried.

'Oh Clara, I'm so happy.'

'Me too.'

She let me go and then picked up Tabs and hugged her.

'Thank you, Mum, for helping make this happen.'

'Nothing to thank me for, I want to be there for my daughter and my grandchild. Anyway, we have time in the future to celebrate, all the time we want, but right now, let's make sure she gets on that plane. Where are we at?'

'About a hundred and seven,' I said.

'It's a lot.'

'It is, and yet still over a hundred and twenty away.'

'We will get there,' she said. 'Right, I'd better get ready for work. Hopefully another day's trading will help us.'

'We'll come down with you. If it's quiet, we can work out exactly what we need to do logistically, assuming we raise the money.'

'We'll raise the money, don't you worry about that,' Mum said confidently.

I followed her down the stairs and then made us both a coffee whilst Mum fussed Tabs. As she did, I quickly prepared the banking run. I smiled as I totalled up the latest takings from the shop and café. Things were going well. After covering bills, stock and staffing, there was almost four grand we could put into the fund – if Mum wanted to, of course. After all, it was her money. It was mostly from the café, though some was from bookshop sales and a small amount was the money I had taken from Tesco, accounted for as additional cups of coffee, an idea given to me by none other than Henry Mantel.

I showed Mum the paying-in book and she smiled. 'It's been busier. We might have to start banking daily. As soon as its banked, I'll transfer it all into the fund.'

'Thank you,' I said, fighting back a tear.

'As I said, nothing to thank me for.'

Above us I heard the flat door open. George must be back.

'Go see him,' Mum said. 'I'll open up, this little one can help me.'

'No, it's okay,' I stood, clearing away our cups. As I washed up, I heard Mum speaking to a customer, a man, who must have been waiting outside. As soon as I heard his voice, I knew exactly who it was. My heart raced and I made my way quickly towards the front of the shop, instinctively feeling the need to move my daughter as far away from him as I could. As I reached Mum and took Tabs, Henry Mantel was browsing the crime section, but I could see he wasn't interested in the books at all. His attention kept flicking to the back of the shop.

Mum approached him before I could tell her to leave him to it.

'Is there anything in particular you're looking for?'

'No, just browsing.'

'Well, I'm at the till if you need any help.'

Mum continued setting up, turning on the till and readying for a potential sale. She smiled, happy that the customers seemed to be coming earlier and earlier. I managed to smile back, but remained wary. Mantel moved along the shelves, from crime fiction to true crime. He picked up a few books, smiled, put them back, and continued to work his way down the shop. Keeping Tabatha with me, I walked towards the café, making myself look busy by grabbing a cloth and wiping the tables. Tabs was heavy in my arms, but I didn't dare put her down. If George was right about everything, there was an extremely dangerous man browsing our bookshelves.

Another customer walked in, a lady Mum knew, and they both headed towards the café. The woman was a similar age to Mum and she took a seat and chatted as Mum made her a coffee. I recognised her as one of the regulars, though I didn't know her name. Mantel drew ever closer to the café, and then quietly took a seat himself.

'I'll be just a sec,' she said, smiling his way as she walked the black Americano to the other table. He didn't smile back.

'It's okay, Mum, I'll help.'

I handed Tabs to her and the two women started fussing over her as I walked over to Mantel.

'What can I get you?'

'Oh, a cappuccino would be fine. To go, I'll not be staying.'

'Of course,'

Making his drink, I kept an eye on him. Two more people walked into the shop and came over to the café. They took seats, and Mum put Tabs down in the children's area, then took their order. I made Mantel's coffee and handed it to him.

'Is there anything else I can get you?' I asked.

'You know I own the Bean Hut, right?'

'Oh,' I said.

'I'm sure you know, it's closed at the moment.'

'Yes, I saw something online. I'm sorry about the break-in.'

He waved me off. 'And I've heard a lot of my customers are coming here now.'

'Yes, we've certainly seen more coming over the last couple of days. I'm sure once you're open and trading again, they'll come back.'

Mantel didn't comment and instead looked over to Tabs on the play mat. It took every ounce of strength not to grab his face and force his gaze away from my daughter.

'She sick?'

'I beg your pardon?'

'Your daughter, she looks sick.'

'She has cancer,' I replied, making sure I didn't blink, making sure he saw in my eyes not to fuck with me.

'I know,' he said, and I had to wonder if he knew, why did he ask? The answer was clear. Cruel prick.

'What do you want?' I asked, trying and failing to hold back my anger. I couldn't work out what kind of person you'd have to be to know someone is poorly but ask about it so indelicately.

'The paper says you need to raise a lot of money.'

'Yes.'

'How's it going?'

'We are getting there.'

He took a sip of his coffee. 'It's good.'

'Mr Mantel, what do you want?'

'You know my name?'

'Everyone does.'

'Well, Mrs Goodwin, or rather, DI Goodwin,' he said, stressing the DI. 'I want to help you.'

'Help me?'

'Yes.'

'Do you know who my husband is?'

'Of course, good old George,' Mantel said.

'I don't need your help, Mr Mantel.'

'Your FundMyCause page, which is still not even halfway to your target, says otherwise.'

I wanted to ask him to leave, to remind him that although I wasn't an active police officer, my husband, who was upstairs, above our heads, was. Mantel knew George was investigating him and I should have told him to fuck off. But I was curious as to what he was going to say in case it was anything that would help my daughter, anything at all.

'So, do you want my help?'

'Fine, I'll bite.'

Mantel stood, picked up his coffee and went back to the crime section to browse the books. I followed. Mum looked up, and I gestured that it was okay, that I would help the customer. Making sure that neither she nor anyone else could hear me, I spoke first.

'You know I shouldn't be talking to you?'

'And yet, here we are.'

'Only because I want to hear what you have to say that might help my daughter.'

'They say that you are red-hot at profiling criminals.'

'Who's they?'

'Doesn't matter, are you?'

'I've done a bit.'

'Now don't be modest, neither of us have the time.'

'Fine, yes. I'm good at profiling people.'

'Including me?'

'Yes, including you.'

'So tell me, what kind of man am I?'

'How is this relevant?'

'Call it a test.'

He looked at me, enjoying himself. But if it helped my daughter, I'd do anything. 'Fine, you are a man who is used to getting his own way. You naturally control a room, and understand how to manipulate people to your liking. You are smart, educated, although not traditionally, and making money comes easily to you.'

'Go on,' he said.

'You take pride in what is yours. I'm guessing your house is immaculate, your wife is younger than you and your children are model students in school.'

'How can you be sure?'

'Because for you, your name isn't just a name, it's a brand.'

He nodded, a small smile catching the corner of his mouth. I had passed the test.

'I have a problem, Mrs Goodwin.'

'If this has anything to do with my husband . . .'

'No, this isn't about him.'

'What's this about then?'

'As you know, someone robbed me.'

'And?'

'Last night, a club of mine was hit too.'

'I'm sorry to hear that. I hope they catch whoever did it,' I said, trying my best not to look nervous as I was sure Mum was now watching.

'I don't know who it is.'

'So, find out.'

'I was thinking this morning,' he continued, ignoring me, 'who would know how to find a criminal better than a copper?'

'What is it you're saying?'

'I want to offer you a job.'

'You've got to be kidding? You know I am still a police officer?'

He picked up a book, thumbed the pages. 'I do, but on maternity leave. So, I won't tell anyone if you don't.'

'I want you to leave.'

'And I want you to help me find whoever is doing this. I don't like being robbed.'

'Ironic.'

'No, Mrs Goodwin, no. I'm many things, but I am not a thief. I will pay you well to help me. I will add to the little pot of money you are trying to fill.'

'The investigating police officers, my husband, will find out who is behind the thefts,' I replied, hearing my own conviction waver.

'Maybe, but your husband won't tell me, will he? And I want to know first.'

'Why?'

'Call me curious,' he said. 'Anyway, thanks for the coffee. Here's my number. If you have a change of heart, you can call me any time.' He handed me a business card with details of the garage he owned, his personal number scrawled in biro across the bottom. He didn't say any more and I watched him walk away. He stopped at the entrance, lit a cigarette, blew out his first drag inside the shop and left.

'What was that about?' Mum came over when she noticed he was smoking inside the shop.

'Nothing, Mum, it was nothing,' I said, trying and failing to keep my heart rate steady.

CHAPTER TWENTY-SIX

George

After my visit to Stockport, I slept late into the afternoon, and despite needing it, I felt guilty for it, too. I knew how little Clara was sleeping. I should have set an alarm, helped her more. I tried to make amends by bathing Tabatha, so Clara had some time to herself. My wife looked exhausted; her eyes were heavy, her skin looked washed-out, grey . . . she looked on the edge of falling apart. I wanted to ask her if she was okay, if I could do more, but I didn't.

Once Tabatha was bathed, I read her a bedtime story then kissed her goodnight. Clara came in shortly after and sat with her for a while, stroking her head, singing a lullaby. I'd never seen my wife so low and I felt powerless to help.

Clara caught me watching her, and I offered a smile.

'Do you want something to eat?' I asked.

'No, thank you,' she replied before turning back to our sleeping daughter.

I went into the kitchen and grabbed a beer from the fridge. As I cracked it open, I heard Clara padding into the living room and thought about joining her, but I only made it as far as the doorway. I watched her, engrossed on something on her phone, no doubt researching what was needed for the America thing to happen.

'What are you doing?'

'Updating the FundMyCause page.'

The screen lit her face in a way that reminded me of when we were younger, when we first met. A camping trip in the Lakes before we got married. That weekend we talked for hours under the stars, her face illuminated by the firelight. I remembered how I ached to touch her, to stroke her hair, to hold her hand. That night under the stars, warmed by the flames, we spoke until the sun began to crest the horizon. That night I knew I loved her. Recalling it made me feel compelled to tell her that I loved her again, but as I opened my mouth, the words wouldn't come.

'I've got to do some paperwork, I just wondered if you wanted a cuppa before I get to it.'

'Are you going back in?'

'No, I'll work from the spare room so you can rest. Need anything?'

'No, thank you.'

I nodded before I shut myself away to work. I grabbed my laptop and sat on the mattress as I logged in and dug up the images saved in a folder under Mantel's name. I just needed to find something I had overlooked, something that would help.

I looked through the crime scenes in chronological order. Hunter's place didn't lead to a new line of enquiry, though even now it shocked me how much we found in drugs and cash. Next I looked at pictures of Hunter's injuries and the scene where he was dumped and left to die. Forensics had taken over a hundred photos of the golf course and I meticulously looked through every single one. I was still waiting for confirmation, but I knew Mantel's DNA wouldn't be anywhere. If they did happen to find something, it would implicate someone else. I suspected Mantel didn't do his own dirty work anyway. With nowhere else to go, I turned my attention to the café and then the newly robbed club in Stockport. If it had been money in that box, what I needed to know, was how much. The staff at both crime scenes were adamant nothing had been taken besides the small cash floats in the tills, but I didn't believe a single word of it. I didn't think the staff were lying, just that they didn't know what Mantel was getting up to. If the café alone had been robbed, you could have put it down to being bad luck, but two of Mantel's businesses in quick succession had to be more than just coincidence. And with the disguised cash box clearly being forced into at the club, it seemed the thief had found what they were after. As I scanned image after image from both scenes, finding nothing new, a message came through from Mike.

They found CCTV footage of the back of the café, taken from a nearby business. I'm sending it over now.

I waited impatiently for the follow-up email, and when it came, I tapped the attachment immediately, pressing play on the video link. The camera quality was fair, but the angle of the lens focused primarily on the back of the bookies next door and not the café itself. However, shortly after the video began, a person came into view. I couldn't make out their features, and they didn't come close enough to the back door of the gambling shop to trigger the motion sensor light. If I had to guess, the person was five foot six or seven. Someone Mantel knew? I got the sense of him being young. Early twenties given his frame. Taking out my notepad, I jotted down the approximate height and build of the man in the video. He was thin, probably an associate of Mantel's who was also a user, maybe one of his young mechanics in his garage. Next time I popped in, I would make a note who worked there to see if any of them fit the profile. I would also have a word with Ethan, tell him to keep his eyes open. The boy was desperate to rebuild his reputation and relationship with his mother, so I knew he would do his bit.

Scrolling back, I paused the footage and took a screenshot of the man, saving it with the other pictures in my file. I needed to find him before Mantel did.

No sooner had I closed my laptop, than I heard Clara calling out.

'George! George!'

She sounded panicked, afraid. I jumped up, my stomach squeezing so tight I thought would be sick, and ran towards her call. She was in Tabatha's room, holding our baby in her arms. Even in the low light, I could tell something was wrong. Tabatha's arm was limp, dangling towards the floor.

'What is it? What's happened?' I asked.

'George, she's not waking up. I can't wake her up.'

25TH JULY 2023

6 days until the deadline . . .

Help for Tabatha

We are raising money to send our daughter, Tabatha, to the US for treatment to help her overcome neuroblastoma.

50%

£115, 760
raised of £230,000 target

Donate Now

---

6 days remaining to reach required target

Important update

Late this evening, I found my daughter unconscious in her room. There was swelling that affected the blood flow to her head, and she was rushed to hospital, where thankfully, they have managed to stabilise her.

She was lucky I found her when I did, she was lucky that the doctors could help swiftly. However, we are beginning to believe that the treatment here will not be enough to save her.

But we still have hope.

News has come to us from Philadelphia and Tabatha has a place on the Floxiline programme as we hoped for. We need to leave the UK, in 6 days to make the window for this programme, and we are only halfway there to reaching our target.

If you are reading this page, thank you, if you have or will donate, we are more grateful than you could ever know. You are helping an innocent little girl have the chance for a better future.

What we need now, is more people to find us and learn of Tabatha's battle. So please, share us as far and as wide as you can. She needs more help than ever.

Clara, George and Tabatha x

Supporters

 G. Thompson
£10

Max Clover
£20

S. Pyrat
£20

H. Calamara
£50

Ms Locke
£20

K. Holt
£20

M. Klein
£20

Andy Burrow
£10

CHAPTER TWENTY-SEVEN

Clara

The constant beeping sound of the heart rate monitor was both hypnotic and terrifying. I sat silently, powerlessly, watching my daughter. If it wasn't for the canula in her hand, you would think she was just sleeping. The trauma of finding her unresponsive had left my extremities numbed and robbed me of my voice, and every time I tried to move, I felt I would faint. Every time I wanted to say something, I couldn't find any words. George sat on the other side of the bed, neither of us speaking, neither of us knowing what we could possibly say to make anything better. In my hand was the tiny one that belonged to my daughter. She was too small for this, too small for any of it, and I wished with everything I had that I could take it away from her.

With every slight variation on the monitor, every slight increase or decrease, fear tried to push its way forward, tried to consume me, to drag me down to a dark place, cold and damp and eternal. I forced myself to keep calm, reminding myself the worst was over.

From discovering Tabatha unresponsive to when we were

told she was going to be okay was just a handful of hours. Hours that felt like years, hours that would haunt me for the rest of my life. Hours that would likely cause me to die younger. There was something about seeing your baby helpless and fearing the worst that changed part of you somewhere deep inside. I couldn't say out loud how seeing Tabatha that way had changed me, but it had; the world spun differently now, and it would never go back to what it once was. The sea was still the sea, the sky was still the sky, and from the outside it all looked similar – and yet all of it had altered. My senses were now both heightened and dimmed, tuned and distorted. I was still a woman, a mother, but I was now something else, too, something more primal. If George had picked up on it, too, this shifting in my identity, he didn't comment. But the tiny candle I held inside, the one I fought to keep burning, nearly went out.

'Clara,' George said, snapping me away from my thoughts. 'She's going to be all right.'

He was right. She was, the paramedics and doctors had made sure of that. They had relieved the pressure, increased the blood flow, reduced the swelling.

'I know, but for how long?' I asked quietly, looking up to hold George's eye, waiting for an answer, one that didn't come. 'How long will she be all right for?' I asked again, tears clouding my eyes so I couldn't see his features clearly.

'Clara, you have to keep faith.'

'Faith? Like some holy intervention will occur?'

'No, faith that the medicine we have on offer will work, faith in our daughter's strength. Faith in raising the money.'

'I'm not interested in faith, George, or hope, or any of that. I'm interested in our daughter being well.'

'Don't you think I am too?' he said, raising his voice before catching himself and lowering it again. 'Don't you think that this breaks my heart, that I would rather die than have her suffer any more? We both want the same things, Clara.'

Tabatha wriggled, drawing our focus back to her, and I stood up and leant over, stroking her head, humming to her until she settled. When I sat down again, I looked at George to say something more, but his attention had shifted from us bickering to Tabs. I watched my husband. His face was still the same face I had fallen in love with, his cheekbones, still his cheekbones, his nose, unchanged – and yet everything about the face I saw was alien. He was like a stranger. I didn't know my husband any more.

'George, remember when I said to try and see her fifth birthday?'

'Yes.'

'Can you see it yet?' I asked, hoping he could because the image I had of it had faded, like an old photograph exposed to the sun. He shook his head.

'I can't.'

'I need you to try.'

'I just can't.'

'George.'

'Clara, stop. I need to focus on the here and now, not what might be in the future. I don't want to drift off into dreamland.'

'You just talked about hope.'

'Yes, I did.'

'But you can't see her future.'

'Clara.'

'Why can't you just try, for me?'

George drew a breath to say something else, but before he could, Dr Bhari walked in and I felt my stomach flip.

'Hello Mr and Mrs Goodwin.'

'Hello Dr Bhari,' I said quietly.

'Doctor, is she going to be all right. Do you know what happened?' George asked.

'Yes, with the type of cancer Tabatha has, it picks a side of the body to attack and can cause swelling in that area. Hers is the right side. The combination of the cancer, the treatment, her weakened immune system. The swelling on her right side focused on her neck muscles, it's a common side-effect, but in her case, it was quite extensive and it influenced the blood flow to her brain.'

'Oh God,' I said, my voice coming as a whisper.

'You did exactly the right thing, and although the reduced blood flow was enough to cause unconsciousness, we don't think it was enough to cause any permanent damage.'

'What if I hadn't checked on her when I did?' I asked.

'Well, we don't have to worry about that, try not to dwell on it.'

I nodded, though I couldn't help but think what might have happened if I'd waited another hour before kneeling beside her cot to stroke her tiny and precious face. What if I'd fallen asleep as I so desperately needed to? What if we'd been too late?

I knew it wasn't healthy to think that way, but I couldn't stop myself. And I knew I'd likely never let myself sleep properly ever again.

'We also have the results of her blood work from the lab.'

'That was quick,' George said.

'We wanted to move fast for Tabatha. The good news is,

the episode experienced tonight is only down to the swelling I mentioned, and this has now been managed. Before you leave, we'll give you some medication to assist in keeping further swelling down to a minimum.'

'So can she come home?'

'We don't see there being any more complications, however, to be safe we want to keep Tabatha in for the rest of the night and monitor her oxygen levels.'

'Of course,' George and I echoed.

'We'll be transferring her to the open ward shortly, and we can monitor her effectively from there.'

Moving Tabs from the high dependency unit to the open ward really did mean she was on the mend. George knew it too and sank back in his chair with relief. We exchanged a small smile, though as soon as my lips curved, that same question came back. She was all right, but for how long?

'Is this likely to happen again?' I asked.

'Possibly. Tabatha is a very poorly little girl, and with her immune system compromised, she might have some challenging times ahead.'

'Doctor, I need you to tell me,' I said, pausing to take a breath before asking the question I had never wanted to utter. 'Is my daughter going to die?'

Dr Bhari paused for a beat too long before he replied.

'We are doing everything we can for her. There are children who are more unwell who go on to make a full recovery. She is in good hands.' But despite his words sounding reassuring, the pause spoke louder. The pause said it all.

Dr Bhari said his goodbyes and we thanked him. Soon Tabs would be transferred onto the open ward, and I knew that when she was, only one of us would be able to stay with her. In the past, it has usually been me, and George never contested it, we never really discussed it either. Tonight was different, though. Because in that brief pause, I understood I needed to do more. I knew I needed to raise more.

And there was someone I knew who had money and was willing to give me what we needed if I did a job for him. Against my better judgement, I needed to speak to Henry Mantel.

CHAPTER TWENTY-EIGHT

Clara

George was stunned when I suggested he stay with Tabatha for the night instead of me. I blamed exhaustion, a need for sleep, and in part that was true. But I couldn't help feel guilty that I was about to leave my baby in hospital. George pacified the obvious struggle I felt by telling me that it was his turn, and he wanted to be with her. That I needed to try and sleep.

'Don't feel bad. I want to stay with her, I've always wanted to stay.'

'Why didn't you say before? We could have taken turns.'

'Because I didn't want to get between a mother and her daughter.'

'Is that all?' I asked, and he shook his head.

'No, because I've been afraid, too. I feel safer at work with drug dealers and murderers than I do in a hospital room. Jesus, saying it out loud I realise how pathetic that sounds.'

'It's not pathetic,' I said.

'Clara, you carry the weight of our hospital visits most of the time. I want to stay tonight, I want to do this for our daughter, for you. I'm gonna try to see her fifth birthday, I'm gonna try and see us being a normal family with a little girl who isn't sick.'

'Thank you.'

'So you should go home, get your Mum round for company, tell her what's happened then try and get some rest. And if you really can't sleep, come back and we'll swap, okay?'

I nodded, knowing I needed to go, but not for the reasons George assumed.

Despite it being the middle of the night when I called Mum, she answered on the third ring.

'Clara?'

'Hey Mum. We've had a scare with Tabatha.'

'What? What's hap—'

I cut her off. 'She's okay, she's in hospital. But she is fine. It was just a scare.'

'Tell me what happened.'

'She had some swelling, they're treating it now,' I said, omitting the fact I had found her unconscious and for a moment, thought she had died. 'She's staying in overnight, George is with her. Can you come and get me? I don't want to drive home alone.'

'Of course, give me an hour.'

Thankfully, despite visiting times being over, the nurses on the general ward let me stay until Mum came. She messaged me when she arrived, and I grabbed my things. Leaving Tabatha was hard, but I knew George would call me if anything changed.

In the hospital atrium, I paused outside WHSmith so I could send a text to Mantel. I hoped he was awake and would message back soon. I had a small window to speak with him without George being around to find out.

Still want to talk?

His reply came back within a minute.

Yes. When suits you?

Anytime after 2.30a.m.

Another message came through giving me the address of where and when to meet and I memorised it before deleting the text so George wouldn't find anything. Then I went outside to see Mum waiting.

'God, Clara,' she said, giving me a hug. 'Can I see her? I want to see her.'

'No, not now. George is with her, she's fine.'

As Mum led me to her car, I knew I needed to talk to her about it all but I didn't know where to start. I felt like a kid who had done something stupid and was trying to tell her mum before she found out from one of the neighbours. Suddenly I was no longer a 32-year-old woman, a mother myself. I was a little girl again.

'Mum, I need to talk to you about something.'

'Okay.'

'I need your help.' I looked out onto the quiet A34, the tail lights of night owls and lorry drivers blurry in the distance.

'Of course, what is it?'

'Before I ask, I need to tell you something, something bad.'

'Right . . .'

'Remember when we spoke about what we would do to help someone we loved?'

'Yes, I remember,' she said, her eyes focussed on the road.

'And we said we would do whatever it took.'

'Yes.'

'And remember when you told me that Dad might have done things to put food on the table?'

'Yes. Clara, where is this going? You're worrying me.'

'I asked because that night I stole some money.'

'Where from?'

'After the robbery at Tesco, there was some cash on the floor. The thieves had dropped it and I took it.'

'I see,' Mum said, remaining impassive. 'Is that why you asked me about what I would do if it were me?'

'Yes. Am I a bad person?'

'I said to you that night, your dad did what he needed to keep a roof over our heads. From where I'm sitting, you needed to take that money more than he needed to do what he did.'

'What did Dad do?'

'Nothing major, and he never told me the details, but I suspect he was involved in selling stolen goods.'

'Dad broke the law?'

'He never said it out loud, he wasn't that kind of man, but I think so, yes.'

'Were you angry with him?'

'I was, but his heart was in the right place. Clara, I feel like you're not telling me everything, talk to me.'

'Mum, I might have to ask for help from someone I shouldn't. Someone who isn't a good person. It's something I know I really shouldn't be doing, but I need to do it for her.'

'Will it risk you getting hurt?'

'I don't think so.'

'Will anyone else get hurt?'

'I hope not.'

'Will it help Tabs?'

'Yes.'

'Do I know this someone who is bad?'

'Have you heard of Henry Mantel?'

'Hasn't everyone?'

'It was him, in the shop yesterday morning.'

'And?'

'He is being targeted by some bad people and he's offered me money to help find out the thief's identity.'

'But . . . isn't George investigating him?'

'Yes.'

'And he still wants to offer you a job?'

'Yes.'

'What if George finds out?'

'I have to hope he won't. Mantel has a lot of money, and we need money.'

'I can't be your moral compass, but if it was me and it wasn't going to hurt anyone and it would help Tabs, I know what I would do.'

'Even if it's wrong to work for him?'

'Yes. Because Tabatha being well is all that matters, right?' Mum said.

'Then I need you to do something for me.'

'Anything.'

'I need you to lie for me. I've arranged to meet Mantel but George has to think I'm at home and asleep. That's why I asked him to stay with Tabs tonight, that's why I wanted you to pick me up.'

Mum was quiet for a moment.

'Are you sure this will help?' she asked.

'I don't know, it might not. I have to try anyway.'

'Yes, I think you do.'

'I'm sorry for putting this on you.'

'You put nothing on me. I'm glad you can come to me.'

'Always.'

'So tell me what you want me to do.'

'When we get home, I need to borrow your car. I need you to text George, tell him I was exhausted and passed out on the couch.'

'Clara, I can't imagine how stressful this is, having to think three steps ahead and with Tabs being so unwell, too. Are you sure you should be doing this?'

'I haven't got a choice, have I?'

'Well from now on in, I'm with you. When it feels too tough, you can lean on me.'

'I already do.'

Mum took my hand in hers and gave it a squeeze. I was shocked at how easy it had been to tell her and for her to agree to help. But then she loved Tabatha unconditionally, too. Once back, we headed up to the flat and I got changed. As I put on my dark jacket, I struggled to do up the buttons; my hands felt numb. Mum helped and again, I felt like a child.

'Are you sure you're up for doing this?'

'I have to be.'

'Clara, please tell me again you're going to be safe?'

'I'm going to be safe, I promise.'

'All right,' she said, giving me a hug. 'Ring me if you need me?'

'I can't take my phone, it's easy to track.'

'You're making me nervous. It doesn't sound as safe as you keep telling me.'

'I know, and I'm sorry. I just need to cover my tracks. No one but you and me can know I'm meeting with Henry Mantel.'

'Just be careful, love,' Mum said kissing me on the cheek as I opened the door to leave. I flashed her a nervous smile. And walked down the stairs, into the night.

CHAPTER TWENTY-NINE

Henry Mantel

Mantel unlocked the door and made his way through the salon. He didn't turn on any of the lights. His brief conversation with Clara the day before didn't tell him either way if she would agree to help. Her message this evening was direct and again, didn't give anything away. He wasn't surprised she had messaged, though. He had baited her and he knew that she was in dire straits. She had something he wanted, but he had something she needed – and need superseded any sense of right and wrong. Also, by agreeing to meet him, she was already involved. She was now in his pocket. It was just the matter of the terms. He'd instructed Clara to enter via a side door located down the dead-end alley, which backed onto a narrow corridor between residential properties and had high fences on either side. He told her to be at the door at 3 a.m., and he knew she wouldn't be late. She would enter and exit the same way. It was the safest choice. Mantel didn't care about them discovering that Clara Goodwin was working with him, but he needed her to find the fucker responsible for robbing his businesses first.

Looking at his watch, and seeing it was time, he left the salon floor, walking down a corridor stacked high with haircare products and cleaning materials. At the end was a fire door and he pushed the bar to open it. On the other side stood Clara Goodwin. Mantel didn't say anything, but walked away, and Clara followed, closing the door behind her. On the salon floor once more, he pulled out a chair for her.

'Please, sit.'

Clara did as she was asked, and Mantel sat opposite her.

'Is she all right?' he asked. 'Your girl?'

'Do you care?'

'I'm a parent too, Clara.'

'She's in the hospital.'

'Will she be okay?'

'I'm not here to talk about her.'

'Fair enough.'

'If I do this, George can never know.'

'Fine.'

'No one can.'

'Agreed.'

'NO ONE,' she said louder.

'Agreed,' he replied again, calmly.

'If I do this, how will you help me?' she asked. Mantel smiled, approving of her direct approach. She was afraid of him, she knew what he was about, but she hid it well, deciding it was best to show no fear and not to back down.

'I'll pay you for your time, for agreeing. And then, when you help me identify whoever is robbing me, I'll pay you more.'

'How much?'

'Don't you trust me, DI Goodwin?'

'No.'

Mantel laughed, enjoying the no-nonsense attitude that Clara was displaying.

'I need to know whether or not it's worth the risk. I could just get a normal job.'

'Ten grand over the next few days, in small deposits. Another fifteen when you find him.'

'How do you know I won't just take the money and run?'

'We both know you are not that stupid. You have more to lose if anyone finds out we've spoken. So, do you agree to the terms?'

'It's a lot of money,' she said.

Mantel waved his hand dismissively. 'Money isn't a concern, The fact that someone is taking it from me is.'

'Is it clean?'

He laughed again. 'DI Goodwin, I'd not be offering it to you if it wasn't.'

Above them, coming from upstairs, was a bang and Mantel watched as Clara jumped.

'It's okay, just one of my staff staying in the flat upstairs to keep an eye on the place.'

'Will he be joining us?' she asked.

'No, this arrangement is strictly between you and me.'

He watched her weigh it up. 'How will I know you have made the deposits?'

'Each transaction will be for a set amount, £500, and the name will begin with B and the surname will start with a C. I'll put £500 across now, so you can see what I mean.'

'Why BC?'

'Bent Copper,' Mantel said, smiling at Clara. 'There, £500 has gone across now, from Mr Barry Clark.'

He turned the screen and watched as Clara squinted to read it.

'I'll do it.'

'Good, though I have to ask, DI Goodwin, why the sudden change of heart? You wouldn't be trying to stitch me up, now, would you?'

'My baby is currently in hospital and I have less than a week to raise the money I need for her treatment in the US. This isn't about you, I just want to save my child.'

'You and your husband, what a complicated relationship you now have.'

'Leave him out of this.'

'I will if you will,' Mantel said.

'I need to know what's been taken so far.'

'My café and the club both had money taken that I haven't disclosed to the police.'

'Why not?'

'I think you know why not. I am in debt because of your husband's raid.'

'He is just doing his job.'

'I don't bear George a grudge, I just wish he would piss off.'

'Who do you owe?'

'I don't know.'

'Sorry?'

'They remain anonymous. I've always worked this way. I do things for my clients, they reward me financially. It's a system that's worked for a number of years. We've never had a problem.'

'Until now.'

'Yes, until now.'

'Is it a new client?'

'Yes.'

'And they aren't happy you lost their drugs and cash?' Clara said.

'Exactly. I have asked for time; they clearly haven't wanted to grant it.'

'I see. How much did you lose?'

'Just shy of sixty.'

'How much have they taken back?'

'Fifteen or so.'

'So, they will likely come back for more. That's why you need me to profile them?'

'Again, it's not about the money,' Mantel said, enjoying the fact that the copper in front of him was growing into her role. He had allowed her to have the power in the conversation so she could feel like she wasn't doing too much wrong. That she still had choices. It was all a lie, of course. This made Clara Goodwin just as much of a criminal as he was, and he owned her now.

'If it's not about money, what is it about then?'

'It's about the message,' he replied, locking his phone and putting it back in his pocket. 'If I allow someone to rob me, unpunished, what does that tell everyone? Sixty quid, or sixty thousand, the number doesn't matter. What I do about it does.'

'And what will you do when I find them?'

'Send a message back.'

'I can't be included in anything if someone is going to get hurt.'

'No, I don't want to hurt anyone.'

'What about Hunter?'

'That wasn't me,' he said, holding Clara's gaze, knowing she didn't believe him. 'I just want whoever it is to know I won't be intimidated.'

'Where do you want me to start?' Clara asked quietly.

'Take this,' Mantel said, pulling a phone from his pocket and handing it to her. 'Only person it calls is me, no one else. Got it?'

'Yes.'

'Keep it out of sight.'

'You don't need to tell me.'

Mantel smiled. 'Start with finding out what your husband knows, who he thinks is involved.'

'I'll not do anything illegal, and I won't compromise my husband.'

'I'm not asking you to, I just want you to listen.'

'I will need a list of everyone in your employment, past and present.'

'I'm already looking into this.'

'You want my help or not?'

Mantel nodded and sat back in his chair, again allowing her to believe she still had some of the power. 'I'll get the list to you.'

'I'm going back to my daughter soon. When the list comes through, I'll get to work.'

Mantel didn't reply. It was clear the conversation was over, and not waiting for him to dismiss her, Clara left the way she'd come, the burner phone in her hand.

Mantel had two officers in his pocket now, and he felt this one would be of more use than the first. DI Clara Goodwin was now a bent copper. The only way he liked them.

CHAPTER THIRTY

Clara

Mum was waiting for me anxiously when I got home from my meeting with Mantel. I had been gone longer than I thought so I smiled to reassure her I was fine. Kicking off my shoes and dropping my bag beside them, I followed her into the kitchen. She noticed I was walking a little slower than usual.

'Love, you okay?'

'Yeah, just tired.'

'How did it go?'

'If I help him, he will give us twenty-five thousand.'

'Twenty-five! Jesus, what does he want you to do?'

'Just find someone for him.'

'And then what?'

'That's it, just a name,' I said, leaning against the kitchen counter, arms crossed, my head low. Mum poured the water, added milk, wrung the bag and then handed me my mug.

'Have you heard from George?' I asked.

'Yes, everything was fine. I told him you were asleep. Want me to message him again?'

'No, I'll message him later, make it look like I've slept.' I yawned.

'When did you last sleep?'

'It's been a while.'

'You need to rest.'

'How can I?' I asked.

'I don't know.'

Mum and I drank our teas and fell into a weary silence.

'Clara, I'm worried about this. I mean, twenty-five is a lot for just one name? Aren't you worried there will be some strings attached?'

'Yes,' I answered honestly. 'But, it's a risk I have to take.'

'Yeah. It is,' she agreed and I smiled. I was so glad to have her in my corner.

'Mum, when I go back to the hospital, would you mind if I took your car?'

'No, of course not. Do you want me to come?'

'No, stay here, get some sleep.'

Despite wanting to go back to Tabatha's side straight away, Mum told me I couldn't leave until I rested, as I would be no good to her if I was sick, or crashed the car due to tiredness. So reluctantly, I took myself to bed and drifted off. Mum was asleep in an armchair when I woke, so I took her car keys and left the flat. As I made my way along the quiet roads, I knew that I had to make another video, to put my face out there again, to try and go viral once more, to speak to more papers, and radio stations. If I got the money promised from Mantel, if I found him that name, we would be only seventy-five thousand from our target. We might actually do it.

CHAPTER THIRTY-ONE

George

I couldn't quite articulate my gratitude towards the staff on the night shift. Despite being a key worker myself, struggling through the past few years without a break or much thanks, I knew the NHS staff couldn't have done more.

Through the night and into the early morning, every time someone came in to check Tabatha's vitals, they offered tea, asked if I was warm enough, reassured me she was okay, and I should get some sleep. But of course, I couldn't sleep. I wanted to be there for her when she woke up. I owed her that, and so much more. So despite the hours of sitting in an uncomfortable chair, despite how tired I was feeling, how the beeps and sounds of the hospital were strangely hypnotic, I forced myself to stay awake, keeping my attention on my little girl. I was just glad that I could do my bit and that Clara was getting some much-needed rest. She'd done so much lately, especially with driving the fundraising efforts. I always knew she was a strong woman, it was part of the reason I loved her, but she was even tougher than I could have imagined, a hero to our family. She was forward-thinking, decisive, brave. I just wished I could tell her as much. I wanted to, but I couldn't, and I didn't know why.

Clutching my fourth or fifth cup of coffee, I watched the sun rise. The day looked like it would be warm, the kind of day you packed up and went to the seaside or found a country park to explore. I had no doubt hundreds of families would be doing exactly that. I wondered if they understood how lucky they were. I was so wrapped up in my thoughts, lost in something other than the life we were living that I didn't hear someone approaching until I was gently tapped on the shoulder. It made me jump. I turned to see Clara smiling.

'You're back?' I said.

'Yeah, I didn't want to be away for too long.'

'How did you get here?'

'I borrowed Mum's car.'

'And you've slept?'

'I have, but as soon as I woke, I wanted to be here.' Clara said, placing a kiss on Tabs' forehead before sitting on the other side of the bed to me. 'How is she?'

'She's good,' I replied. 'Calm.' I noticed that something was off, that as Clara sat, she did so with a slight grimace. 'Are you all right?'

'Cramp,' she said. Lack of sleep would do that, but she seemed on edge, too.

'Has she been asleep this whole time?' she asked me.

'Yep, they said to expect as much.'

'Have you slept?'

'Nope. How could I?' I replied. Before I could say any more my phone started ringing, although I was too slow to answer before it stopped.

Seconds later, a message pinged though. It was from Mike, and as I read, I knew it was bad.

'Shit.'

'What is it?' Clara asked.

'There's been a third Mantel robbery.'

'What?'

'Three robberies in as many days.'

'God.'

'Yep, and it gets worse, this time someone was hurt.'

CHAPTER THIRTY-TWO

Clara

George asked if he could step outside quickly and ring Mike. I told him he should, it was important to get in the loop. I waited by the window to see him walk outside the hospital into the warm morning air. As soon as he did, I pulled out the burner phone and turned it on. Within seconds, a text arrived.

Ring me

Stepping away from the window, in case George looked up, I dialled the number linked to the text and waited. Three rings and he picked up.

'I assume you know?'

'I've just found out from George.'

'Where are you?'

'At the hospital with my daughter. George mentioned someone was hurt?'

'Yes.'

'How bad?'

'Why does that matter?'

'All the details you have will help with the profiling I'm working on.'

'Shoulder is fucked, concussion, he'll live. I need this to stop.'

'And I want paying, so this is what I want you to do,' I said.

'I'm listening.'

'I want you to gather all of the staff currently on your payroll. Call a meeting. And I want to be able to watch without anyone knowing I'm there.'

'Why?'

'I want to see how they react to you calling them all in. If it's someone on the inside, this will catch them off guard.'

'I employ a lot of people, I can't close my businesses either, it will look suspicious.'

'The meeting isn't for you regular employees, Henry. I'm not interested in your nail technicians or mechanics. The meeting is only for those who know your other streams of income.'

'I see. I'll arrange it.'

'My daughter should be discharged at some point this morning. When she is and I have her back home, I'll message. I'm not leaving her while she's in hospital, that would look suspicious.'

'I understand.'

'If I find your thief, and you set me up . . .'

'I'm a man of my word, DI Goodwin. If you help me find this person, you will be rewarded.'

I hung up. I reckoned I could trust Mantel on this, but that still didn't make me feel any less uncomfortable about what I was doing to raise money to get Tabatha to America.

Putting the burner away again, I leaned against the cool glass and took a deep breath. I was working for a criminal, possibly a murderer. What had I become?

203

CHAPTER THIRTY-THREE

Clara

Happy with how she was doing, the doctors discharged Tabatha and we were back home by mid-afternoon. It was just me and her in Mum's car as George took ours and went straight to work. I was glad of it, I needed time to work, too. He was trying to catch Mantel, and I was trying to help Mantel. The irony wasn't lost on me.

As I arrived home, Tabatha was still asleep in her car seat, so I went to the flat via the outside door rather than parading her though the shop. I messaged Mum so she knew we were back and she said she'd pop up later when we were settled.

Once we got upstairs, with the door firmly closed, I lay Tabatha in her own cot, changed into fresh clothes to remove the smell of the hospital, and then messaged Mantel so he could call the staff meeting and put the plan into action. Mum agreed to sit with Tabs from half-past five, so I could be wherever he wanted me to be by six. If George came home, she would say I'd got upset and gone for a long walk to clear my head. She would lie for me – again – all for the greater good of raising that money for Tabatha.

Mantel texted me the location and I turned the phone back off, burying it in the bottom of my bag. When Mum joined us, I had a chilli bubbling on the kitchen stove. She'd finish cooking it, and we would eat together when I got home.

'Clara, the reason you've asked me to come and stay with Tabs, are you doing something for him, for Mantel?'

'Yes. But I won't be back late.'

'Right, right.'

'I have to leave my phone here, but I'm going to give you a number. Mum, you cannot ring this phone ever, unless it's an emergency with Tabatha.'

'Clara, I really don't like this, the sneaking around, the lying to George. Are you sure you should be doing this?'

'It's twenty-five grand, Mum. Now please, promise me, don't ring that number unless—'

'It's an emergency. Unless I need you back urgently, I'll not call. Why can't you just take your own phone?'

'Because I have Find My Friends on. George might look and I don't want to be traced to this meeting with Mantel.'

Before Mum could say any more, I took her mobile, punched in the number and called it. The burner vibrated in my bag.

'It's the last call, don't save the number.'

Handing Mum her phone back, I went back into my daughter's room and kissed her on the head, whispering that I loved her before making my way towards the door. As I put on my shoes I looked back at Mum who was standing nervously in the kitchen doorway.

'Whatever it takes, right? That's what you said,' I reminded her.

'Yes, Clara, I did. Just . . . be careful.'

'I will, I promise,' I reassured her, hoping I sounded more convincing than I felt.

CHAPTER THIRTY-FOUR

George

'Who is the man who has been hurt?' I asked Mercer after she filled me in on the latest crime.

'Baz Wright. He's on Mantel's payroll, but as far as we can see, he's clean. He's a mechanic at his garage.'

'A mechanic? What was he doing at a beauty salon?'

'He says Mantel paid him to look after the place, he needed the extra money.'

'Has he always done that?'

'No, only since the Bean Hut was broken into.'

'So Mantel was worried the salon would be targeted.'

'It seems so,' Mercer said.

'Ma'am, I'm going to head down there now. I want to get a look at it.'

'Of course. Mike is there already. George, I just wanted to say I saw, we have all seen your video.'

'Yes,' I replied, unsure of how else to reply.

'We are having a whip-round here, it won't be much, but—'

'Thank you, Ma'am.'

'Are you sure you should be here right now? You look tired.'

'I am tired,' I said honestly. 'But I'm all right. Work is a good distraction. Tabatha is comfortable, Clara is with her. We decided that we need to keep pushing on, as a family, because if we stop, if we give up then . . .' I trailed off.

'I understand, but George, if it becomes too much, you need to tell me.'

'I will. Thank you.'

Leaving Mercer's office I made my way towards the car park, but as I walked through the station, I couldn't help but wonder who Mantel's inside man was. Someone had to be. I scrutinised everyone I passed, glancing at their computer monitors where I could, listening to their conversations when I was in earshot, assessing whether they seemed the type to be working for him. But everyone was acting normally, working as you'd expect. I began to wonder if I had got it wrong about the insider. But I wasn't sure who else would have been able to tip off Hunter the day of the raid.

When I arrived at the salon, Mike was outside talking to a uniformed officer. He waved my way and pulling up as close as I could, I sighed and heaved myself out of the car. My legs felt heavy and my energy depleted after the sleepless night at the hospital.

'George? Wasn't expecting you in today. Have you even slept?'

'No, mate. But I'm good.'

'And Tabatha?'

'She's home with Clara, discharged a little while ago. We were lucky.'

'Thank God. Shouldn't you be at home?'

'No, there's nothing more we can do at the moment. I'd rather be here where I can be of some use.'

'Is Mercer all right with that?'

'She is for now.'

Mike nodded before leading us under the police tape outside the salon. The front window had been knocked out, and glass was scattered everywhere.

'Think this is the same person as the coffee shop and nightclub?' I asked.

'Without a doubt,' Mike said, looking inside the salon from the street. 'The takeaway next door had footage, we've seen it and looks like the same guy to me. But you know something?'

'What?' I asked.

'Mantel was here too, he left only twenty odd minutes before the break-in.'

'Are you sure?'

'A hundred per cent. It was him. He arrived at just after 2.45, left just after 3.15.'

'And the time of the break-in?'

'3.27.'

'Why was Mantel here in the middle of the night?'

'You're guess is as good as mine.'

'And it can't be a coincidence right? That the salon is targeted just after Mantel leaves?'

Mike shrugged. 'Maybe Mantel is being followed?'

'Yeah. I think so too. And the thief's MO is changing,' I added, looking at the damage.

'Yeah, front window smashed in, man hurt.'

'How is he, the victim?' I asked.

'Broken shoulder, a sore head. Nothing serious.'

I nodded. 'Let me guess, nothing has been taken?'

'We'll know soon enough; the manager is inside right now,' Mike said.

'The manager?'

'Kimberly Watts. Previously Mantel.'

'Why is she only checking now? She must have known hours ago.'

'She was at a spa retreat, was quite pissed off to be having to come home.'

No sooner had her name been mentioned, Kimberly bustled out of the salon looking very disgruntled. She looked at Mike, not registering me at all. Ms Watts had a glamour about her which exuded wealth, an arrogance born of knowing she led a lifestyle most could only dream off. I didn't like her.

'Nothing has been taken,' she said, her tone annoyed rather than concerned.

'Are you sure nothing is missing, Ms Watts?' Mike asked.

'Not a bloody thing.'

'Ms Watts, why would someone break into your shop and steal nothing?' Mike asked.

'I don't bloody know. It's a salon, we don't keep cash around. Most of our clients pay by card. Besides, you work it out, you're the police officer, not me.'

'Excuse me, Ms Watts?'

'Yes?'

'I'm DS Goodwin. Ms Watts, are you still close to your ex-husband?'

'What's that got to do with anything?'

'Does he still have a stake in this business?'

'Yeah, not that it is anything to do with you.'

'Humour me. How would you say that the two of you get on?'

She sighed as if the mere effort of talking to me was beyond her. 'We get on fine. Just on a professional basis now. I run this place, staffing, customers, all that. He oversees stock and the accounts.'

'I see. So does he visit you often? Here, I mean?'

'Once a fortnight. Sometimes he comes in late at night to do the books.'

'Would it be unusual for him to come in the early hours of the morning?'

'For anyone else, yes. Henry, no. That man never sleeps. What's this got to do with the break-in?'

'Oh, it's probably nothing, thank you.'

I gave Mike a look as Ms Watts started to ask if Mantel was up to no good. He deflected her question by asking if she could take him around the salon to assess any damage that may have been caused. She went in first, and Mike hung back.

'Got to be connected, right?'

'Yep. Mike, can you find a list of personnel? I want to know the name of everyone who works for Mantel.'

'Sure, why?'

'I think whoever is doing this, whoever Mantel owes, they're either seriously smart, or, more likely, they know exactly where to look for whatever it is that's been taken.'

'You think they work for Mantel?'

'Yes. But, they are also working for whoever Mantel owes. We need to find that go-between.'

'Gotcha. Leave it with me. I'll stay here, see if Ms Watts has a database she'll grant us access to.'

'Thanks. We know that it has to be someone close to Mantel, all we gotta do is find out who it is.'

'I worry more people might get hurt in the meantime.'

'Me too.'

'Do you still think he has someone in his pocket from the force?' Mike asked.

'Yeah, I do,' I said. 'So keep the fact we are trying to find this link quiet for now.'

Leaving Mike to carry on digging, I headed back to the office, fighting the overwhelming sense of exhaustion and trying to focus on the job I needed to do. As I drove, I recapped the timeline of this ever-evolving case, starting with the raid. Hunter was sloppy, a lot of drugs and cash was seized, but he'd been tipped off somehow. He ended up dead for it. Prime suspect was Henry Mantel, yet we couldn't prove it, then Mantel's places were targeted by a series of break-ins to recoup what was owed. The case had three strands to it. The raid, Hunter's murder, and now the thief. There was a link from Mantel to Hunter, but I now needed to find someone who linked them all. Only then would we have grounds to bring Henry Mantel in for questioning. We knew how dangerous he was; Reece Hunter had found that out the hard way, Connor was in hiding and I knew that Mantel could kill again, would kill again, if he found out who was robbing him.

By the time I was back at the office, Mike had messaged with the list of employees from the salon. There were eight in all, and one name leapt out. Billy Garrett. I didn't know who he was, but it looked familiar. I messaged back asking Mike to find out how he was involved with the salon. A few minutes later, he replied. Ms Watts had confirmed Garrett oversaw installing security, as well as maintaining it. He was paid on a retainer, by Henry Mantel. I looked through the coffee shop and nightclub records, and discovered that Garrett was connected with the other two sites as well.

'Yes!' I said quietly so no one in the office heard, before getting up and making a beeline for Mercer's office. Closing the door behind me, I told her what we had just found. She didn't need any convincing to authorise us paying Garrett a visit and congratulated me on finding a name that plausibly linked all three robberies. Back at my desk, I sent two messages. The first was to Mike, telling him to get back as soon as he could so we could make a move on Garrett, and the second was to my wife, telling her we had a breakthrough on the case. She didn't reply. She was likely napping. Or with Tabs. For a moment, I worried about my daughter, but if something had happened, Clara would have let me know immediately. I had to focus on getting to Garrett and not letting this new lead slip through my fingers.

My phone pinged again and I opened another message from Mike telling me to check my emails. Attached was a shot from the takeaway's CCTV camera. It showed our man stood with a hammer mid-air moments before he smashed the salon window. I zoomed in and the image became pixilated. I couldn't make out much, and most of his face was dark as he was wearing a mask of some kind. However, it was definitely the same guy I had seen in the grainy CCTV from the café. And now I had a name.

I was quietly confident I was looking at an image of Billy Garrett.

Garrett was once Mantel's man. Now he had turned and was working for someone else. It told me he was an opportunist, and given a little pressure and a chance to avoid serious jail time, I was sure he would turn again – but this time for us and he'd help me put Mantel away for good.

CHAPTER THIRTY-FIVE

Clara

I parked the car half a mile from the location sent by Mantel and decided to walk the rest of the way to be on the safe side. The easiest route would be to head back to the main road, and then turn left onto the slip that lead down to the builder's yard and scrap metal facility, but I couldn't risk being seen, so I jumped over a small drainage dyke beside the layby and walked along the edge of the farmer's field, masked by the trees. Thankfully, those trees surrounded the entire field, so I was able to draw close to the warehouse I had been instructed to arrive at without anyone being able to spot me.

Squatting beside a wide alder, I watched men drifting into the warehouse via the large dock door at the front. Inside there were stacks of old metal, remains of ruined cars, corrugated iron. A scrap heap. I could see Mantel there talking to another man, one I didn't recognise. He stood a good four inches taller than Mantel and was several stone heavier – a big man, no doubt capitalising on his genetics for financial gain. Whoever he was, he was clearly someone

Mantel trusted. I had no doubt I was looking at the two men responsible for the death of Reece Hunter, and one of them was now my employer.

I took out the burner and sent a text.

I'm outside.

I saw Mantel take his phone out of his pocket, read my message, and begin to type.

Approach the building from the north. There is a door, it will be unlocked. After the meeting, come to me.

Keeping low, I made sure I was far enough away that when I broke cover, the huge building would hide me from the gathering men at the front. Taking a few deep breaths, forcing more oxygen to work its way into my underused muscles, I sprinted away from the trees towards the side entrance. It was only perhaps eighty metres at most, and yet I felt exposed for an eternity. When I reached the building, I lowered myself to the ground and pressed my back against the warm metal, listening. I could hear Mantel talking somewhere close by, but more important than that was what I couldn't hear. There were no footsteps, or voices coming my way. Satisfied I'd not been seen, I moved towards the door Mantel had mentioned. It was open a crack and gently I pulled it wide enough to slip inside. Mantel's voice boomed as he spoke to his staff about security and how it needed to tighten up, that it wasn't just him being attacked by those responsible, but all of them. Until that moment, I never understood how people like Henry Mantel could rise up and do so well, but listening to him, I now knew. The man was a monster, there was no doubt, but he was also a charismatic leader, rallying his troops.

I made my way towards the sound of voices murmuring in

agreement with their boss's words about protecting the family they were, and hid behind a huge shelving unit stacked high with pieces of refrigerators, car panels and copper pipes. From my vantage point, I could see the crowd, but I was confident that if I kept my movements to a minimum, I would remain unseen. Besides, all eyes were looking at Mantel.

There were over thirty people in the group, men and women who were under Mantel's employment. I watched for anything that might alert me to any discomfort, a rub of an eye, the covering of a mouth by way of scratching a top lip, shifting of feet, wiping of palms, but it was harder than I thought it would be. All of them looked uncomfortable, afraid. At the back of the group, I recognised a face I had never expected to see here. PC Lee Sharman.

I was stunned, but more than that, I was torn about what I should do. George suspected Mantel had an inside man, but telling him who would mean betraying my own involvement. And I couldn't do anything to jeopardise the money Mantel had pledged.

I felt a sudden urge to leave, to tell Mantel I had made a mistake, that I couldn't do this. I wasn't a criminal, I wasn't a bent copper, I was just a mum who wanted to help her daughter. I wasn't built for any of this. I wanted to go home. But I also knew Mantel would not let me simply stop. I was his now, and I would have to see it through or face the consequences. And my daughter, she needed me to be brave, to finish what I'd started and get her on the plane to Philadelphia. She needed me to dig deep, despite every fibre of my being telling me to run away.

As I watched the meeting, I felt my hands begin to tingle

and my chest tighten. My breathing became sharp and I felt as though I wasn't getting enough air into my body. The anxiety came from nowhere, fast and aggressive, and I had to look away for a moment, pleading with myself to stay calm. If I had a panic attack now, someone would find me and Mantel would not be pleased.

'Get a fucking grip, Clara,' I whispered to myself, and it seemed to do the trick, or at least just enough for me to be able to look and listen to the meeting once more.

Focused on the group again. Everyone listening knew their boss wasn't a happy man. They feared him, so I had to rule out fear as a tell. I had to rule out discomfort, too, so instead I looked for someone who had a smugness about them, a slight smirk, a curl of the lip. Someone who was afraid, but still believed they were smarter than the man before them. Sliding the burner out of my pocket, and with shaking hands, I texted his number, not caring about the typo.

Talk aboht the robberies

Mantel paused and looked at the phone. He didn't explain to anyone what he had just read, he didn't need to. No one dared ask.

'Three of my businesses have been hit, three of the businesses we have all worked hard to build with our bare hands. Three of our homes, and in total, just over thirty thousand pounds of our hard-earned money has been taken.'

Mantel continued to talk about how the robberies happened, and he mentioned someone called Baz, who had been lucky. I assumed Baz was the man injured only hours before. As he spoke, I continued to watch the men, my phone ready to take pictures of anyone who stood out. And then two

217

men did stand out. I couldn't put my finger on it at first, but as I looked more closely, I soon realised why they drew my attention. While everyone else was shifting, wiping sweaty palms – PC Lee Sharman included – they stood still, one with his hands in his pockets, the other arms crossed. Both were a similar height, similar build. They were either not afraid of Mantel, which I didn't believe was possible, or maybe they knew something he didn't. I snapped two photos, and having seen enough, I sat quietly and waited for the meeting to end.

As people began to leave, I dared to look up and as I did so, I was sure one of the men I had photographed saw me. But he didn't pause, didn't say anything, so I decided he must not have. Still, not wanting to take any risks, I didn't look again until I heard Mantel speak a few minutes later.

'They are all gone.'

Standing up and moving away from my hiding place, I looked round to see that not quite everyone had left. Beside him stood a bear of a man.

'This is Tony.'

'Hello, Tony,' I replied, hoping my voice didn't show how nervous I was feeling to be in such an isolated place with these two men.

'Tony and I go way back. Whatever you have to say, he can hear.'

I nodded and pulled out the phone. 'I can't be sure, not without looking into it more, but on first glance, two men stood out.'

'Why?'

'They seemed too composed.'

'Composed?'

'Like they knew something the others didn't. Again, it's just what my first glance said. To be sure, I'll need a little time.'

'I didn't see nothing,' Tony spat, crossing his arms and looking at me suspiciously.

'Tony,' Mantel warned.

'And I don't trust a fucking word that comes out of your pig mouth,' he continued, looking like he wanted to hurt me.

'Tony, DI Goodwin isn't a police officer right now.'

'No? Then what is she?'

'Someone who works for me.'

The sound of those words felt hot in my head. Like a fire poker, glowing and searing to the touch. But it was true. I was exactly that. Someone who worked for Henry Mantel. Someone who was now in his pocket. And again, the only thing that stopped me running away in that moment was my daughter.

'So, Mrs Goodwin, who were the two that caught your eye?'

I unlocked the phone and went to the photo album. There were only two pictures in there. I handed Mantel the phone and he looked at them carefully. I tried to read his expression, the micro movements that told the story of what he was thinking. But he was unreadable. That frightened me.

'Again, I'm not a hundred per cent. I need some time to dig.'

'How long?' he asked, the charm in his voice dead.

'Two days.'

Mantel agreed and handed the phone back.

'When you are sure, you ring me.'

'Who are they?'

'Mitch Tower and Billy Garrett.'

I repeated their names so I didn't forget and turned to leave, catching Tony's eye as I did. Whereas I couldn't read Mantel, Tony's distrust was written all over his face.

Back in the car, driving away as fast as I safely could, I struggled to breathe properly, wondering again what I had got myself into.

I wanted to spend the rest of the evening hiding, composing and centre myself, to try and manage the guilt and pressure I was now under. But I knew this was impossible and I needed to appear together. To eat with Mum as planned, as though it was just another day in our tricky lives and nothing more. As I arrived home and parked Mum's car, I saw George was back from work.

CHAPTER THIRTY-SIX

Clara

'Hiya,' I called as I walked into the flat.

'Clara?' George said, coming out of the living room at the end of the corridor.

'Is Tabs okay?' I asked.

'She's fine. Where have you been?'

'I went for a walk, I needed some air. Cuppa?'

Before George could answer, I nipped into the kitchen and stood beside Mum who was washing up at the sink.

'I told him he'd just missed you when he got in, so you've been out for half an hour on your walk,' she said quietly, but I could see she wasn't happy having to lie.

'Thanks, Mum.'

George walked into the kitchen. Mum focussed back on the washing-up bowl, and I faffed with mugs, teabags, and milk, hoping George didn't notice the slight shake in my hand.

'Everything all right?' he asked, clearly seeing that something wasn't.

'Fine,' Mum and I said together, too quickly.

'What's going on?'

'Nothing,' Mum said. She sounded angry, and as she had finished washing up, she excused herself from the kitchen.

'Clara?'

'Hang on.'

Following Mum, I saw her putting on her shoes by the internal door that led down into the shop.

'Mum?'

She didn't say anything but disappeared down the steps. Behind me, George saw her leave and looked stunned.

'Clara. What's going on?'

'Just . . .' I shouted, before catching myself. 'Just give me a minute, please?'

'Yes, of course,' he replied, shocked.

Going downstairs, I walked through the stock room and into the main shop. Mum was by the till, writing something down. Busying herself. I slowed my approach.

'Mum?'

She ignored me and continued to write. She was pressing down so hard on the paper I was sure she was going to tear through it and ruin the countertop.

'Mum, I know you don't like lying.'

'You're right, I don't but it's not that.'

'What is it then?'

Mum paused her scribbling on the paper and looked at me, suddenly serious.

'What, Mum?

'I heard a rumour about Mantel and the golf course. Is that true?'

'Yeah. I think it is.'

Her mouth fell open and she stared at me in such a way I knew I was in trouble.

'I didn't know it was this heavy, Clara. I can deal with him being a criminal, I can. It's wrong, but you're doing it for the right reasons. But if he's a killer, you have crossed a line that you shouldn't have. Not only does it mean he's the worst kind of criminal, but it also proves he is too dangerous to be around.' Her voice was rising, and I begged her to quieten down. George was just above us, no doubt trying to listen.

'Mum, we need money to save Tabatha, we need more than we are making at the moment. You said to me whatever it took.'

'But I meant, take a shitty job, beg strangers. Jesus, even stealing that money from Tesco is better than working for a murderer. He wants a name from you. Have you thought what he might do with it?'

'Mum, do you know how much money he has?'

'Blood money.'

'Maybe, but are we above that? You didn't seem to mind when it was Tesco's money.'

'Not the same.'

'Yes, it is. Mantel has a brand-new Range Rover; he lives on Sycamore Road in a million-pound house. Should we care about where his money is coming from? Or should we just be glad it could help to save Tabatha?'

Mum didn't reply.

'He is paying us twenty-five grand, and I know the risks, but it's worth it.'

'Be careful, Clara, there will be a price to pay for being involved with someone like him,' she warned.

'I know, but I also know what we can gain.'

Mum knew it too. We could gain a well child, a cancer-free baby. We could gain a future that was getting harder and harder to see. We could make sure her fifth birthday, the one I fought to see, came true.

'I don't like any of this, Clara,' she said.

'Nor do I.'

'And once this job is done, you're out? Yes?'

'Yes, Mum, I promise,' I said, though I didn't believe Mantel would let me go just like that. 'What do we tell George?'

'Tell him I'm just upset about everything with Tabatha.'

'Not sure he'll buy that.'

'He has to, we can't tell him the truth, can we? Go up, tell him everything is fine. I'll be up soon.'

'Don't be angry with me, Mum.'

'I'm not angry, I'm afraid.'

She looked down, continuing to write whatever it was she was writing, only this time the anger in her scratches was gone. I wanted to tell her I loved her and I hated that I was making her worry for me. We all had enough to worry about right now. But I didn't. I couldn't bring myself to. Tabatha being well was the focus, and once she was well, once she was in America receiving treatment, everything else would heal.

Leaving Mum to it, I walked back up to the flat. George was sat in the living room, perched on the edge of the sofa, Tabatha asleep beside him.

'What was that about?' he asked as I came in and sat down on the chair opposite.

'Mum's just having a moment, it's tough for all of us.'

'And you?'

'What about me?'

'Are you okay?'

'That's a stupid question,' I said scoffing. I regretted it immediately. 'Sorry.'

He waved it off. 'Jo told me you went for a walk?'

'I needed to clear my head.'

'But you took her car?'

Shit.

'Yeah, I wanted to get out of the town, feel the fresh air. Anyway, want that tea?'

'Sure.'

Making my escape, I went back to the kitchen and reboiled the kettle. To distract myself from having to lie to George, I checked the FundMyCause page. The total was climbing and it was now over £147,000. It had shot up very quickly. I clicked on the details of the donors and saw that there had been several deposits, totalling over twenty-four grand, all of which had come in a short space of time from Bernadette Clooney, Brian Cookson and Beatrice Coleman, all names with the initials BC. I was confused, Mantel had paid me for a job I hadn't yet finished. It didn't seem his way to trust anyone with an advance, but then I realised, it wasn't an advance at all.

'Oh shit.'

Mantel had closed the deal, which meant in his mind, I had done my job. But I hadn't. I had only given him my initial thoughts on two men who looked suspicious. Nothing more. That money being there told me that in his mind, my suspicions were signposting their guilt.

Shit, what had I done? What had I done?

Walking quickly to the bathroom, I locked the door and

pulled out the burner phone, turning it on and waiting for it to come to life.

'Hurry, up, come on . . .'

'Clara?' George said from outside.

'I'm on the loo. Make the tea, I'll be back.'

I didn't hear George walk away and I held my breath. After a beat, I saw his shadow disappear through the gap under the bathroom door.

Eventually the phone fired up and going to the messages, I tapped the only thread in there and hoping to God it wasn't too late, began to type. As I did so, Reece Hunter came to mind and I had to wonder whether I had just indirectly signed a death warrant on two men.

CHAPTER THIRTY-SEVEN

Henry Mantel

As the old British Racing Green Land Rover drove along the lane towards him, Mantel stepped through the warehouse towards it. He'd barely moved since his meeting took place, just stood there mulling over how he could have been so blind. He didn't trust coppers as far as he could throw them, and he wondered if Clara Goodwin was leading him into a trap of some kind. Perhaps she was working with her husband to bring him down. But he had approached her, and she had taken money from him. Dirty money. No, he didn't trust coppers, but he did trust a mother who would do anything to save her baby. He trusted that because it was a primal need; protecting a loved one was something that resonated with most people, even someone like him.

Also, he reasoned that despite her gaining twenty-five grand by highlighting Garrett and Tower, she knew what would happen to those who crossed him. She wouldn't just say anyone's name to get her money. She was the type who wouldn't be able to live with someone's else's blood on her hands.

Clara Goodwin was telling him the truth.

It was Tower or Garrett, or both.

After Goodwin left, he had told Tony to find both men and bring them to him. But as the Land Rover stopped in front of him and the door opened, only Mitch Tower got out. He gingerly walked over to Mantel, his hands in his pockets. His fear was palpable.

'Henry,' he said, giving a tight nod once he was inside the warehouse and close enough for Mantel to see the sweat breaking on his brow. Tower turned to look behind him. Tony stood a little way back, blocking the exit. Tony smiled at Tower, but it didn't reach his eyes.

Mantel looked past Tower and beckoned Tony with a nod of his head. Tony brushed against Tower as he passed then turned away from him. Both he and Mantel knew full well Tower wouldn't dare move.

'Where's Garrett?' Mantel asked.

'Not at home. But he was before I got there. I asked his neighbour. Seems like he came back after the meeting and then left again quickly. The guy said he was in a panic. That's why they noticed.'

'I see,' Mantel said as his phone pinged with an incoming message from Clara Goodwin.

'Want to find out from Mitch where he is? I better take this.'

'Leave it with me.'

Mantel walked away, further into the warehouse, away from a terrified Mitch Tower, and looked at his phone.

I have only said I suspect they could be connected. I need more time to investigate

She was bright. He had transferred the funds, as promised,

and she understood exactly what that meant. She had seen that in his mind, they had concluded their business agreement.

There's no smoke without fire. Thank you for your services, we'll take it from here

Three dots immediately pulsated on his screen, and he waited.

You said you would give me two days. I want to be thorough

We both know time is a precious commodity. You've done your job; unless you were lying

No, of course not. They stood out in the meeting.

Again, no smoke without fire. We're done here

Thee more dots appeared, but Mantel locked his phone and put it away. Their conversation was over.

Walking back towards Tony and Mitch, he saw Tower on the floor, struggling to get to his hands and knees just as a ferocious kick from Tony landed against his ribs.

'Tony,' Mantel said calmly, stopping him mid swing from delivering another vicious blow. Panting, Tony wiped his face where some of Tower's blood had splattered on it, then walked over to his boss, trying to catch his breath.

'Says he doesn't know anything.'

'And do you believe him?'

'He's taken quite a kicking boss.'

Mantel approached the coughing and begging mess that was Tower and stood over him.

'Henry, please,' he spluttered.

'I'm a forgiving man, Mitch. I just want to know who you are working for.'

'You. I work for you.'

'And who Garrett is working for?'

'I don't know anything, I swear. Please, Henry.'

Mantel lowered himself to the floor, his left knee cracking, and placed his hands on Mitch Tower's cheeks.

'Mitch, talk to me. I can't help you if you don't.'

'Please, Henry. I swear, I don't know . . .'

His words were cut short as Mantel slid his left thumb into his eye and pressed hard. Pain robbed Tower of his ability to speak, and his words morphed into a scream. He thrashed and clawed at Mantel, who simply pressed harder until Tower didn't thrash or claw any more.

Kneeling back, Mantel wiped his thumb on Tower's limp body before getting to his feet.

'Boss?' Tony said uncertainly. Even he was shocked by what he had just seen.

'Clean up this mess, then find Garrett. Find him and kill him.'

'And then?'

'Leave their bodies to be found. We need to send a message.'

FundMyCause™   Menu   Log In   Sign Up   Search 🔍

Help for Tabatha

We are raising money to send our daughter, Tabatha, to the US for treatment to help her overcome neuroblastoma.

68%

£156, 125
raised of £230,000 target

Donate Now

---

5 days remaining to reach required target

 Supporters

Following the news of Tabatha's scare, and us being accepted into the Floxiline programme, we have been stunned by the support shown. In just one day we have gone from 50 per cent of our target reached, to almost seventy. Thank you everyone.

We are so close, not only to our deadline, but now, our target too.

Only one week ago, we were heartbroken with news of our daughter taking a turn for the worse, now, we are beginning to believe we will hear that bell toll when she beats this disease.

Tabatha is continuing her treatment here, she is staying strong. And despite how frightening it is, how frightened we are, George and I are hopeful, because of the kindness of strangers. Because of people like you.

We need you to keep sharing, keep telling Tabatha's story. You are making such a difference her life.

You are helping us see her 5th Birthday.

Clara, George and Tabatha x

Supporter	Amount
Miss B Killorn.	£35
Justin Markson	£50
Issy Morris	£15
Kelly Sharpe	£50
Ms Henley	£20
Jamie Pallister	£20
Y. Hussain	£50
B. CLay	£500

CHAPTER THIRTY-EIGHT

Clara

Every time I closed my eyes and tried to go to sleep, I was haunted by the sight of Tabatha's limp body. The spark in her eyes fading. I was worried that if I did fall asleep, I could be too late if Tabatha had another turn. I'd been told it was a good job I'd checked on her when I did, but really it was just luck that I happened to at that moment. What if my luck had run out? I'd not sleep until my daughter was on a plane to the US, in the care of their doctors and receiving the life-saving treatment she needed. That had always been the goal. But now I realised that although we were making progress to reach our target, none of that would matter if Tabatha wasn't well enough to travel. I had to get my daughter on that plane whilst I still could. There might come a point when she would be too ill to fly. I couldn't help but fear that moment was quickly approaching.

Time was running out.

I needed one final and definitive push. But even though all I wanted to do was focus on the money, the world needed to carry on, I needed to carry on, especially now

I had done something terrible for a terrible man. No one, George included, would find out I was involved with Henry Mantel. So I got myself ready to go to the support group. As we usually met only once a week, something had to have happened for Gary to message saying an extra session was on. I'd still not heard from Sadie and I didn't know what that meant, so as I moved around the flat getting ready to leave, I felt anxious.

I hoped the walk, the fresh air on the way to the meeting, might help both me and Tabatha. I hoped being around others might help, too, and I hoped I would learn that Sophie, and Sadie were okay.

Tabs and I were early and as we walked in, Gary was still getting chairs out ready for the session to begin.

'Hi Gary, we're early, is that all right?'

'Yes, of course. Hi Clara,' He said, but his usual smile was replaced with a more downbeat expression.

As I lifted Tabs from her buggy and took my place in the circle, others began to drift in. When everyone had arrived, Gary addressed the room.

'In the ten years I have run this group, there have been countless victories. Forty-nine times our bell has been rung by children who've come here. Forty-nine times cancer was beaten. We have all seen someone ring, haven't we?'

I hadn't, but others in the room had.

'And when it does, we hug them, celebrate with them, cry happy tears for them. But sadly sometimes that bell doesn't ring.' He paused, took a deep breath and my heart dropped. I knew what he was about to say.

'And our job is the same, when the family is ready. We are

there to wrap around them, hug them, hold them, just as we would if it went the other way.'

'Who?' asked James, one of the dads, his voice tight with anxiety.

'Sadie's little girl, Sophie,' Gary replied before lowering his head for a moment, trying to compose himself. Sophie had passed away, Sophie had lost her battle. I started to cry. Sadie was so confident they would beat it. Sophie had looked to be doing so well only a few weeks ago. It happened so fast. Sophie had the same form of cancer as my baby. Sophie was diagnosed a few months before my daughter was. Sophie was a similar age to Tabatha. But most frightening of all, Sophie had been responding, Sophie had been fighting the cancer in a way that Tabatha couldn't. And Sophie still died.

I tried to listen as Gary continued speaking but his words faded into the background. I hugged Tabatha tighter as her little chest rose and fell, she made her little coos and noises and movements in my arms. And then my baby looked at me in a way that was different, like she was desperate to tell me something and didn't know how. I knew I needed to move. Apologising to Gary, I stood up and got ready to leave. He said he understood and that when the worst happened to a family, the group met several times to ensure everyone felt supported, and that the next session was in a few days' time. I nodded, although I had no plans to return. The group used to be synonymous with hope, but that hope had died with Sadie's little girl.

There was only one thing to do. I'd have to go back to Mantel. If he was willing to pay me, I would help him avoid being arrested. I would protect him from the police.

When I got home, I went straight to see Mum in the shop. She was smiling at a customer, but as I walked over to her and she saw my face, she knew immediately that something was wrong.

'Clara, what is it? Is it Tabatha?'

'No, she's fine. Thank God.'

'Yes, thank God.'

'Mum, I've got to go and do something tonight. George is on a late, are you able to stay with Tabs?'

'Of course, what do you need to do?'

'There's one more thing I have to try.'

'I thought you were done with that man?'

'Not quite,' I said, not lifting my gaze from my sleeping daughter to meet hers. I didn't know for sure what was going on as Mantel wasn't returning my messages, but I knew that it was just a matter of time before I discovered either Garrett or Tower – or both – had ended up in a hospital, or worse. And it would be my fault entirely for telling Mantel I suspected they were behind the robberies. I wasn't thinking of the consequences properly when I agreed to help. I knew both the men I'd identified were bad men, but if anything happened to them, I would have to carry that forever. Then again, looking at my baby I wasn't sure I cared what burden I ended up shouldering. I would always carry the weight of thinking my baby had died, and I would carry the weight of whatever happened to those men. I would be Atlas, condemned to carry the entire world on my shoulders, but if Tabatha survived it would all be worth it.

'Clara?'

I looked up, having missed whatever question Mum had asked me.

'Sorry, I was miles away.'

'I asked, why do you need to see that man? He's paid the money, you've done your part.'

'We need more, Mum.'

'Then we go back online, we ask for kindness.'

'Yes, we need to do that, too. But I just don't think we'll be able to raise what we need that way in time.'

'Clara, please, please don't go.'

'I have to, Mum.'

She could see that I wasn't going to back down. 'When?'

'I don't know,' I said. I wanted to go there and then, but I could hear noise from above us, which meant George was home. I didn't want to see him, I wasn't strong enough to continue the lie. But I also knew I had to. The lie needed to live on so my daughter didn't end up just like Sophie.

'Clara . . . if, when you go back to that man, promise me you will be safe. Promise me you won't do anything stupid.'

'I promise,' I lied.

CHAPTER THIRTY-NINE

Clara

George took one look at me when I walked through the door and knew something was wrong.

'You're not all right, are you?

I shook my head.

'Is it Tabs?' He was clearly worried, looking at her with concern.

'Tabs is fine. It's Sophie.'

'Who?'

'My friend Sadie's baby.'

'Oh?' he said, wondering what was wrong – and then he understood. 'Oh, shit.' George looked down at our daughter again. 'Oh, God.'

I knew in that moment he was thinking exactly the same thing as I was, that it could so easily be Tabatha in her place. George enveloped me in a warm hug, relief that it was not our daughter uniting us.

For the afternoon, we moved quietly as one and as Tabatha rested, George and I sat close together on the sofa. Tabatha wasn't getting better, she was sleepy more often, she was losing weight, her hair was all gone and her eyes carried dark circles that weren't there a week or so before. She was losing this battle. She was losing, just like Sophie had lost.

'George, I feel like we're running out of time.'

'No, Clara. You've raised so much, you have done what I thought was impossible. What are we at? A hundred and sixty thousand? I didn't think you'd be able to surpass ten. We still have a few more days. We can do this.'

'I don't mean until the deadline.'

'What then?'

'I mean, I think Tabatha is running out of time. She has to be well enough to fly out there, and I can't shake the feeling that five days is too far away.'

'Clara, love, I'm sure it feels like that with everything that's happened. You've had a shock but—'

'No.' I cut him off. 'No, I mean I'm understandably shaken about Sophie and Sadie. But I can't explain it, I've just had this feeling that won't go away. That we need to move faster, we need to get her there quicker.'

'I know I wasn't very supportive of this idea when you first suggested it,' George started.

'Understatement,' I muttered.

'No, okay, I deserve that. I wasn't supportive because I was scared. You seemed so clear on what to do and I was floundering, lost, like a little boy. But I'm here now. And if you say we need to move faster, then that's what we do.'

'Really?' I asked.

'Yes, I trust you, Clara, I always have.'

George lifted my hand and gave it a kiss and I smiled at him before looking away and back to our sleeping daughter.

The guilt pressed harder on my shoulders. One day he would know I had lied, stolen, committed crimes, and that trust he had in me would be gone.

George was about speak again when his phone vibrated beside him. He reached down and picked it up, and his expression immediately changed.

'George?'

'You know I said we've been looking for a man who connects the dots in the Mantel case.'

'Yes?'

'We might have found him.'

'If you need to go, you should.'

'No, Clara, I should stay.'

'It's okay. Go catch him.'

'Are you sure?'

'Yes, you're due to be at work later anyway, if they have a lead, you should be there.' I said, sensing that a window to speak to Mantel was beginning to open.

'Thank you.'

George got up, and as he readied himself to leave, I stayed in the living room, listening as he spoke to Mike. Just before he hung up, he said a name. One I knew.

'Mike, send me the address for Garrett, I'm leaving home now.'

Shit, both George and Mantel were looking for Billy Garrett.

George left, and I watched him climb into the car and drive away. He was going for Garrett, but I didn't know why. Mantel wanted him because I had said he looked suspicious but George didn't know that, so he clearly wanted Garrett for something else. And if Mantel thought for a second I had spoken to George and tipped him off, everything would fall apart.

I needed to speak to him, I need to warn him my husband was coming.

Running back into the bedroom, I grabbed the burner phone and turned it on. I dialled his number and it rang six times before disconnecting.

'Shit.'

I tried again and again, but he didn't pick up, so I quickly tapped out a message.

Henry, I know you said we're done, but I'm in this now and I want to show I can do more, if you are willing to give more. George is also looking for Garrett, I don't know why, I've not spoken to him, but I wanted to give you the heads-up. George is heading to an address now.

I waited, desperately hoping he would see it. He eventually replied.

Received and yes, I have a use for this sort of information. And if you can keep your husband off my scent, I will reward you as I did before. We need to meet. Come to my garage in town in thirty minutes.

Understood

CHAPTER FORTY

George

Tracking down Garrett had been challenging. After meeting Mike, we went to the addresses linked to him. There were several in the area, friends, family members, but no one had seen him. Word had got around that the police were looking for him, and as this was all linked to Mantel, no one was willing to speak to anyone in a uniform, at least until Mike received a message that Billy Garrett's ex-girlfriend, Melanie Caldwell, was willing to talk. Her address was just out of town, and Mike and I drove to meet with her.

'Christ, it's muggy,' Mike said as we got out of my car.

'Rain's coming,' I replied yawning and looking at the darkening sky. Evening was drawing in, thick black clouds too.

'You're tired, mate, you sure you wanna be here?'

'I'm sure. Now let's find this prick.'

Knocking on the paint-stripped front door, we could hear a dog barking inside, and then Melanie's voice calling out.

'Shut up! Fuck's sake, dog. Hang on.'

Mike gave me a look as if to say, 'This will be interesting.'

And moments later, the door opened, and Melanie stood before us, a cigarette in her hand, her hair scraped back into a messy ponytail.

'What do you want?'

'I'm DS George Goodwin, this is DS—'

'Oh yeah, it's you. You got my message then?'

'We did.'

'You're looking for Billy, aren't you?' she said jumping in.

'We are. You mentioned you might be able to help?'

'I shouldn't, I mean, word gets round, you know? Apparently Henry's not happy.'

'Henry?' I asked.

'Yeah, Mantel. You know him. Everyone knows him.'

'Who told you this? That Mantel isn't happy?' I asked.

'Don't matter. So, you want him, yeah? What's he done?' she asked, taking a long drag on her cigarette.

'Nothing, we just want to have a friendly word.'

'Bullshit,' she said. 'Your type don't want friendly words with his type. I ain't stupid.'

'We wouldn't suggest you were.'

'But I'll tell you where he is.'

'Will you?'

'Yeah, one condition.'

'What is it?' I asked, looking at Mike.

'You make sure he knows it was me who told you.'

'Yeah?' Mike said. 'Any reason?'

'He's a little shit, that's why. Finds out I'm pregnant and fucks off with another slut.'

'I see,' I replied, fighting the urge to comment on how she'd said 'another slut', implying she was one, too. I flashed another look at Mike, who was deadpan and serious other than a glint in his eye which told me he'd noticed it as well.

'So, where is he?'

'You promise to make sure he knows I dobbed him in?'

'Of course,' Mike said, and I saw Melanie perk up at the very thought of helping us find him. She even showed us the exact house on Google Maps.

'Oh, Melanie, one more thing,' I said just before she closed the door.

'Yes?'

'Has anyone else been round to ask for Billy?'

She hesitated. 'No, no one.'

'Thanks for your time,' I said, turning and walking away. The door slammed shut. 'She's lying about that last bit,' I added quietly as we walked back to the car.

'Yeah, she is,' Mike echoed.

The location Melanie had given us was only a few miles outside town, a farmhouse near Tomthorn. As we headed over there, Mike following me in his car, the sun began to dip on the horizon as the evening drew in. On our arrival I kept one eye on the house, and the other on the land around it. We were in an unmarked police car, but if I was Garrett, I would run from anyone I didn't know. He was living on the edge, robbing his boss or helping someone else to do so. He surely knew how dangerous Mantel was, everyone did.

We got out of the car and approached the house, a weather-beaten old manor that could have looked incredible if it was cared for. The windows were stripped of paint from decades of exposure to the elements. The garden was weed-ridden and the roof had tiles missing, revealing dark gaps like an ageing boxer's grin. It wasn't until we drew closer that we saw the front door was open, the hinges broken at the top. Forced entry.

Inside the house was dark and lifeless.

'William Garrett, this is the police.'

I waited for a sign of movement but there was nothing, so I stepped over the threshold. Although it was a warm day, the pre-rain humidity off the scale, the entrance hall felt damp, like the walls were breathing a sickly-sweet vile stench.

'William Garrett?'

I moved along towards the end of the dark corridor.

'Come on, mate, let's keep looking,' Mike whispered.

We went through to a living room, sweeping through and checking the corners and dark spaces in case he jumped out and tried to attack us. But there was still no sign of life. The place was a mess, old food containers and empty bottles strewn around. When we got up the stairs, we noticed signs of struggle; there was a door that had been kicked or barged open. Entering the room, we saw a bed, the covers in a heap on the floor. I looked beyond, to the gap between the edge of the bed and the radiator, and instinctively took a step back. The bloody remains of a man lay in a heap. His dead eyes were wide open, staring back at me.

CHAPTER FORTY-ONE

George

'Mike, look,' I said, pointing to a pair of white Nike trainers, the left one with blood on the toe.

'Jesus.'

I stepped around the edge of the bed, moving closer to the corpse of Billy Garrett. There was no point looking for a pulse, no point administering CPR. The man was long gone. Mike recoiled when he saw him. He stepped backwards and as he did, he spotted another body, this time behind a chest of drawers. I looked at the second man. His left eye was missing. I didn't know who he was, or how he was connected.

'Fuck's sake!' I shouted.

'George, calm down.'

'I want Mantel now. I fucking want him in custody.'

'George.'

'He's fucking with us now. Enough is enough.'

I stormed out of the room and back downstairs. Mike followed and grabbed me as I stepped out into the warmth of the evening.

'Where are you going? We have to call it in.'

'You call it in. I can't fucking stand to be here.'

'George. Please try to calm down.'

'I don't want to fucking calm down, Mike. I'm done being calm, I'm done pretending this shit isn't getting to me now. I'm done being patient and hoping for the best. I'm done.' I stopped speaking, unsure whether I was just talking about Mantel, or Tabatha's illness, or both. 'Fuck this.'

'George.'

'I'm going home, Mike, to be with my little girl. I can't do this any more. She needs me. I need to be with my baby.'

I walked to the car and climbed in. Mike didn't follow, instead getting straight on the phone to call in the grim discovery. I drove off, pulled out of the lane then turned right, and as the heavens opened, I began to cry. Death was everywhere it seemed, and I was powerless to stop any of it. I wasn't crying for Garrett. I was crying because today, before I left the flat, I felt that something was different. That the news of Clara's friend's baby somehow confirmed the worst was happing to our own daughter.

'I just want my life back; I just want my fucking life back,' I shouted, driving hard into the storm. But even as I calmed, that same thought I'd had returned. I was losing my case, I was losing my daughter.

CHAPTER FORTY-TWO

Clara

It only took me ten minutes to get to the garage. I wanted to be early, earlier than Mantel; I felt it was important because I needed him more than he needed me now. Standing to the side of the building, I did my best to shelter from the pouring rain but it was pointless, I was soon soaked to the skin. The smell of wet, warm tarmac took me somewhere else, somewhere easier, a different time before all this – somewhere in my youth, with bicycles and friends and long summer days, and although I wanted to stay there and remember the innocent times, the ease of my childhood, I knew I couldn't. There was work to be done.

My thoughts shifted as the phone vibrated violently in my pocket and I struggled to pull it out. I looked at the caller ID. It was Mum's number. She knew only to ring in emergencies, so as I pressed to accept the call, I thought I was going to be sick.

'Mum?'

'Clara, sorry, I didn't know what to do.'

'What is it? Is Tabs okay?'

'She's fine. Someone called Mike just messaged you asking where George was.'

'So Tabatha is fine?'

'Yes, love, she's fine.'

'Shit. You scared me.'

'Sorry, love. I shouldn't have rung.'

'No, it's fine. Who did you say messaged?' I asked.

'Mike?'

'Mike. He's George's partner. George should be with him.'

'Well apparently he's not.'

'Mum, open the Find My Friends app and see where George is.'

'I've done that already; it says he's on Sycamore Road. Clara, didn't you say that's where Mantel lives?'

'Yes.'

'I panicked. I thought if you're going to Mantel and he's also going to Mantel, George might see you with him.'

'Thanks, Mum. Message Mike back straight away and tell him where George is.'

'What's he doing there?'

'I don't know, but I doubt he has a warrant, so it can't be good. Tell Mike to hurry.'

'What about you?'

'Don't worry, George won't see me,' I said, and hanging up. I sent Mantel a hurried text. I knew if I didn't, he wouldn't trust me, and I needed him to trust me so he would pay me. I had to warn him that my husband was going to his house, and if he hadn't already left, he needed to stay at home, so George didn't follow him, and bring him to me.

CHAPTER FORTY-THREE

George

I slowed down as I pulled into the quiet street where Henry Mantel lived. My self-pity had worn itself out; all that was left was rage. I knew that unless I took a stand, unless I did something, he would get away with everything he had done. I wasn't sure if I was going to wait outside and watch or knock on his front door and kill the man. All I knew was my daughter was dying from a terrible disease and for me, Mantel had become the face of that illness.

The houses on Sycamore Road were known for their size and immaculate design. Each house was slightly different to the others, though they were all detached with long drives that swept up to their pillared front doors. Tidy lawns and double garages and children's toys, bikes, basketball hoops and trampolines. None of them locked away. It was a suburban paradise. The dream that most people had, including me. And someone like Mantel had all this. The house, the wealth, the healthy children.

I hated him for it.

As I moved slowly along the street, I couldn't help drawing

comparisons. All I wanted was to do good, be good. A good copper, a good husband, and a good daddy. I was failing at them all. Life felt so unkind, so unfair and drawing up outside Mantel's house, that sense of unfairness compacted. For a man who only cared about himself, only did terrible things, wrong things, he had it all.

I stopped at the bottom of his drive and stayed in the car. I could see Mantel in his kitchen, staring out of the window directly at me. Like somehow he knew I was coming to his door. I kept my eye on him as I got out of the car. The rain was pouring down, but I didn't rush as made my way up his long drive towards his house. I was not backing down. And then, at the front door, I waited. I didn't knock, I wanted him to expect it, and for it not to come. I wanted him to worry why it hadn't. After a minute, the door opened.

'Can I help you?' Mantel said as the door swung open, and I couldn't find the words to speak. 'What the fuck do you want, DS Goodwin?'

I opened my mouth to say something and again, nothing came.

'Get the fuck off my doorstep.'

Mantel stepped back to close the door, but I stopped it with my hand and pushed back. I didn't know what I was doing, or what I would do next. All I was thinking was how unfair it all was, and if I let Mantel shut his front door, I would somehow lose something.

'I strongly suggest you leave; this won't end well for you.'

'I know it was you who killed Hunter.'

'Hunter? I don't know a Hunter.'

'And I know you killed Garrett and the other man.'

'Again, I don't know who you're talking about.'

'I'll find the evidence.'

'Good luck with that.'

Behind me, I heard a car pull up and the engine stop.

'DS Goodwin.' It was a voice I wasn't expecting; DCI Mercer. I turned to see her and two uniformed officers approaching.

'Your boss is here to stop you from doing something stupid. Now given you don't have a warrant, get the fuck off my property.'

Mantel again tried to close the door and this time I stuck my foot in the way to stop him.

'You've got a death wish,' he said, smirking at me.

'Is that a threat?' I hoped it was, I hoped for a fight.

'Go home to your kid before the cancer kills her.'

I saw red and before he could close the door, I grabbed him and dragged him out of the house. Slamming him against the wall, my hands found their way to his throat and I pressed hard. As I squeezed and watched Mantel's eyes start to bulge, I was grabbed by the two uniformed officers and dragged away from him. Mantel dropped to the floor, coughing and struggling to draw breath.

'Let go of me, let go.'

I wanted to kill him, to end him. I wanted to wipe him off the planet. But the two uniformed officers didn't let go and despite my struggle, they managed to drag me away. They left me with Mercer before going back to make sure Mantel was unharmed. I was expecting a bollocking, but as Mantel was still within earshot, Mercer just told me to go home.

'I'm sorry, boss, I'm so sorry. He killed those men, I know it.'

'Maybe. However, this isn't the way we go about solving it, or anything else. Go home, George, that's an order.'

Mercer waited for me to get into my car, then she turned and walked towards Mantel, her hands held up, palms showing. Even with the door closed I could hear Mantel's smug tones. I'd fucked the case, ruined the months of work, the late nights, the stress. All for nothing. Whatever evidence I put before a court now, his solicitor would be able to bat away because I had just assaulted him.

I took one last look and resigned to the fact I was in a lot of trouble, I fired up the engine and left.

As I headed back into town, I had to turn my car lights on as the thick clouds were directly overhead, rendering the waning evening sun powerless to hold back the night. The rain drummed on my car, and to drown it out I listened to chatter playing through the police radio. The static easing the dread I was feeling, I wasn't really listening to what was being said until someone in dispatch stated there was an alarm sounding, asking who was closest to have a look. I didn't think anything of it as it was likely a false alarm. Then they mentioned the address. It was a garage on the outskirts of town. Mantel's garage. Which meant he was being robbed, which meant we were wrong about Garrett and the link to catching Mantel was still out there. I knew I'd been ordered to go home, I knew I should leave it. I was in no fit state to do anything properly. I knew I was in deep shit for assaulting Mantel and this was going to be taken care of – over the radio I heard another officer confirm he was already driving over to investigate. But when they gave their current location, I also knew I was closer, much closer. And I couldn't let it go.

CHAPTER FORTY-FOUR

George

The high-pitched alarm screeched above the sound of falling rain. Its shrill piercing noise made it difficult to hear any movement coming from inside the building, but I knew he was there, somewhere. The side door to the garage was smashed open and the shards of glass scattered over the floor shimmered in the reflection of the streetlights. He was there. He was inside, and he would have to come out through the broken door I was standing next to; I just had to be patient and wait for him to make a run for it. He would come to me, and I would use the cover of night to surprise him. However, even knowing I had the advantage, I was nervous. He was proving to be slippery, resourceful. If I screwed this up, I knew I'd likely not get another chance. If I fucked this up, I might get hurt, or worse.

Forcing myself to steady my breathing in the hope it would lower my heart rate, calm me, and stop me from acting on impulse, I stepped back against a wall ten or so feet from the door and pressed myself against it, feeling safe in the knowledge that no one could sneak up on me.

I looked into the building, trying to make out any movement in the darkness, hoping I wasn't mistaken in the belief he was still inside. For too long I had wanted this man – he represented the keystone to bringing down Henry Mantel, the man who had caused so much pain and suffering, the man I had fought to bring to justice for over a year. Right now, Mantel's associate didn't know I was here, waiting. Finally, I had the upper hand.

Just as I began to doubt myself, I heard a noise coming from inside the garage. It was nothing more than a shuffle, but it was enough. Moments later I saw movement and the surge of adrenaline flooded from my stomach, into my arms, legs, head, readying my muscles for a fight. For so long I had wanted to find a way to Mantel, and the person who was the crucial link to enable an arrest was about to step out of a crime scene in front of me. As a police officer I didn't often feel on edge, but as I waited, I struggled to contain my nerves. The man, the thief, climbed through the broken door and out into the rain. I sprang out of my concealed spot and tried to grab him, though he twisted out of my grip and began to run.

I had to stop him escaping.

'Stop! Police!' I shouted, stepping out into the light, blocking his way. The man looked back, his face obscured by a baseball cap and a shroud of mist from the pouring rain.

'I said stop!' I shouted, giving chase.

But the man kept running, and he was fast, the distance between us continuing to grow. In a straight sprint, I wouldn't stand a chance – but this was no ordinary race. I'd been to this garage many times, and I knew that the thief was heading towards a dead end, a self-made trap. I would catch him, arrest him, and finally I'd have Henry Mantel for his crimes. For too long Mantel had been one step ahead, for too long he'd acted like he was untouchable. But not any more. Once I had the thief in custody, the truth would spill about Mantel and the robberies, the drugs and – more recently – the murders he had committed. Who this guy was, beyond a thief, I didn't care. I only needed him as leverage, to land the bigger fish.

Although the wall behind the building did form a dead end, I knew the man would likely be able to scale it, but to do so, he would have to slow down. I'd gain a crucial a few seconds to close the gap, grab him, and drag him to the ground. This man, this thief, was the key to it all, every single crime, every single death.

Soon I would finally have my answers.

I didn't shout again to tell him to stop, it was pointless. Instead, I used that energy to propel myself forward, to push vital oxygen into my leg muscles which were now beginning to slow. The suspect rounded the corner and I knew this was my moment. If I could catch him before he got over the wall, I'd be able to drag him down and hold him until another officer arrived. The man looked over his shoulder, saw me advancing and then in a panic began to run straight for the wall. He jumped, grabbed the ledge and began to heave himself over. It slowed him, just as I hoped, and although my lungs were burning, I gained considerable ground. As the thief swung one leg over the top, I lunged and grabbed the other, pulling him back onto the ground. Both of us landed heavily, my shoulder taking the brunt, but from the sudden huff of air that was forced from the thief's body, I knew he had landed more awkwardly than I had and was now winded. But he didn't give up trying to escape; he began to resist, struggling to get free, and soaked through, holding him became difficult.

'Stop resisting!' I shouted, but the man didn't, and he managed to slip free. As he scrambled to his feet, turning to run in the other direction, towards freedom, I swiped at his left leg, smacking it into his right and sending him over again. He cried out in pain as he hit the floor, and the sound of his voice stopped me in my tracks.

The suspect rolled onto his back and then sat up knowing the chase was over. In the struggle, his baseball hat had been knocked off. As the thief lifted his head, his gaze meeting my eyes, I struggled to understand who I was seeing.

It wasn't a man as I had always assumed. Panting, with rainwater running into her eyes and mud covering half of her face, sat my wife.

'George, I have to go,' she said as I sat there speechless, frozen in shock. 'George, you have to let go of my arm.' She had to shout over the rain slamming onto the tin roof of the garage behind us.

'Clara?' I said, unable to let go.

'I can't explain, not now, but I will. I have to go, before someone else gets here.'

I felt myself tighten my grip.

'George, you have to let me go.'

'Clara, I don't understand. You're the one who's been robbing Mantel? You're the thief?'

'Yes, please, let me go.'

'Fuck.'

'I'll explain everything, I promise.'

My eye was drawn behind us, as approaching blue lights flashed through the trees.

'I know this is a shock and I'm sorry you had to find out this way. But you have to make a choice right now.'

As I struggled to speak, I let go of her arm and Clara pulled herself up onto her feet, offering her hand to help me up too. The blue lights were drawing closer.

'Clara? How involved are you in this?'

'George, I promise I'll tell you everything, no more secrets, no more lies. But I can't be seen here with you. The people I'm working for, they won't like it if I'm seen with police.'

'But you are the police,'

'But right now, I'm not.'

'Then what are you?'

'A desperate mother,' she replied before turning and making her way back to the wall. She didn't look back as she scaled it and disappeared.

I stood there for a little longer before making my way back towards the front of the garage where the police car was pulling up. A young PC called Witherall got out and approached.

'DS Goodwin? What are you doing here?' he asked, looking me up and down, confused as to why a senior officer was standing there soaking wet and covered in mud.

'I heard on the radio there was an alarm and as I was passing, I swung in to have a look. I'm afraid that whoever it was, they got away,' I said, still stunned by the truth.

'Are you hurt, sir?'

'Nothing more than my pride.'

'Which way did they go?'

'Back this way, the way you just pulled in, about a minute ago. You didn't see him?'

PC Witherall turned and dashed off in the direction I'd suggested, the opposite direction to where my wife had just made her escape.

CHAPTER FORTY-FIVE

Clara

I practically fell through the flat door and fumbled to close it behind me, the commotion causing Mum to dash from the living room into the hall. As soon as she saw me, confusion and panic flashed across her face.

'Jesus, are you all right?'

'Shit, Mum, shit.'

'Clara, what's going on?'

'Where's Tabatha?'

'She's in her cot in your room Clara, you're scaring me.'

Ignoring Mum, I peeled off my sodden coat and went to see my daughter. She was asleep but restless, twitching and fidgeting, her little body trying to fight off the evil disease in her body. She was wrestling with it, holding on until I achieved what I needed to do, what I was failing to do. My eyes filled, and as a tear dropped onto Tabs' bedding, Mum took me by the shoulders and guided me out.

'Come on, love, let's get you sorted,' she said.

I complied, too tired, too broken to argue.

'You need to talk to me; I want to help. Has this got something to do with Henry Mantel?'

I couldn't speak, but I nodded and Mum took a deep breath. She led me into the bathroom and sat me on the edge of the bath, helping me to undress. I was soaked to the skin and bruises were beginning to appear from my struggle with George.

'Jesus, Clara, what happened?' she asked again.

I didn't answer her.

Once stripped down to my underwear, I shivered.

'Jesus, you're hurt,' Mum said, noticing my injuries.

'I'm fine.'

I could see she didn't buy it, but she didn't press me on it. 'Come on, love, swing your legs over.'

I did as she instructed, on autopilot, like when I was a child and I acted on command to my mother's tender tones. With my feet flat on the cold bottom of the bathtub, Mum turned on the handheld shower and checking the temperature, she turned it onto my legs, washing the dirt and blood down the drain. She washed my arms, hands, hair, and I watched as my crime swirled and vanished down the drain – and with it my hope, too.

'Clara!' A voice came from the hallway as the front door slammed.

'Shit, it's George. Clara, what do I say?' Mum asked.

'It doesn't matter,' I replied.

'He knows?'

I nodded, too exhausted to say any more.

'Clara?' George called out again.

'She's in here,' Mum said and a moment later the bathroom door opened. George stood there; he too was covered in mud.

'Clara, what the fuck is going on?'

'George, calm down,' Mum snapped.

'Calm down? What's going on? Jo, do you know what she's been doing?'

'Yes. George, I know she is working for Henry Mantel.'

'Working for Mantel? What do you mean working for Mantel? Clara, what the fuck is going on?' Despite the fact George sounded angry, I could see he was more afraid than pissed off.

I sighed, and inside, the candle that was my hope, that was Tabatha's future, began to flicker once more, the flame threatening to go out. I wanted to be able to wrack my brains and come up with some other explanation as to what I had been doing, but I was too exhausted to even try.

'Clara? Answer me. You told me you were the thief, what do you mean you're working for Mantel? Don't you know the amount of shit you're in, the amount of shit we are all in.'

'Is it any more shit than we're already in with Tabatha?' I asked quietly, looking him directly in the eye.

He didn't reply, the anger in his eyes burning out at the mention of our daughter's name.

'I'll explain it all, I promise. Just give me a minute. Someone put the kettle on, make us all a cuppa. Once I'm dressed, I'll tell you everything.'

'How can I trust you, Clara?'

'I'm too tired to lie any more.'

George left the bathroom, Mum too, and the room fell into a silence, like the walls themselves were judging me for what I had done. I felt them pressing in, the weight crushing my already bruised and battered body. This past week, I had seen more conflict than I had done in my last year of being a detective before I went on maternity leave. My ribs ached, my head throbbed and now, thanks to George, my left arm felt dead. Not that it was his fault, of course. But the guilt, the aches and pains, they all evaporated like early morning summer mist when I snuck out of the bathroom and went in to see my daughter. I didn't take my eyes off her until my nerves were placated and my resolve was reinforced. She was fighting for her life; I needed to match her grit and tell the truth about what I had done. It was nowhere near as hard as what she was having to do. Not even close. Leaning over, I kissed Tabs on the head.

'I love you.'

I got dressed and hobbled my way into the kitchen. Mum had made three cups of tea, and I picked one up.

'Thanks, Mum.'

She didn't reply, but sipped her own as we waited for George to come back. When he appeared, he looked at me like I was a stranger, like he didn't know who I was. I had felt that George and I were going to be okay, that despite our challenges we were going to find a way to reconcile, save our marriage. Now I knew that we would likely never recover. Not from this.

'Well?'

'George, take a breath.'

'Take a breath? I should have arrested my wife at a crime scene tonight.'

'George, please. I am going to tell you everything, but you need to listen and try to understand.'

George opened his mouth to say something and stopped himself. 'All right, I'm listening.'

'Mantel offered me a job, helping him to find whoever is robbing his businesses. I agreed.'

'When?'

'Only a few days ago.'

'And you knew about this, Jo?'

'Yes.'

George sighed heavily.

'I made Mum promise to keep it a secret. She wanted me to tell you. But it was a lot of money, George.'

'How much?'

'Twenty-five grand.'

'But it's Henry Mantel.'

'I know, George, but it's also a lot of money, for our daughter.'

'So Mantel has employed you to find the thief. But you told me you were . . . oh fuck,' he said, working it out. 'Clara? Surely not?'

'I'm working for Mantel to try and find his thief, but I am also the one who has been stealing from him.'

CHAPTER FORTY-SIX

Clara

'George, I never meant to get so deeply involved in anything, believe me. When we set out to raise money to help Tabs, the thought hadn't even entered my mind,' I pleaded.

'No?'

'No, George. It's me. Of course not.'

'And yet, here we are,' he replied cuttingly.

'Please, just let me explain. This is hard enough as it is.'

'Clara, you cannot expect me to be okay with any of this,'

'No, but we can at least listen,' Mum interjected, silencing him.

The two of them sat dumbfounded as I tried to explain how I had simultaneously been stealing from Henry Mantel while also helping him. I could see George couldn't comprehend how it was possible that neither he nor Mum had clocked that I was behind the crimes.

'Clara, just slow down,' Mum said. 'We're struggling to keep up.'

'Sorry,' I said, taking a breath. Now the truth was out,

I wanted to get everything out as fast as I could, but I knew I owed them a proper explanation.

'It began that night, at the Tesco robbery, I saw those two men get away with a lot of money. I knew they would get caught, they were sloppy, amateurish, and when I took some of the money they'd dropped—'

'What?' George said.

'Let her continue,' Mum interrupted.

'When I took that money, a thought struck me. If I did something similar, if I stole to raise money for Tabatha, I didn't think I would ever get caught. I have built a career on arresting criminals, I know where they go wrong. Every time. And I knew because of that, if I stole . . . I knew I would get away with it. The thought only lasted a moment, but the idea was there.'

'Oh, Clara,' Mum said taking my hand. I wished George would do the same, I wished he would reach over, hold my hand, hold me, support me. But he didn't.

'I didn't think any more about it, of course. I felt guilty enough about the few hundred pounds I'd picked up off the floor.'

'Then how . . .' George started.

'Then I overheard that recording, the one from Mantel's office, when he stated that he needed time to process money.'

'Yes,' he said, in a way that made it look like I was trying to make him shoulder some of the blame.

'George, it wasn't your fault. None of it. In that recording, he didn't say raise the money or move the money. He said *process* the money, which told me he had dirty money that he was trying to clean.'

'I don't understand?' Mum said, but I could see George did. He knew exactly what I was talking about.

'When someone is laundering money,' I continued, 'they need to get illicitly gained income clean. They can't just walk into a bank with a ton of money earned in the sale of, say, drugs without anyone raising an eyebrow. If Mantel banked all of his dirty cash, the police would be onto him – and without being able to account for that money, it would be used in the case against him.'

'So the money needs to look legal?' Mum asked.

'Yes.'

'How does someone do that?'

'By processing it through a company or business,' George said quietly. 'Cash-heavy trade. Like coffee shops and salons.'

'I still don't understand,' Mum said.

'Say a coffee shop sold a hundred cups of coffee in a day,' he continued. 'It would be hard to disprove that it didn't sell five hundred. And if each cup is £2.50, you could take a thousand pounds of dirty money and process it as those extra cups. Then it could pass through the banking system and become clean.'

'After that call,' I continued,' I knew Mantel had money somewhere waiting to go through the system. I wasn't 100 per cent sure, but hearing him saying he needed to process the money in that recording . . . it meant it was worth a try.'

'The night of the Bean Hut . . . how?' George asked.

'Tabs was asleep. Mum, you were here with me, George, you were at work. I snuck out for an hour, came back before dawn, and then worked down in the shop.'

'You snuck out leaving me and Tabs?'

'I figured if she woke, you would look for me downstairs,

and I would either be back already and if not, there was note saying I couldn't sleep and had gone for a walk.'

'And the club in Stockport?' George asked. 'How did you do that?'

'That time you were asleep. I moved your phone so it didn't wake you, and then when I was back, I came to you and I woke you up as Mike had called.'

'You woke me with messages about your own crime?'

'Yes.'

'You do know I went to the scene that night?' George asked, and again I nodded.

'I assumed you would.'

'Fucking hell, Clara. What about the salon? How did you do that?'

'Mantel had offered me the job to try and find the thief. I wasn't going to do it, but then with Tabs being rushed in and taking a turn I was panicking that we were running out of time. So I agreed to meet him, to find out what he had to say. I had no intention of robbing the place.'

'Is that why you suggested I stay at the hospital with her?'

'Yes.'

'So you could meet with Mantel? Jo, you said she was asleep?'

'I told her to say that, George.'

'How does that explain the salon robbery?' he asked.

'I met Mantel there, and it gave me the opportunity to scope the place. After he left, I broke in.'

'And attacked a man,' George added.

'What?' Mum said.

'Yes, but I didn't mean to hurt him as much as I did. I figured if I robbed it there and then, Mantel would never think it was me because in his mind, I was back at the hospital with you. I did it because I knew it would strengthen my alibi.'

'Jesus, Clara. Do you know how dangerous this is?'

'Yes, George, I do. But I'm trying to save our daughter,' I replied.

George looked me in the eye, our anger meeting on a level playing field. 'Can we have a minute, Jo? Clara and I need to be alone.'

Mum looked at me to make sure I was okay, and I nodded. George was right, he and I needed to be alone to work out what we were going to do now the truth was out.

'Of course. I'll go home. If you need me, just call,' Mum replied.

CHAPTER FORTY-SEVEN

Clara

Before Mum opened the door to leave, I ran after her.

'Mum, I'm so sorry. I hated lying to you. I just didn't want to drag you into anything.'

She nodded. 'Just . . . I worry, you know.'

'I'm okay, Mum. Please don't be angry with me.'

'No more secrets, though. Ever.'

'I promise.'

She kissed me on the cheek and left, and for a while, I stood with my head pressed against the back of the door. After telling the truth, I felt more exhausted than ever. I walked back into the kitchen where George was waiting for me. He sat at the kitchen table, fiddling with his wedding ring.

'George, I wanted to tell you—'

'Did you?'

'Of course.'

'Clara, I know you're lying.'

'Fine, no I didn't, is that what you want to hear?' I said honestly. 'I hoped you'd never find out, both you and Mum.'

'Well that hasn't worked.'

'No, it hasn't. But I didn't want to hurt you, or jeopardize your career.'

'I'm not sure I believe you on that either.'

'That's not fair.'

'Fair? *Fair*? Clara, you've been lying to me, working for that man, stealing from that man . . . You're a police officer for fuck's sake. I'm a police officer. Don't you realise the shit we are in?' George said, his voice rising.

'It's not about us though, is it?' I replied, matching his level. 'Us . . . is that even a thing any more George?'

'What is that supposed to mean?'

'Since our daughter got sick, you have slowly withdrawn. You and I are barely in the same room unless we're at hospital. Our relationship is failing. I didn't want to have to do what I've been doing, but you're not here, even when you are.'

'So this is my fault?'

'I'm not saying that, George, but maybe, maybe if we were stronger, we would have found a better way to make this money together.'

He didn't reply, and I had to assume it was because deep down he knew I was right. 'You could be arrested,' he said eventually. 'And now I've helped you, I could too. Who would be there to look after our baby then?'

'Look after our baby? What do you think I'm trying to do? I'm not doing this to line my pockets, chase a thrill. I'm doing this for our daughter. This is about Tabatha; this is all for Tabatha.'

'You don't have to, though. No one is forcing you to do this. We have the NHS, we don't have to pay a single penny to get her well. Christ, I bought into your fundraising thinking you were doing something incredible.'

'I have been doing something incredible.'

'You've been stealing, and people are getting hurt.'

'George, Tabatha is seriously ill.'

'Don't say that.'

'She is not getting any better, and she won't, and it's fucking well time you saw this. George, our little girl is not going to make it, unless we get her to America.'

'You don't know that.'

'Yes, I do.'

'How, how do you know?'

'I just feel it. Our little girl is going to die.'

'Stop, Clara.'

'No, George! No. It's time we said it out loud and faced facts. She won't make it unless we do something. Our baby is going to die.'

'You don't know that, Clara, you don't,' he replied, but without much conviction.

'When we couldn't wake her, do you know what I thought?'

'Clara, I don't want to talk about that right now.'

'I thought that was it, I thought we had run out of time – and don't stand there and tell me you didn't think the same, too.'

He didn't respond.

'Surely you understand why I'm doing this? Between the FundMyCause page, Mum taking out a loan and what I've been doing, we're getting closer and closer to our target. Closer to our baby being able to get on that plane, fly to Philadelphia and take part in the trial that will make her well again.'

'Clara, there's no guarantee Philadelphia will work.'

'No, there isn't. But one thing I do know, one thing that's guaranteed, is if we don't try, if we don't do everything, and I mean absolutely everything for her, I won't be able to live with myself. Could you?'

George didn't answer and lowered his head.

'I don't like what I'm doing any more than you. I hurt someone at the salon, badly. I have to live with that for the rest of my life.'

'Clara, don't you understand how bad this is? Don't you see that Mantel is dangerous? Hunter is dead, and now two more have been killed.'

'Two men?'

'Yes.'

'What are their names?'

'Why?' George asked, his expression morphing into worry.

'Just tell me,' I snapped.

'One was called Garrett, the other we don't know yet.'

I felt the world shift. Gravity felt thicker, and it forced me to sit.

'You know that name?' George asked.

'Yes.'

'Well, he's dead. Mantel thought he was the thief, like I did, and he killed him.'

George looked at me and he could see the guilt on my face.

'Clara?'

'I didn't mean for anyone to get hurt.'

'Shit, Clara, please don't tell me you set that up for us to suspect him instead of you? Clara, please, please tell me that's not true.'

'George, I didn't want anyone to get hurt. I just wanted to raise some money.'

'Clara, tell me, please. Tell me you didn't do anything to lead us that way?'

'I didn't, of course I didn't,' I said, because that much was true. I hadn't led George to think Garrett was involved, but I had led Mantel that way, and now he was dead. 'The other man was called Wayne Tower.'

'Shit, shit!' George said, horrified at the extent of my involvement. He threw his coffee cup and it hit the wall. The sudden outburst made me jump, and from our room, Tabs began to cry; it had scared her too. Despite feeling weighed down with guilt, I moved quickly and picked her up, trying my best to soothe her. It felt like it would be impossible to offer her any comfort given the realisation I was responsible for two men being dead. I was now complicit in murder.

However, she didn't know that, and after a few minutes she began to settle once more. I lay her down and went back into the kitchen. George stood up from where he had crouched down to sweep up shards of exploded mug.

'Clara, I need to know, did you lead Mantel their way? Did you tell him that Garrett and Tower were the culprits?'

'No.'

'Thank God.'

'But I did suggest they looked like they were involved.'

'Shit.' George put the pieces of the broken mug on the side. He couldn't look at me, but stared down at the sharp shards of porcelain.

'Why those two?' he asked.

'I had to watch a meeting Mantel held. Those two were

a similar height to me. I figured, knowing I'd be on CCTV, I could look like either of them.'

'Oh, Clara.'

'Don't, George. I know what I've done. I'm going to have to try and live with it.'

'Mantel will kill you if he finds out.'

'He won't find out.'

'Clara, I'm scared for you.'

'Don't be,' I said walking towards him. 'I know what I'm doing.'

'Do you?'

'Yes.'

'You're in deep, Clara.'

'I know, but I'm not thinking about that.'

'What are you thinking about then?'

'Her fifth birthday,' I said, looking up at him.

'Is there anything else you need to tell me?'

'Yes.'

'I'm listening,' he said, still unable to look at me.

'It's about Lee.'

'Who?'

'PC Lee Sharman.'

'Right, what about him?'

'Just . . . he isn't to be trusted.'

George stared at me for a long moment. 'I need some air,' he said eventually.

'George, please don't go, we need to talk about—'

'You lied to me, Clara.'

'I know.'

'We're supposed to be a team.'

'I know. Please, let me—'

'We are fucking police officers,' he shouted. 'And you are knee-deep in the case I'm working on.'

'I know, George, I didn't want to put you in this situation.'

'Well you have. And you know the worst bit? Worse than knowing my wife is a thief, worse than knowing she is working for Henry fucking Mantel. Worse than knowing my wife is possibly culpable for the death of two men?'

'George, please.'

'Worse than me now having to think about what I do with this information, worse than all of that?'

'What?' I asked.

'I don't even know who you are now. You look like my wife, you sound like her, but you're not her, not any more.'

I wanted to argue the point but stopped myself. He was right, I didn't know who I was any more either and I had never felt so lost.

CHAPTER FORTY-EIGHT

George

I walked away from the flat, heading in the direction of the nearest pub, hoping to grab a pint before last orders. I needed time to think, to work out exactly what I would do. I knew I had been harsh and hurt Clara. But finding out that she had lied to me, what she had been doing, had hurt me. My words were cold, but her actions were unforgivable.

The rain had eased, but it hadn't fully stopped and by the time I got to The King's Head, my T-shirt were soaked through. As I walked in, a few people looked up but quickly returned to their business as I approached the bar.

'Pint of Guinness, please.' The bartender looked too young to be pulling pints. He tried to engage me with small talk but I wasn't interested and once I had my drink, I found a small table in the corner, beside a window that overlooked the street and sent a message to Mike.

I can't explain why, but I've been thinking about Mantel's informant, can you keep an eye on Lee Sharman

His message came back quickly.

Mate, what have you done? You're in the shit. You shouldn't have

left the crime scene. You shouldn't have lied to me about where you were going.

I know I shouldn't have and I'm sorry, And I know I'm in the shit. I'll deal with that later. But I'm not messaging about that right now, I need you to keep an eye on Sharman

Mike didn't reply straight away and I thought for a moment I had either got him into trouble or he was too pissed off at me to message back. I sipped my pint anxiously. Then, my phone pinged.

Sharman, is he the type?
I've just got a gut feeling
I'll keep an eye on him.

I put my phone down, knowing Mike would have questions as to why I thought Lee Sharman was a dirty copper. I needed a lie to cover the fact my wife was inside the Mantel organisation. As I tried to piece one together, I still couldn't process what Clara had told me. She was in real trouble. I wanted to understand, to be on her side, and if she'd been confessing to only the stealing of money from the robbery at Tesco, as much as it was wrong, I think I would have forgiven her. But working for Henry Mantel, fully aware of what kind of man he was and how hard I had been trying to bring him to justice over the past year . . . I didn't think I could. Clara had betrayed me, and then there was the business with Lee, too. She knew we had a leak, and she didn't tell me, her own husband, what she had discovered.

I took a long sip of my pint, and as the cold liquid washed down my throat, I sank back into my chair wondering when life had got so fucking hard. But I knew the answer; it got hard when Tabatha was diagnosed.

Picking up my phone again, I went to my photos and scrolled back over a year to when Clara and I first found out we were having a baby. I looked through them, at Clara progressively growing in size as the due day marched ever closer. In the photos we were happy, smiling, cheek to cheek in selfies. Our eyes had a sparkle, a lightness that spoke of a future where the three of us would move though life as a unit, unbreakable and hopeful and full of love. Our eyes spoke of our unified commitment not only to one another, but our family, too, and now I knew that the sparkle we once had was gone.

And then I came to the first photo of our daughter in Clara's arms, tucked under her hospital gown, her cheek against Clara's chest, with me beside her, red-eyed from crying. I scrolled on, feeling my eyes prickle with tears. One fell and I wiped it away quickly, not wanting anyone to see. I looked at hundreds of pictures of Tabatha sleeping and smiling and in the bath, bubbles all around her. I looked at pictures of my wife holding her and feeding her, and I missed that time. Truth be told, I missed them both. The child and the wife from that time. When life made some sort of chaotic, sleep-deprived sense.

I stopped at a picture of Clara on the sofa, Tabs asleep in her arms, and I zoomed in on the expression on my wife's face. She looked at Tabs in a way she never looked at me, her expression showing a kind of completeness.

The bartender called last orders and draining my pint, I ordered another one, again trying to avoid catching his eye.

'You okay, mate?' the young man asked as he pulled it.

'I just need a quiet drink.'

I took my drink and returned to my table. Family was everything, it had been since the day I met Clara, but still I had to ask, could I forgive her? Could I even keep what she was doing a secret?

I went back to scrolling through the early pictures of my family, before Tabatha first became unwell. In one, I was sat on a sofa with Tabatha, who must have only been a few weeks old, in my arms. Beside me was my mum. I was looking at the camera, smiling, but Mum was looking down at my daughter, her smile almost bittersweet. I thought about what she had had to endure as a parent with my brother, how she lost him to drugs, how once he was gone, for a while she had wanted to die, too. My own mum, just like Clara, changed because of her child. And even though my mum and I never talked about Steve, sometimes, when I saw her, I knew she was thinking of him. I knew, even now, she would do anything to get him back.

And that was all Clara was doing, she was trying to get our daughter back.

I got up and left. I tried to make sense of everything on my walk home, and I knew I would forgive Clara because she was doing it for our girl. But as for us – as a couple, a partnership, I didn't know if we would make it after this.

CHAPTER FORTY-NINE

Clara

I wanted to make George understand but I knew that he needed some time to come to terms with what he'd just found out.

Part of me wanted to climb into bed and try to forget what had happened, but I knew I couldn't. Regardless of what George thought – or did – I needed to keep going. So despite being clean already, I went and ran a hot bath. I ached, my muscles were bruised and battered, I needed heat to try and soothe them. But it was more than that. I felt such guilt, I wanted to try and wash it off my skin. I turned the taps on and once the water was deep enough and steam had covered the bathroom mirror and the broken woman who looked back at me from it, I got in. For a while I didn't do anything other than lie there and let the hot water work its magic. It soothed my aches, but stung my fresh cuts and grazes, though pain was welcome, pain meant I was still going, still moving. Pain, ironically, kept me wanting to do more. But even though I wanted to, knew that I had to do more, I couldn't help myself wondering how much I would have to do. People were now dead because of me. And George would want to solve the case, use whatever I knew to bury Mantel. But doing so would mean I would have to stop, and Tabatha needed me not to stop. I was in too deep to turn back now, it had to count for something.

Quickly rinsing my hair, I pulled the plug and got out of the bath. As I turned to grab a towel, I jumped. George stood in the doorway. I hadn't heard him come in.

He was looking at my naked body, but not with lust or disgust. It was shock.

'Clara, what happened to you?'

George looked at the deep purple bruising on my left thigh, my ribs, my right arm and stepping closer, he gently touched the latter.

'Did I cause all of these?'

'No,' I said quietly.

'Thank God.'

Turning, I showed him my back and he gasped. It looked horrific, but in truth the pain was subsiding.

'Jesus, Clara.'

'That one is from where I fell off a wall behind the Bean Hut.'

'Before or after the robbery?'

'After. The money was in my bag, I lost my balance.'

'And this?' he asked, touching my thigh.

'Getting into the club in Stockport.'

'This?' He stroked my ribs. His touch sent goosebumps across my body.

'The salon. I was punched.'

'Oh Jesus, Clara,' he said again.

'It's okay, George, all of it.'

'And these?' This time he touched my arm, the grazes, the fresh bruising.

'The garage.'

'Tonight?'

'Yes, tonight.'

'I did this?'

'Yes.'

'I'm so sorry,' he said, stepping closer to me.

'You didn't know.'

'But now I do.'

'Yes. Now you do,' I echoed. 'Question is, what are you going to do about it?'

George looked at me with an expression that reminded me of a long time ago, before all of this, and then he stepped closer and almost kissed me. I wanted him to, but we didn't force it, stopped only centimetres apart. I dipped towards him, glancing my lip off his, and the touch sent a hot flash through my body. I could feel my skin tingle, my body wanting him. He grabbed my arms, squeezed them, and our lips brushed each other's once more. I needed to kiss him. He kissed me back and I felt a wave of relief that he didn't pull away. I wrapped my arms around his neck, held him as tight as I could, and he pressed his body into mine. It had been so long since my husband and I had touched each other, it almost felt like the first time. George's hands explored too, grabbing my hips, pulling me in, and I felt him grow hard against me. I knew this wasn't about us mending or fixing our relationship, this was about us finding a release for the pressure we both felt. A release for the crimes, the hurt, the lies and secrets, a release for the fear. It seemed almost certain George and I weren't going to be together after all of this, but, neither of us cared. I think he knew it too, this was our goodbye sex.

He pulled away from me, took my hand and without talking, led me to the spare room. I pulled at his belt, wanting it undone but so excited, so caught up in the moment, I couldn't free the buckle. I was nervous and started to giggle and he laughed too and took over the task. As he did, I lay down. George took me in, looking at my naked body, the shock gone, no sign of disgust, just a lustful gaze that told me he wanted me badly. Seeing him that way, my body responded, aching for him. For the first time since Tabs was born and despite feeling self-conscious for it, I let him stare. He dropped his trousers to the floor, his underwear too, and pulled his T-shirt off. Lowering himself onto me he kissed me again, his skin on mine. I opened my legs wider, and with our lips still pressed together, he guided himself inside me.

CHAPTER FIFTY

Clara

George lay with his head on my stomach, his arm wrapped around one of my legs, holding it close to him, and I stroked his hair as I looked at the ceiling. Relief and joy and release worked in harmony, and for a brief but wonderful twenty minutes, neither of us spoke. We just existed in the moment, no past, no future. Just us. For what it was worth.

Getting up I went to the bathroom to freshen up. When I returned wrapped in my towel, George was sitting up, his underwear back on. As he looked at me I could see that the calm, the closeness was gone.

'George?'

'Clara, I need to know, how much have you taken from him?'

'Over six from the café. Twenty-two from the club, and four and a half from the salon.'

'Shit, that's over thirty grand!'

'Yeah.'

'And the garage, tonight?'

'A hundred pounds, if I'm lucky. I hoped to find more. I hoped it would be over. I hoped tonight was the last.'

'Is it all added to the FundMyCause page?'

'Some, yes.'

'And the rest?'

'Here, in the flat.'

'How much is here?'

'About twenty-seven.'

'Shit, how are you going to get it clean and add it to the rest?'

'I don't know. I haven't got that far.'

'Where is it?'

'In our room. In the base of the wardrobe. I'll have to pay it into my personal account on the day we go to Philadelphia but I figured by the time anyone is aware, it will be long gone.'

'But then you might get caught?'

'I won't, not if I'm careful. There is no link back to us.'

'How have you got so good at this?' he asked me, and I didn't know if he was impressed or horrified.

'Because I have to be.'

'So including that twenty-seven in the bedroom, how much are we short?'

'Thirty thousand or so.'

'You think he has that much at his office, just lying around?'

'No, not as much as thirty. Our page is still trickling money in, but I hoped to find at least as much as I did at the bar. Then, I'd have felt like it was almost over.'

'Clara, putting the money in the wardrobe, wasn't that risky? I mean, I could have found it at any time.'

'George, our room is probably the best place to hide it from you. You're always in the spare room.'

My words stung, I could tell, but he didn't say anything back. Instead, he nodded and looked down at his feet.

'Show me.'

I got up and walked into our room where Tabs lay asleep in her cot. George followed behind and I quietly opened the wardrobe and moved a jumper I had placed over a shoebox. Pulling the box out, I removed the lid and showed George the stacks of stolen cash. I expected him to say something about the risk, the danger, the stupidity of my actions. But he didn't.

I hoped he was going to say he was going to try harder to save us, so I could too, but he stayed silent. It seemed our fate was sealed.

'So what's next?' he asked, unable to look at me.

'We have to do something online, as a couple again, to try to find new supporters. We have a little over four days. But George, she has to be well enough to fly. We need to get her on that plane before that.'

'So we make a new video.'

'And I need to find one more place, one more business. One more job.'

'There has to be some at his garage.'

'I looked; I couldn't find anything. But it doesn't make sense.'

'Why? he asked.

'Mantel would want it close. I've no doubt he might have some at his home but . . .'

'But?' George asked.

'But after the break-ins, he's afraid. He has a family, right?'

'Yeah.'

'He has kids, too,' I said quietly. 'That's why I was so sure he would have some at the garage rather than at his place.'

'Wait,' George said, his mind racing.

'What?'

'I know where it is. I'm sure of it. He has a hatch in the floor of his office.'

'A hatch?'

'Yes. I couldn't work it out before, but I'm convinced it's a storage space.'

'How do you know?'

'The day I took the car to book it in, I saw Mantel getting up from the floor in his office. I didn't know what he was doing, but what if he had a secret compartment somewhere.'

It made sense. He was there the most and would want his money nearby.

'George, it's possible, but even if you're right, he'll be waiting. We need to find another place.'

'Clara, I'm sure of it.'

'But I've been there. If there is money there, he'll no doubt move it.'

'He can't, not yet anyway. It's a crime scene. There are too many people watching.'

'The police won't stay long. And then he can do what he wants.'

We both fell silent, thinking, and in the silence he sat beside me, so close our thighs touched. His warmth acted like hope.

'I've got it,' he said, moving away. 'I'll get 24-hour surveillance on him, but somehow we'll make sure he knows the police are watching. He'll think he is smarter than us for it. Like we are waiting for him to do something that incriminates him. I suspect he'll stay away from the garage when he's not working. He'll not move anything knowing we have eyes on him.'

I thought about it; it might work.

'George does this mean you're going to help?'

'You say you can see her fifth birthday? I can't see past the cancer, but I want to be able to.'

'Me too.'

'You started this for her. Together we'll finish it. We need a final video to try and keep the donations flooding in. It will get us closer and then we'll have less to find from Mantel.'

I nodded; it made sense, we had a plan. 'And us? What about us?' I asked. He didn't answer and as I was about to say something more I heard the ping of a message from my burner phone, which was still in my coat pocket.

Retrieving it, I saw there was one new message.

'Who is it? George asked.

'Mantel.'

'What does it say?'

'It says he and I need to talk. There's an address.'

'What are you going to tell him?'

'I don't know, but I need to tell him something.'

CHAPTER FIFTY-ONE

George

'I don't like it, Clara.'

'Me neither, but what choice do we have? We have to see this through, for her. I'm going to have to go and meet him.'

'When? Now?'

'What choice have I got?' she said.

'Yeah, I guess so,' I agreed.

Clara began to type. She sent the message and one came back within seconds.

'He was waiting for you.'

'Yeah, he was.'

'What does that mean?'

'He's desperate,' Clara replied. 'He wants me to meet him at the warehouse.'

'Is it safe to go back to the warehouse?'

'I don't know, I hope so.'

'I'm not sure about this. It's remote, isolated. It feels too risky.'

'Then what should I do?'

'What if . . .' I started, an idea forming. 'What if you tell him we are watching. I said we would need him to find out we had surveillance on him. What if you warn him about it.'

'Me?'

'Yes, tell him you need to meet elsewhere, as the police are watching the warehouse.'

She thought about it for all of a second and then told me it was a brilliant plan. Mantel would see she was working for him, in deep, and warning him that he was being watched would only make her seem less likely to be a suspect in his eyes. She could get Mantel to trust her, and then we could use it against him.

Her fingers moved fast as she messaged him, and I leaned in to read it.

It's not safe to meet there, George has you under surveillance

He pinged back quickly.

Why are you telling me this?

Because I have to help my daughter. I need money. If you and I are seen together, it won't do either of us any good. You said you would pay me to keep him off your scent

He didn't message back as fast this time and we waited an agonising two minutes.

'Why isn't he replying?'

'He is weighing up his options,' Clara said.

Finally, it came.

Where?

Come to the bookshop tomorrow morning. Come inside, like you are shopping, we'll find a place to talk in there

Won't your husband be there?

No, he'll be at work

Another agonising wait, an unbearable wait.

I'll be there at 11

She showed me the message and I looked at my watch.
'That's a little over eleven hours from now, that gives
us time.'

27TH JULY 2023

4 days until the deadline . . .

FundMyCause™ Menu   Log In   Sign Up   Search 🔍

Help for Tabatha
We are raising money to send our daughter, Tabatha, to the US for treatment to help her overcome neuroblastoma.

£169, 541
raised of £230,000 target

Donate Now

---

4 days remaining to reach required target

We are now hovering around 75% of our target. We didn't dare to dream only a week ago of reaching such a huge sum of money. Thank you everyone. We are so close, not only to our deadline, but now, our target too. And as George and I begin our final push with the media outlets to spread the word, and Tabatha's story, we are asking for more help from you

If you cannot afford to donate, by spreading the word, sharing this page with your network, you will still be making a massive difference to her life.

Tabatha is continuing her treatment here, she is staying strong. And despite how frightening it is, how heartbroken we are, George and I are hopeful, because of the kindness of strangers. Because of people like you.

We need you to keep sharing, keep telling Tabatha's story. We need you to help us find this final 25 per cent to save our child.

You are making such a difference her life. You are helping us see her 5th birthday.

Thank you.

Clara, George and Tabatha x

Supporters

Peter Marks
£20

Sean Hubbard
£30

Lena Jankowski
£20

Victoria Cooke
£50

Sue Blyth
£30

Buxton C. Church
£300

Adam Boland
£25

Vanessa Boland
£25

FundMyCause™
Terms of Use   Privacy Policy   Cookie Policy

About Us
Careers
Help & Support

CHAPTER FIFTY-TWO

Henry Mantel

Mantel had hoped that dealing with Tower and Garrett would make those he owed money to step back, understand he wasn't to be messed with. But no sooner had the pair met their ends, someone had tried to rob him again. Tried and failed. He wondered if Clara had got it entirely wrong, or was misleading him. He could have asked her on the phone, but he needed to see her face to face, eye to eye.

From outside the study door, Mantel heard two little voices shriek with delight.

'Uncle Tony!'

'Hey girls. Where's your daddy?'

'In his room.'

There was a knock, three gentle taps.

'Come in.'

Tony came in, closing the door behind him, much to the protest of Mantel's daughters. 'Your girls, Henry, they're getting bigger every day.'

'I can barely keep up,' Mantel said.

'You've got your hands full, that's for sure.' Tony spotted Mantel's bruised neck. 'Boss, what happened?'

'I had a visit from DS Goodwin last night.'

'He grabbed you?

'He did.'

'I'll fucking kill him.'

'No, no need. Let it go.'

'He's got some fucking balls.'

'Tony, let it go. After what he did last night, he won't be sniffing around any more. He'll be off the case, it will eat him up.'

'Okay boss.'

'Did you get the CCTV from the garage's hard drive?'

'Yes, about that, there's something there. Something you might find interesting.'

'I'm listening.'

Tony pulled a tablet from his bag, opened an app, and handed it to Mantel. The screen was divided into quarters, each showing a grainy image from one of the four CCTV cameras within the garage. One showed the inside of the dark empty space, one showed the inside of Mantel's office and the other two showed the exterior of the building front and back. Mantel pressed play and watched as a person came in through the rear. He saw them break the door, get inside, and move quickly towards the reception area first. They disappeared off camera for a while.

'Where have they gone?' Mantel asked.

'Just keep watching boss.'

Within a minute, they were back, dashing fast and low through the workshop towards the stairs at the rear.

'Fucker,' Mantel hissed as he watched them head up the stairs. 'Do you think it's the same man as before?'

'Maybe, it's hard to tell.'

Mantel watched as the camera inside the office caught them pressed against the glass. They tried to open the door, and when that failed, they smashed their way in. Mantel didn't blink as he watched them rummage around his private space. It was clear this person was neither Garrett nor Tower, but they were soon to end up like them. Having seen enough, he handed the tablet back to Tony.

'Find this fucker, find them and bring them to me.'

'Boss, keep watching. It gets weird,' Tony replied, pushing the tablet back into his hands. Mantel wasn't in the mood for cryptic clues or games, but took the tablet back anyway; it wasn't often Tony thought anything was out of the ordinary. He saw the thief leave the office and run down the stairs, out of the building and around the back. A car approached, and a man climbed out.

'Is that George Goodwin?'

'Yep.'

Mantel watched as Goodwin gave chase to the thief and in the bottom corner of the quartered screen saw him grab the thief and pull them back down from the wall they were trying to climb. They began to fight, rolling in the mud, and in the struggle they disappeared around the side of the building, out of shot.

'I can't see anything.'

'Just keep watching.'

After a minute, Goodwin staggered to his feet and into the view of the camera once more. He was out of breath, and he had stopped moving. Mantel leant into to watch more closely. Goodwin was saying something. He turned away from the thief, and Mantel saw from a different camera angle a police car approach. Goodwin then ran in the direction of the police car.

'What the fuck?' Mantel said.

The officer got out of the car, and Goodwin pointed in the opposite direction to where the thief had just stood.

'What is he doing?'

'I don't know, boss. But it looks like he let them go.'

'Why would he do that?'

'I don't know.'

'Do we have sound from the video, can we hear what he is saying?'

'No, boss.'

Mantel sat back in his chair. Goodwin knew who the thief was, and instead of doing his job, he had let him go. 'Why did he not arrest him?' he said to himself. Processing the information, he tried to find a reason.

'Boss, what are you thinking?'

'Goodwin let him go because he is using him to get to me.'

Tony nodded.

'Which makes me think that whoever this thief is, we know them.'

'But it's not Garrett or Tower.'

'No, not them. Maybe it's someone Goodwin knows.'

'Who?'

'Where's Lee Sharman?' Mantel asked.

'I've not heard anything, so I assume he's at work.'

'Keep an eye on him.'

'I'll see where he is. Do you think it could be anyone else Goodwin knows?'

'Like who?'

'I don't know boss, someone else from the force?'

'If anyone else there was inclined to want to raise extra funds, I'd know. And they would work for me.'

'What about Goodwin's wife?'

Mantel laughed. 'Clara? No, no. Didn't you see how afraid she was when she came to the warehouse. No, she ain't got it in her.'

'But she needs cash.'

'And I'm paying her to work for me now. When I first met her, she was a rabbit in the headlights. She's a desperate mother, nothing more. She ain't got it in her. I'm going to meet her this morning.'

'Is that a good idea?'

'She's with us now. She gave me a heads-up that her husband was placing surveillance on me.'

'She did?'

'Yeah, she did. She overheard him saying he was getting people to watch me, and she told me.'

'Why?'

'She's on the payroll now, for information.'

'Boss, she was one of them. You can't trust her.'

'She needs me to keep quiet about how she's earned some of that money for her daughter. And she wants to earn more. She isn't one of them, not now. She's one of us.'

'Want me to come with you?'

'No, go to the garage, make sure everything is as it should be. See what Lee is up to.'

'And if I see George Goodwin?'

'Don't speak to him, just carry on with your business.'

Tony nodded and left the room, and Mantel listened as his kids made a fuss of Uncle Tony before he left. Once he had, Mantel got ready to leave. He would tell Clara about the video, about what her husband did, see what she had to say. If she wanted him to keep quiet, she needed to do more than warn him about whatever George was doing. She was going to have to find out who that man was her husband had let go.

CHAPTER FIFTY-THREE

Clara

I checked my phone; three minutes to eleven.

My heart pounded and no matter how often I wiped my palms, I couldn't stop them feeling clammy. I needed to calm down, Mantel would see straight through me otherwise. Mum was nervous too. She didn't say as much, but I could tell by the way she chatted with the customers in the shop. Her usual flowing conversation was clipped, polite but short, and she still couldn't look me in the eye. She stayed by the till at the front and I sat at the back, with Tabatha, nursing a cold cup of coffee. George had wanted to stay nearby, quietly waiting in the flat, but I told him to go. If Mantel discovered he was there, we would come unstuck. It was better to be safe, so he reluctantly left for work. The police were at the garage, investigating the scene, and he agreed to go there, show his face, stay if he was allowed.

Two minutes.

I fussed with Tabs, but she was tired, and falling asleep in her pushchair. I rocked her gently. A customer came over and took a seat in the café area and Mum bustled over to serve

301

them. I heard the front door to the shop open, and watched as Mantel walked in. I stood and pushed the buggy to Mum, handing over responsibility for Tabs.

'I'll be quick.'

She didn't respond, and as I walked towards the door which led to the staffroom, Mantel followed and without saying a word, came inside. No one saw, no one cared. To customers, strangers, nothing seemed out of place. With the door fully closed behind us, I walked towards the small table.

'Want to sit?' I asked.

'No, I'm not staying long,' he said, leaning against the wall. 'You know someone tried to rob me last night?'

'I heard something about it this morning.'

'Think it's connected?'

'I don't know, I hope not.'

'Why do you hope not?'

'Because then I was wrong about Garrett and Tower.'

'Do you think you were wrong?'

'Honestly, no,' I said, hoping the fact I was lying didn't show.

Mantel studied me, his eyes hard and unreadable. It unnerved me, and he knew it. 'Mrs Goodwin. Last night, your husband was at my garage.'

'What?' I said feigning shock.

'This surprises you?'

'Yes. He didn't tell me.'

'Seems you two have some major communication issues.'

'We're going through a lot.'

'Yeah, I suppose you are.' He still held my eye. 'I got some CCTV from outside my garage. It shows your husband let the thief go.'

'Let him go? You saw that?'

'He misdirected other police officers, sent them the wrong way. I'm wondering why he would do that, why he would let him go?'

'I don't know. Can you send me the footage so I can take a look?' My heart was galloping in my chest. I needed to check exactly how much Mantel had seen. I needed to look like I was trying to understand what my husband was doing, but more than that, I needed to know what he knew.

'I can get it to you,' he said. 'DI Goodwin, why did you tip me off about the surveillance?'

'Because if you get arrested now, I've no doubt you'll drag me down with you.'

He nodded. 'Glad we're on the same page. Find out what your husband is up to, find out who he was speaking with. And find out who he let go last night, and why.'

'I'll try my best.'

'I don't want your best, DI Goodwin. I want your word. We both have things to lose here. You more than me.'

'You have my word.'

Mantel lingered a tad longer than I would have liked, and for a moment I was sure he knew something. But he didn't say anything else as he left, other than that the CCTV would come to me shortly.

Once he was gone, I walked back out to the shop floor and straight over to Tabatha. Mum looked at me for the first time that day, and I smiled weakly at her.

'Clara, please tell me you've got this under control,' she said quietly. 'Now I know who he is, I don't want that man in my shop again.'

'I know, I'm sorry, there was nowhere else to meet.'

'Please tell me this is all going to be all right,' she implored again.

'It's fine mum, I've got this,' I said, but I could tell she didn't quite believe it, and neither did I. I had been way out of my depth since the night of the Tesco robbery where I committed the first of what had now become many crimes. It had spiralled out of control, and I couldn't find a way out of the mess I was making. And yet when I felt close to cracking, as soon as I looked at Tabatha, it mattered less. Nothing mattered now, besides getting on that plane. I had to keep going and make a start banking some of that stolen money, and moving it into the fund. I'd start small, maybe only five of the twenty-seven grand I had stashed above my head, and tomorrow I would add a little more. Some into my bank, some into George's and Mum's too. I'd rob and lie and cheat and risk the lives of others and myself, for her.

CHAPTER FIFTY-FOUR

George

I hated that I had to leave the flat knowing Mantel was about to arrive to speak to Clara, but she was right, if he even got a sniff of me being there, he would come for us both. So I left for work, and even though I knew Mercer would probably have to suspend me for losing it with Mantel, I didn't go to the station straight away. I should have, but my wife needed me to do something for her, for our daughter, first. So I made my way to Mantel's garage instead. If Mercer was at the crime scene, Clara's crime scene, I'd be sent away. I just hoped she wasn't, because I needed to discover if the hatch in the floor of his office was really there.

Arriving at the garage, I saw a police car sat outside. Mercer's car was nowhere to be seen, so I had some time. As I got out of the car, I saw a handful of Mantel's staff were being spoken to by officers. Outside, hung a crude sign written on card using a sharpie saying that due to unforeseen circumstances, the garage was shut. I approached the officer taking statements and he shot me a quizzical look as if to say, 'What are you doing here?'

Word got around fast.

I ignored him and made my way over to the scientific support officer.

'Morning. I'm DS Goodwin.'

'Morning, Sir. I'm Jake,' the scientific support officer said.

'Have you found anything?'

'Nothing yet. There are hundreds of prints on everything, so until we can rule out employees, this is a waste of time.'

'And when will that likely be?'

'For this, a botched break-in, nothing of value stolen? Probably never.'

'I see. Is there anything else to go on?'

'There's CCTV by the front, and inside the building, too. We are waiting for that now.'

'Who has the footage?'

'The owner of the garage.'

'I see. Well, if you get anything, let me know?' I wanted to know what they found in case anything incriminated my wife. I knew that if it did, I would have to tamper with the evidence.

'Of course,' Jake replied.

I moved through the workshop, recalling what had happened last night. My eye was drawn to everything Clara had turned over or looked inside. I tried to recreate what she had done, but even knowing the truth, I couldn't see her doing it. Clara smashing these things, Clara committing this crime.

I heard a car arrive outside and turned to see Mantel getting out of his black Range Rover.

'Shit,' I whispered under my breath. I had hoped I would have more time. He must have only spoken to Clara for a matter of minutes, and raced here after. Ideally, I'd wanted to be in and out before he saw me. I needed a diversion. Whistling, I caught the attention of the PC who was taking the statements outside and he came over.

'I need you to stop the owner and get his statement.'

'Now?'

'Please.'

'Sure thing, DS Goodwin. But is it a good idea you being here? I heard that—'

'Never mind what you heard, just keep him outside, I need to look at something.'

'I'll try,' the officer said before heading back outside and approaching Mantel. I didn't hear what the young PC asked, but I did hear Mantel's response, two words which bought me just enough time.

'Be quick.'

Without looking back, I slipped up the stairs and into his office. From the forecourt, it looked like I was investigating the scene, and I was – but only to find out if I was right and Mantel had a secret space in the floor. It didn't take long; looking at the spot I thought I saw Mantel that day, I noticed a slight difference in the carpet tiles. Dropping down, I carefully peeled back the edge of one of the tiles, and underneath I could see a wooden hatch. Satisfied I could describe it to Clara and she'd find it in the dark, I left and began to make my way back down the steps. As I hit the ground, Mantel turned from the officer, and we made eye contact. He smirked and I felt my confidence waver.

'Well, good morning DS Goodwin, fancy seeing you here.'

'Morning Mr Mantel. I'm sorry for your circumstances.'

'Are you? I thought you lot were sure that Garrett was the crook.'

'You mean Billy Garrett, who was murdered?'

'That's the one. I heard about his death.'

'Or maybe it was Wayne Tower?'

'Maybe.' He smirked again.

I leant into him, so no one else could hear, though I saw the officer twitch, no doubt thinking there would be another altercation.

'I'll prove what you have done one day.'

'Good luck with that, George. After last night I'm pretty confident you'll be off this case and out of my hair.'

'Maybe, but I will still come for you, Henry.'

'That sounds like a threat to me.'

'It's a promise.'

Mantel laughed out loud and those around looked over. He shook his head and mock wiped a tear. 'I cannot fucking wait for that day, George. You know where I am. Now, you wanna fuck off? I've got a business to run, and as you pigs are too incompetent, I've also got a thief to find.'

Mantel stared me down for a long moment before turning to talk to one of his staff. Before yesterday I would have brushed off his last comment, but knowing now he was talking about finding my wife, I felt myself panic. I needed to throw in a curveball to keep him guessing.

'You think you're smarter than us?'

'I know I am.'

'So you can clearly see what I can see?'

That caught his attention, and he looked at me. 'Fine, I'll bite.'

'This isn't connected,' I said, hoping he'd take the bait.

'What do you mean it isn't connected?'

'I've read up on the other robberies. This one is different.'

'What makes you say that?'

'It's too chaotic, too rushed. The other crimes, the guy took his time. This was a botched break-in. It isn't the same person.'

'So, who the fuck is it then?'

'That's what I'm trying to find out.'

I tried to walk away; being this close to the man made me uncomfortable. But I'd only managed a couple of steps when Mantel grabbed my arm.

'Don't you think it's all too much of a coincidence, DS Goodwin?'

'Let go of my arm, Mantel.'

He did, raising his hands in mock defeat.

'And to answer your question, not really. Work it out. The town knows you've been targeted, everybody knows. You're on the ropes, your power is fading, and if you're a common or garden thief, it presents an opportunity.'

'Are you saying it's someone taking advantage of the situation?'

'If they knew Garrett and Tower were suspects, if the blame is elsewhere.'

'How would anyone know? Surely that kind of information stays with the police?'

'It should, yes. But you have people everywhere, don't you?' I said, enjoying the look on his face as he processed what I was telling him. I almost told him that I knew he had a copper on his books, but I stopped myself. 'If you notice anything or remember anything that will help, call the office. I'm sure you know the number.'

'You're not holding out on me are you, DS Goodwin? Not got a secret you wish to share?'

'Goodbye, Mr Mantel.'

'See you DS Goodwin, looking forward to when you come for me.'

I didn't reply, instead, I headed back to my car. I didn't know how Clara did it. However, even with her patience, her strength, cracks were beginning to show, and the sense of time running out both for her and our daughter surrounded us.

28TH JULY 2023

3 days until the deadline . . .

FundMyCause™ Menu   Log In   Sign Up   Search 🔍

Help for Tabatha

We are raising money to send our daughter, Tabatha, to the US for treatment to help her overcome neuroblastoma.

81%

Donate Now

£186, 200
raised of £230,000 target

---

3 days remaining to reach required target

Tabatha continues to fight her disease, the treatment is doing what it can for her. But our baby girl is not getting any better.

We now have less than 72 hours until we fly, and a fifth of our target still to raise, we are now fearing we might not get there. And although she is in the Floxiline programme in America, which this funding page is for, unless we have it all, they won't accept her when we arrive.

Please, please, if you are reading this, help us. We need the kindness of strangers, we are doing everything we can to raise this huge sum of money, but without you, we simply won't get there.

If you can spare anything, please donate, if you cannot spare any money, please share our page, tell our daughter's story, help us get her to her 5th birthday.

We are desperate.

Clara, George and Tabatha x

Supporters

Dean Williams
£15

Carl Daniels
£20

L. Morante
£10

Craig Simons
£20

Selma Langdon
£30

Posy Hackford
£10

Ashleigh Giles
£25

Kieran Waters
£20

CHAPTER FIFTY-FIVE

Clara

George came home shaken, and we agreed that we needed to keep a low profile until we knew exactly what our next steps were. Mantel would be watching. Watching me as I was now in his pocket and watching George following the threats he had made. We needed to make sure we had a contingency for everything.

'Clara, how have you been doing this? I'm a wreck.'

'I am, too. I really am. I need this to be over.'

'Yeah, Mantel is dangerous, we need to get out of here as soon as we can.'

'I am worried that he will find the link, though. He knows you let someone go last night, if he finds out it was me . . .'

'Yeah.'

'I don't know what he's capable of, so I want us to be careful. I think we need to get burner phones. Only you and I know the numbers so we can talk without the risk of anyone – Mantel or the police – finding out. We'll get rid of them before we leave.'

'Good idea,' he said.

As George recovered from his encounter with Mantel, I went out and bought two pay-as-you-go phones. I no longer doubted that at some point I would be dragged into the investigation. Before that happened, I hoped we would be out of the country.

I couldn't help but note that I was now a woman who carried three phones, two of which were burners. I was a real criminal.

Safely back inside and sure Mantel hadn't seen me out and about, we kept low profiles, caring for Tabatha and spending the rest of the day and night planning the final push to raise the remaining money we needed. Once we had cleaned the money in the wardrobe, we needed just twenty-one grand. We were so close. As we talked about what we would do, I felt for the first time since Tabatha's diagnosis that we were a real team.

We prepared to shoot one last video asking for help, and we planned our final hit on Mantel. It was ironic – two things, the same end result, polar opposites in approach. We hoped to find enough to finish this, and if we even got close, that was a lot of money to clean before we put it through the FundMyCause page. We looked at the hospital policy and discovered that they would take up to 10 per cent of the money in cash. We just had to get it out of the country. For the rest, we would have to use our banks and the bookshop accounts, to get it into the system. Three days was not long in the grand scheme of things, but too long for us.

The plan was set. We ran over and over it to make sure we hadn't forgotten or overlooked anything. Even feeling as confident as I could, we had to wait for the right moment to act.

'I don't know how we're going to make sure Mantel doesn't come for us,' George said. 'It's not like I can call Mercer and get her to drag him in for questioning.'

'No, she won't see you as being objective,' I agreed.

'No, I still have yet to face her wrath for last night. So what do we do?'

'I tipped him off that he's under surveillance, and I bet he has seen the police around.'

'Yeah.'

'So, let's make sure he knows he is being watched at home, too. That way, he won't want to leave.'

'And then with him at home feeling the eyes on him—'

'I could go to the garage, and get it.'

Tabs was awake for most of our talk, comforted in my arms. She eventually drifted around 6 a.m., and once she was settled, we set her on an activity mat on the living-room floor and perched down there too, our backs against the sofa as we watched her sleep. My head was on George's shoulder, his hand on my knee. When Tabs was better, once she was well, I was going to try and save my marriage. There was hope; we were so close to being able to begin to put this past six months behind us if we could forgive each other, if we could forget what we had lived through.

From behind us, we heard the sound of the internal door between the flat and bookshop open and close. 'Your mum is here,' George said, lifting me from my sleep-deprived thoughts.

'Yeah.'

'We need to tell her the plan.'

'I know.'

'I'll go put the kettle on. Want one?'

'Please, thanks George.'

He didn't reply but heaved himself up onto his feet. A moment later I heard Mum calling softly.

'Hey.'

'In the kitchen,' George replied, and with Tabs sound asleep, I lifted her from the mat, placed her in her cot and joined them. As I walked into the kitchen, Mum smiled weakly.

'Are you okay?'

'Yeah, are you?'

'I am,' she said, and I wanted to hug her but stopped myself. Now was not the time.

'Do you forgive me?' I asked.

'Nothing to forgive,' she replied, her smile a little stronger than before. 'Is Tabs asleep?'

'She was up a lot in the night, finally settled properly about a couple of hours ago.'

'Have you two been up all night?'

'Uh huh.'

'Oh God. You must both be exhausted.'

'We're fine.' It wasn't true, really I was so exhausted that everything hurt.

'Sit down, let me make these.'

'Thanks, Mum,' I said, taking a seat at the kitchen table. George put the mugs down and sat beside me, his head resting in one hand while the other found mine under the table and held it.

'Mum, we need to talk to you.'

'Oh?' she said, looking from me to George and back again.

'Before we do, George and I are going to put out one more video asking for help. Would you film it?'

'Now?'

'Please, Mum.'

'You sure? You both look, well . . .'

'I know we look like shit, but it's important. We want this done. We want our daughter on that plane.'

CHAPTER FIFTY-SIX

Clara

With Mum filming us, George and I got comfortable on the sofa, me holding a sleeping Tabatha in my arms. Once I had wanted to hide her disease from the world, but now I wanted people to see how ill she was. We needed their generosity.

Mum nodded to tell us she was now recording, and taking a final look at George, I began to speak.

'Some of you might know who we are. Some of you have already helped, and to you, I want to start by saying thank you. But lots of you don't know who I am, or why I am posting this video. We need your help. Here, sleeping in my arms is my . . .' I looked at George '. . . our daughter Tabatha. She has cancer, and she needs . . .' My voice began to crack, the emotions I'd tried to suppress coming to the fore.

George stepped in. 'We are raising money to get her into a treatment programme in America. We need to be out of the UK in the next three days to make the window for this to happen; the next window for this specialised treatment is six months away and by then we might . . .' It was George's turn to trail off. He was still looking into the camera, trying to find the words. For the first time in this whole ordeal, I could see him begin to cry, too. 'We need to go now,' he finally said in such a way my heart ached even more than it already was.

'So far,' I continued, 'we have raised a massive £186,000, which is so much money. And we are so thankful to everyone who has donated and given what they can. But it's not enough to save our daughter. We need two hundred and thirty to get her onto the programme. We are proud people who have spent our lives not asking for help.' I had to pause to wipe my eyes. 'But now, we need it, we need so much of it because this disease in my daughter is killing us all. We are doing all we can, and it's not quite enough.'

I looked over to George once more, and he looked back, his eyes red raw.

'This is who we are doing it for,' I said, looking at Tabatha. Mum lowered the camera, so she was on the screen. 'This little girl who is too innocent, too young for this pain she is going through. Please help us, even if it's only a few pence, help us.'

Tabatha wriggled in my arms and began to cry, and as I got up and moved away from the camera, I heard George continue to speak.

'Below this video is the link to our FundMyCause page. If anyone out there is able to donate, please, please, take a look. We have less than seventy-two hours to help Tabatha, to save her. Thank you.'

As Tabatha took a little milk, I watched as Mum stopped recording.

'People will help,' she said quietly.

Within minutes of posting the video, people began to comment and share and over on the page, new donations were coming in. Small amounts, but every penny counted.

Tabs didn't manage to get back to sleep, three hours was all she got in the end, and knowing it would do her good, would help her rest, I got her ready to go out to our *Stronger, Better, Together* session Gary spoke of. I didn't want to go, not after we were told poor Sophie had died, but I knew I needed to. If Mantel was watching, I wanted it to look like I was still the same old Clara, bumbling through and stealing hope from where I could. The support group wasn't that for me now, not after Sophie, but he didn't know that. I had to hide what I was doing in plain sight, anything else might make him suspicious. Thinking of Sadie, I checked my phone. She still hadn't read my messages. I wouldn't either if I was her.

As I was about to load Tabs into her buggy and head out the door, George appeared in the hallway, fully dressed.

'Wait. Let me grab my shoes.'

'You're coming?' I said, trying not to sound too surprised.

'If I'm still welcome?'

'Yes, of course.'

'Great.'

As we walked onto the high street, a black Range Rover approached.

'Shit.' George said quietly, I didn't know why, and by the time I saw, it was too late to do anything but continue.

The car slowed and I came eye to eye with Henry Mantel. He then put his foot down and sped on his way.

'Think he knows?' George asked.

'Nope, you assaulted him, threatened him, he's just trying to be Bertie big bollocks right now.'

'Yes, you're right. Sorry, I don't know how you're not jumpy about it all.'

'We have to try and hold it together, just for a couple more days.'

'Yes,' George said, and with that, we continued towards the church. When we arrived, Gary was there to greet people.

'Clara, it's so good to see you.'

'Hi Gary, this is my husband, George.'

Gary took George's hand and shook it firmly. 'It's great to see you, George, come in.'

I walked in and George followed behind, a little nervous. As I lifted Tabs out of the buggy and showed George where to sit, Gary mingled, speaking to us all. Once the group had assembled, he sat down, ready to begin. There was another family missing, one I didn't usually speak to. I couldn't place their names, but the void was there. Gary was watching me looking for them, and when I met his eye, he held it for a second.

'Good morning, everyone. Thank you for coming today, three sessions in a week is a lot, but I wanted to ensure, following the tragic news, you have the support you need. I'm so glad to see you all here today, and welcome to those fresh faces who have joined us. You may have noticed that we are missing Jennifer, Ross and baby Oscar, and I know, following the loss of Sophie, you might be fearing the worst. They wanted you to know that Oscar rang the bell.'

Around the circle there was an outburst of joy. Some clapped, some cried, all of us grabbed our babies and held them tight. A hug that said, 'One day this will be us.'

'Rang the bell?' George asked.

'They are in remission. They beat their cancer,' I whispered.

George looked at Tabs, and he then smiled at me before turning his attention to the other families, those who were tired and afraid and lost, those who had hope.

Gary then continued with the session, asking how we all felt given the news and there were mixed feelings. We were all so happy that Oscar had rung the bell, but also willing the ordeal to be over for us soon, too. Layered in as well was the feeling of guilt, for Sophie was still gone, and Sadie would be broken. We split into smaller groups to talk and drink coffee and let our children play. Tabs was too tired, and noticing, Gary joined George and me.

'How is she?' he asked.

'She's struggling.'

'Children are more resilient than we give them credit for.'

'Yeah.'

'George, how are you coping?'

George looked stunned to have been asked so directly how he was. And I realised, I wasn't sure I had ever asked him the same question. At no point through it all had my husband or I asked each other how we were coping and maybe that's why the distance between us had grown.

'You don't have to say, sorry, I have a habit of jumping straight in there,' Gary said, steering the conversation away.

'No, it's okay,' George said. But he didn't offer any more, Gary nodded, as if understanding, and wandered off to talk with other parents.

'Gary can be quite direct.'

'It's all right, I can see why you come here.'

'Really?'

'Yes, this place isn't about doom, this is a place for hope.'

The session continued and concluded in the same manner as it always did, Gary talking about hope, the group reflecting. And then we left. Walking home, George and I had one hand each on the buggy, pushing it together, and neither of us said anything for several minutes. We just walked, our stride in unison, our thoughts elsewhere. Then George spoke.

'When he asked how I was feeling, I should have told him I was scared,' he said. 'I should have told him I felt like a failure.'

'You're not a failure, George. But I also understand what you're feeling.'

'You do?'

'Yeah, we have one job as parents, right?'

'Yeah, we do,' he said. 'Clara, when people were talking at the end of the session, I saw it.'

'What?'

'Her fifth birthday. I saw it. I saw her in her school uniform, you know, one of those little chequered dresses, a little pair of white socks pulled up to below the knee.' He had to pause and clear his throat. 'She had a book bag in her hand. She was wearing a big pin badge. Her hair, long and as dark as yours, was tied in a ponytail. She was so excited, Clara, so happy. And she wasn't sick. She was strong, she was healthy and happy, and so smart. When she smiled, two front teeth were missing. She had your eyes, your dimple too. She was so beautiful Clara, so, so beautiful.'

George caught a tear that fell before composing himself, and we continued to walk in silence. His hand found mine and held it tightly.

'Clara, we finish this thing, we get her to America, and then we sing our hearts out on her fifth birthday.'

'Yes, George, we will,' I said, not asking if we would be singing it together, as a married couple, or together as Tabatha's parents.

When we got home, Tabs was asleep, and as George carried her to her cot , I heard the burner phone given by Mantel ping from the kitchen.

I want an update

I told him that George had been threatened outside the garage, that the thief had a knife and would stab him unless he let him go, but he didn't see the man's face. The police were looking into it. It was part of the plan George and I had discussed during the night, and I hoped to God he bought it. He didn't reply. Right now, George was speaking of the future, and I let myself be swept up in it. For one blissful hour, the future was just within our grasp, and the things I had done to ensure that didn't matter. Due to our efforts, my sacrifices, we almost had enough money to send her to Philadelphia.

As George started making lunch, I went to check on Tabatha. She was on her back, her arms above her head, sound asleep. At first glance, she looked peaceful and content and pain-free, but as I watched her, I noticed her breathing was fast. Too fast. I touched her tummy; her Babygro was damp with sweat.

'George!' I called, and hearing my panic he ran into the room.

'What? What's wrong?'

'She's burning up.'

He touched her head and swore. 'Shit. I'll ring an ambulance.'

Picking her up, I ran to the kitchen, wet some kitchen roll and placed it on her forehead. She woke, screamed, then started to shake violently.

'George, she's having a seizure. Tell them to hurry. Please, please!'

CHAPTER FIFTY-SEVEN

Clara

With me beside our daughter and George following behind us in the car, the ambulance drove quickly, blue lights on, to hospital, where a team was waiting for us to arrive. They moved quickly, the paramedics briefing the doctors on what had happened. The seizure was under control, but Tabatha was still unresponsive. The doctors worked fast, inserting a breathing tube and taking her vitals. They placed a canula into the back of her tiny hand and administered medication, too busy trying to help her to stop and tell me what they were doing.

They managed to stabilise her and her heart rate returned to normal.

'Is she okay?' I asked when a nurse turned to speak to me.

'Mrs Goodwin, we are going to take Tabatha straight up for a scan. We need to see what's happening.'

'Yes, do what you need to do,' I said, but she didn't wait for my permission. I followed, watching my baby rushed along the corridor towards a lift. I paced helplessly, desperate for news. I needed someone to tell me what was going on. My phone rang, my real phone, and scrambling, I pulled it out of my bag.

'Where are you?' George asked.

I started to cry. 'She's in for a scan.'

'I'm on my way.'

George hung up and arrived two minutes later. We hugged and after an agonising wait, a doctor came out to us.

'Mr and Mrs Goodwin. Let me start by saying we have stabilized Tabatha enough to move her to intensive care.'

'Oh, thank God,' I said.

'However, she is very ill, and until we can get her vitals under control we'll need to keep her in. We've sedated her now, to allow her body to fight.'

'How long . . .' George started, then stopped to catch his breath. 'How long will she be asleep for?'

'It's hard to say, but she needs this if she is to have any chance. We are doing everything we can for her.'

'Can we see her?' I managed to say before my voice started to crack.

'Of course.'

We followed the doctor up to the first floor and into the PICU, towards Tabatha's bed. She was hooked up to several machines, her tiny chest rising and falling with mechanical help.

'Oh God,' I said, my hand flying to my mouth.

George comforted me, and somehow keeping it together, he asked the doctors questions. I could hear them talking though I struggled to process what was being discussed.

'What do we do now?' he asked.

'We keep her sedated, and we investigate options. But she is comfortable, she isn't in pain. We have to hope she is strong enough to battle, but . . .'

'But? But what?'

'I'm sorry, Mr Goodwin. Tabatha is in a very serious condition.'

Those words hit me like a train and I couldn't hear any more of what was being said. I reached for a chair and slumped into it, looking at my daughter.

My helpless daughter.

George was still speaking, the doctor was still responding, but I couldn't focus on them.

My poor, dying daughter.

The doctor then left the room, leaving us alone with Tabatha.

'Clara. Clara,' George said, stooping down to my level and gently holding me. 'Did you hear?'

'She is comfortable, they can't do any more.'

'No, after that. There is still hope for America. They will help us get her there. They said that it's the best option now, and they will begin the process this end. As soon as she is more stable, we can go, we need to be ready for that.'

'Oh,' I said, still struggling to feel anything but numb.

George squeezed my shoulders, and refocusing, I could see the determination in his eyes. 'Clara, we need to move.'

'What?'

'As soon as it's dark, we need to get this done.'

'Tonight?'

'Yes, tonight.'

'How will you make sure Mantel is out of the way?'

George pulled out his phone, and without explaining anything else, made a call. Putting it on speaker phone as it rang.

'George, I'm not sure you should be ringing me.'

'Mike, I need you to listen. Clara is with me.'

'Hi Mike.'

'Hi Clara, what's going on?'

'I've had a tip-off, and given the shit I am in, I can't do anything about it. Mantel is up to something. I need you to pay his town centre businesses a visit.'

'All of them?'

'Yes, all of them. Go to his garage first.'

'Wanna tell me why?'

'Trust me. You don't need to do anything other than look around, I want Mantel to know.'

Mike sighed. 'George, Mercer is still gunning for you.'

'This is why I need you to help, we are close to getting him Mike. I promise, I won't ask anything again.'

'Fine. I'll go and look around, am I looking for anything specific?'

'No, just make sure Mantels' cameras pick you up. Thanks mate.'

George hung up and looked at me. 'Right, message Mantel, tell him you heard Mike and I talking, and that Mike is snooping around, we want Mantel to watch him. You need to go, get ready.'

'Go? But Tabatha?'

'Is getting the best care possible. But we have to act right now. If we want her in the programme, we need to do this.'

I nodded, he was right.

'Make sure you keep the burner on so we can talk.'

'I will.'

'The car is in car park B. Go home, get ready, and when I message you, get that money and save our daughter.'

CHAPTER FIFTY-EIGHT

Clara

I raced back home, messaging Mantel on my way to the car just as George said I should. He texted back, instructing me to find out what George now knew.

At the flat, I packed my rucksack, changed into my dark clothes and waited for the burner that was my link to George to ring. When it did, I jumped.

'Mike has been to the garage, is now in town at the salon and café before going to the golf course. The garage is clear.'

'I tipped off Mantel. Do you think he's seen Mike on the garage CCTV?'

'We can hope. We can also hope that he will be looking elsewhere when you arrive; he will be able to look back, but by then, hopefully, we will gone. Be careful.'

'I will.'

Hanging up, I put on my shoes and left the flat, locking the door behind me. I walked through the quiet streets, trying my best to avoid the CCTV cameras in shop entrances, checking behind me to see if I was being followed, but all was quiet. It was, for the most part, just like any other night. At the garage

I saw that the door I had broken had been replaced. However, the window beside it remained the same, and knowing I didn't have time to try and get in using subtler methods, I picked up a rock and threw it at the window, smashing it completely. The alarm began to sound, I had to move fast. Clearing the glass, I climbed through and ran for the office. That door was also locked, and again, I smashed the glass.

Inside I crouched on the floor and pulled up the carpet tile George had told me to find to reveal the wooden hatch. That too was locked, but I'd expected as much. I grabbed the hammer from my rucksack and began to smash it open. Wood cracked then split and eventually gave way, making me fall backwards. Using my torch, I shone it into the void beneath and saw what I was looking for; money, stacks of it. Easily as much as I'd found in the club in Stockport. Opening the rucksack, I rammed it all in and just as I was putting the bag back on my back, I heard movement from the garage floor. I looked over the top and saw two officers inside, torch lights shining. I ducked behind the door frame. They were there a lot quicker than they should have been, either bad luck or they were already close by.

'Police. Is anyone in here?' One officer said.

'Look,' said the other, a voice I recognized. It was Mike. If he was there, then Mantel would be watching.

I looked through the smashed window to see a torch beam cutting through the dust. The first officer then radioed in, saying that there had been a break-in and the suspect was still inside.

I heard the first officer say back-up was on the way.

'You look around down here, I'll go up,' Mike said, and I panicked, looking for somewhere to hide.

'This is the police, come out with your hands up,' Mike barked, his voice drawing closer. I half crawled, half ran, to the far window of Mantel's office, wondering if I could break it and jump. The fall was around thirty feet, I would break my legs and I would get caught. I heard footsteps coming up the stairs. Mike was on his way.

On Mantel's desk was an ornament, a large piece of expensive-looking decorative resin on a silver stand. Grabbing it, I hid in the dark corner of the room. It was heavy enough to use if I had no choice. I needed to get out, I needed to take this money, whatever the cost. In my hands was my daughter's future, in my hands was her life.

Torchlight shone into the office and I pressed myself into the wall to not be seen. Mike tried the door, and unable to open it, he started to climb through the window. My hope was he wouldn't see me, and I could climb out and run before he could grab me. I hoped in the darkness, I could have the element of surprise. I held my breath as one long leg climbed in, followed by the other, the torch beam pointing at the floor where I had broken the hatch door. I wanted to move, but he was still too close. If he took just two steps towards the desk, I would bolt. But he didn't, he lifted the torch, and turned it around the room.

'What the . . .' he started when he saw me in the shadows, and before he could shout for help, I ran for him, shoving him hard. I tried to climb out of the window but my hand slipped onto a shard of glass still in the frame, slicing it open. Mike grabbed me, and I turned, hitting him with the ornament. The weight and the adrenaline meant as it made contact with his head, I knew it was too hard. He dropped to the floor in such a way I was sure he was dead.

'Mike?' the other officer called out. 'Mike?'

I wanted to make sure I hadn't killed him, but I didn't have time. The other officer was coming. I looked out of the office to see where he was and could make him out heading across the garage floor. Before he could reach the stairs, I climbed the window and hid in the shadows of the far corner of the platform. He came up and looked into the office. Seeing Mike, he climbed in and began to administer medical attention.

'Mike, can you hear me, mate? Mike! Officer down, I need help,' he called into his radio, and knowing he was on the floor, I ran. He saw me dash past and called out.

'Wait, stop!'

But I was too fast. Before he could climb out of the office, I was down the stairs, running for the exit. Outside I didn't stop. I looped behind the garage to scale the same wall I did before. There was a small but dense woodland area behind; he would take one look over and knowing he wouldn't catch me, he would go back to help poor Mike. Once over the wall, I continued to run, careful to stay in the shadows until I reached the main road. In the thick foliage, I took off my jacket, hat and mask, forcing them into the bag. Then, as I hit the tarmac of the quiet street, I walked as calmly as I could, my head low, hiding my tears. I hoped that I gave off the look of someone finishing a late shift in a local pub. If anyone saw me, they might question why a woman was walking alone at night, but I suspected they wouldn't think I had just committed a crime and severely injured a police officer, a friend. The walk took half an hour, and in that time, despite hearing sirens, I didn't see anyone. Back home, I locked the door behind me, and with my back to it, I fought to calm my racing heart. Unzipping the bag, I spilled the contents onto the floor. I gathered up the bundles of money and counted, and with each passing thousand, the guilt I felt for hurting Mike faded. Blood dripped onto the bed from the cut on my hand, but I couldn't feel it; all I cared about was did I have enough?

We had £192,345 in the FundMyCause pot. I had £22,000 stashed away.

And now I had £18,000 more.

I did the maths. Our new total was £232,345.

We had done it. As the tears began to fall, tears of relief, of exhaustion, tears of shame and pride, fear and hope, I messaged George on the burner.

We've done it, we have enough. We have over 230 grand!

No, Clara, YOU did it. You did all of this. You have saved our baby

CHAPTER FIFTY-NINE

Clara

I hid the money with the rest, unable to fully process that I had forty thousand pounds just sat there in my wardrobe. I cleaned up my hand and got changed, desperate to get back to Tabatha and George. As I was about to leave, I heard noises from the street below; looking out, I saw two officers patrolling. If they saw me, I could say I had to nip home to collect some things, but, then, if one of those officers was Lee Sharman, he might tell Mantel and then Mantel might suspect it was me who was the thief. Even if he didn't, the police might become suspicious as to why I was home. It was too risky. I had no choice but to lay low.

Moving away from the window, I sat on the edge of the sofa. Not being able to go back to my daughter was going to break my heart, but I needed to sit tight, stay in the dark. No one would think to look here unless I gave them reason to.

I messaged George.

I can't leave the flat, too many eyes watching. Please update me every hour, I can't bear not being with our baby

Good idea, lay low for a while. Come later. Clara, she is going

to be OK, you have made sure of that. Tomorrow, we clean what we need to clean, and we get our daughter on that flight

Slumping back on the sofa, I grabbed a notepad and pen and crunched the numbers. If Philadelphia were happy to take 10 per cent in cash, we still had to get a lot of money through the banking system in a very short window. It would be difficult, and it would raise a lot of red flags, but what choice did we have? I would do it all tomorrow, banking some through Mum's business account, saying that our café had an influx of people buying cake and coffee. I'd put another few hundred in as a cash donation for Tabs. I'd have to put some into my own account, and George's, and the joint account and send it across. Small chunks of cash, three or four thousand in each. I knew doing it that way, I might not get caught. For us, it was a lot of money, but it wasn't as much money as some banked daily. I had to hope no one looked hard enough.

I heard more voices, and moving quietly back to the window I saw two police officers walking past, likely the same two as before. They were shining torches, looking for anything out of place. One of them shone his beam up towards the flat, and I ducked away. I went to our bedroom at the back of the flat where I knew I couldn't be seen, closed the door and turned on a lamp. I caught my refection in the mirror. Once, a strong woman had looked back at me, a woman I liked the look of. Now someone else was in her place, someone who carried guilt, shame, someone who knew one day that everything that had happened in the past few weeks would catch up. The weight of her actions this week would haunt her forever. She would have a heart attack at fifty, or a stroke at fifty-five. She would suffer indignity; she would pay her penance.

29ᵀᴴ JULY 2023

2 days until the deadline . . .

FundMyCause™   Menu   Log In   Sign Up   Search 🔍

Help for Tabatha

We are raising money to send our daughter, Tabatha, to the US for treatment to help her overcome neuroblastoma.

88%

£203,755
raised of £230,000 target

Donate Now

---

2 days remaining to reach required target

Important update

Tabatha is currently in intensive care following a seizure. We have been told that the treatments available through our NHS will not save her.

She needs to be on a plane to Philadelphia as soon as possible or she will not make it.

We desperately need your help. Anything you can spare, anything at all, will make a difference.

We have a confirmed place, we just need the final funds to be able to go.

We appreciate everyone's help so far. You have shown us that kindness wins, you have given us hope and we are getting so close. With your generosity, we can get Tabatha onto the programme and change her life forever.

We need her on a plane as soon as we can. We need you to help make that happen.

Clara, George and Tabatha x

Supporters

 M Murdock
£50

Jessica Harvey
£20

Paban M
£20

Natalie Wrench
£20

Louise Compton
£10

Laura Short
£10

Mr and Mrs Jackson
£100

Gary
£50

CHAPTER SIXTY

George

Sitting beside my daughter, I watched the total on the FundMyCause page grow. There was now over two hundred thousand, and it was still climbing. We had a buffer. Two weeks ago, I would have said this was impossible, and yet now we had a buffer. All because of Clara.

I messaged her updates but as the night wore on, her replies took longer and longer to come back to me, until, at just after four, she stopped replying altogether. I was glad she had managed to fall asleep. I wasn't surprised. I couldn't begin to understand how exhausted she must be feeling now it was over.

I hoped she was sleeping deeply, dreaming of our baby on her fifth birthday. A birthday she was now going to have, because of Clara's courage. I had been a shitty husband, I'd let my girls down, but I wouldn't waste this second chance.

My phone started to ring beside me, and I moved quickly so I didn't wake Tabs, even though I knew I couldn't. I saw it was DCI Mercer. I had been expecting the call since the assault on Mantel, but for her to ring in the night? Something was off.

I answered it in hushed tones. 'Hey boss, listen, I know I did wrong, but I can't talk—'

'George, Mike has been assaulted,' Mercer said interrupting me.

'What? When?'

'Last night.'

'Shit, is he okay?' I replied, my shoulders sinking.

'He's sustained a head injury. A fractured skull.'

'Fuck.'

'He's going to make it, but he's been properly banged up. George, what the hell is going on?'

'Ma'am, I wish I knew,' I lied.

'Sorry to call so early in the morning. I know you two are close. I just wanted you to know. When I have an update, I'll message.'

'Thank you, Ma'am,' I said, and she hung up. I kept the phone to my ear a little longer, stunned. Mike's skull had been fractured. By my wife.

'Fuck.'

Surely Clara didn't know what she had done? Surely she was startled, had panicked. If she did know it was him, could I forgive her for it? Mike was our friend, my partner, a good man. She needed to tell me what happened, but I also didn't want to wake her. She had been through so much and I was so torn. I loved my wife, but if she had hurt Mike intentionally . . . It was too much to get my head round.

An hour later, an hour of me waiting to know how Mike was, Clara messaged and I rang her back straight away.

'Hey,' I said. 'You slept!'

'Hey. I did, a little.'

'Clara, Mike is in a bad way.'

There was silence for so long I was sure the line had gone dead.

'Clara?'

'How is he?' she asked.

'Not great, but he'll make it.'

'I didn't want to hurt anyone, I'm so, so sorry. I was cornered, I didn't know what to do. If I let him catch me then . . .' She paused, took a deep shaky breath. 'How do I recover from what I've done?'

'First, you get on the phone to Philadelphia. You tell them we are coming, you pay a deposit or whatever they need and we get the ball rolling, starting with getting those flights booked. Then, when we are there, when Tabatha is well, we can work on the rest together. I'll stay here, ring you every half an hour to give you updates. She's stable, she's sleeping. I'll speak with the doctors here; tell them we're ready to go. We are so close to finishing this.'

CHAPTER SIXTY-ONE

Clara

Being so caught up in the events of the night, I realized now that Mum didn't know that Tabatha was in trouble. I wanted to tell her, I wanted her with me. But the police were looking for someone who had hurt one of their own. If she arrived so early and was seen, the police would want to know why I wasn't with my baby. When I called, it was almost six in the morning.

'Clara?'

'Mum, something happened in the night. Tabatha has been hospitalized.'

'I'll be there in an hour,' she said, her voice resolute.

'No, Mum, I'm at the flat. Come here.'

'OK, I'll be right over.'

When Mum walked in, she rushed over to hug me and we both started to cry. When I gathered myself, I explained how Tabs had had a seizure but was now stable and under sedation. I told her how I'd left the hospital for one final hit on Mantel.

'I've been stuck here all night. Stuck here away from my baby.'

'You should have rung me last night,' Mum said, holding me close again as I cried.

'I know, Mum, I'm sorry, I just . . . the police were out in town. If they saw you and knew I was at home, they might have questions. I didn't want to risk it.'

'I understand. I'm here now. How close are we to our target?'

'We have it.'

'What?'

'We have enough. We just need to finalize the travel arrangements.'

Taking Mum by the hand, I led her to the bedroom and showed her the stacks of money I had stolen, a massive forty thousand pounds, and we both just stared at it. This was blood money, but it was also money that was going to save my innocent daughter's life. With Philadelphia being five hours behind, it was only just after one in the morning there, so we wouldn't hear anything from them until at least 2 p.m. our time, and as soon as we did, we needed to be ready to pay the deposit the minute that call came. We went down to the shop and prepared a banking run, and Mum said she was confident we could put across as much as seven grand into the business account without raising any attention. I grabbed a shower and after that it was nearly time to open the shop and go to the bank. I took seven bundles of twenties wrapped in banking bands, and shoved them, along with the other banking cash and the paying-in book into my rucksack. I put another two in my pocket to bank in my own account, plus one for hers and two for George's. In total, I had twelve grand of the forty from the flat. We would smuggle the 10 per cent deposit between us to America, and the rest, the few grand left, I would work out how what to do with later.

As I prepared to go off to bank the money and get back to my family, I walked onto the shop floor, and the urgency I felt, the hope that powered me, was stopped in a second. For Mum had opened the shop, and as I drew level with the till, I saw Henry Mantel.

'Mrs Goodwin,' he said. 'Fancy seeing you here. I'm sure there is somewhere else you need to be? Isn't there? I heard your baby is unwell?'

'I had to get some things.'

'I see. Well, I'm just looking around. Seeing if anything takes my fancy.'

'I didn't expect to see you today,' I said, hoping I sounded relaxed, calm. Hoping the money in my rucksack wasn't acting like a beacon for him.

'I like a mystery, working out puzzles, catching a crook, that sort of thing.'

'What?'

'Books, I like those type of books,' he continued. 'How's your fundraising going?'

'We are getting there, thank you. Your donation has helped a lot.'

'Just doing my bit,' he said, smiling at me. 'I kind of hope I find one that catches most people off guard.'

'I'm sorry?'

'A book, you know the type, all the arrows point to one character, and then you learn it couldn't possibly be them, then you get that twist,' he said, snapping his fingers and making me instinctively blink. 'I like it when I'm smarter than other readers, seeing what other people refuse to see, you know what I mean?'

'I'll get my mum; she'll be able to recommend a few. Excuse me, I really must be going. I need to get back to the hospital.' I tried to walk around Mantel, but he wasn't making it easy. As I managed to pass, he grabbed me by my arm, lifting it up and revealing my bandaged hand.

'That cut looks nasty. How did you do it?'

'Opening a box out back, the box cutter slipped.'

'Ouch, you should really get that looked at, DI Goodwin.'

'I will, thank you. I hope I was helpful to you last night?'

'You were,' he said, looking at me in a way that made me feel even more uncomfortable.

'Good. I've got a few leads to follow up on. I'll have more for you later, or tomorrow morning.'

'Take care of yourself, Clara.'

Mantel didn't go to the crime and thriller section, but instead turned and left. I was sure he was on to me.

CHAPTER SIXTY-TWO

Clara

After I'd been to the bank, I headed back to the hospital where George and I sat quietly, holding hands. Even after everything we had done, it felt like the candle was fading, the wall paintings that were our daughter's future life moments were beginning to recede back into the darkness. There was no change with Tabatha, she was still sedated, but a nurse told us she was already faring better. She wouldn't wake, but, she might be well enough to fly. God willing. Mum was at the shop dealing with the team at the Children's Hospital of Philadelphia, and at just after three, she called.

'Mum?'

She was crying.

'Mum? What's wrong?'

'It's done. She's in.'

'When can we go?'

'They are ready for her. They are just getting the flight details confirmed now. We should hear back soon.'

'Thank you so much for doing what you have done,'

I managed to say without crying, despite the overwhelming sense of relief.

'You did it all, love.'

I hung up and let the tears come. George hugged me.

'What did she say?'

'As soon as she's safe to fly, we can go.'

'Oh Clara, oh God,' George said, as he too started to cry. A passing nurse heard our tears and came into the room.

'Are you two okay?'

'They are ready to receive her in Philadelphia. When might she be well enough to fly? What do we need to do?'

'Let me get Dr Bhari,' she said smiling.

'Thank you.'

Dr Bhari came shortly after, and he agreed that despite the risks of moving Tabatha, it was now her best option. He informed us he had set up a call with the specialized travel operator who would support us on the flight, but as Tabs was now sedated and needing extra support, the cost would be much more. Fifteen thousand more. We looked at the page. As it had climbed to almost hit our original target, we could cover that extra money from what we had stolen. Again it would be tight, but we could do it. We'd agreed that Tabatha could be on a plane within twenty-four hours. I sank into a chair beside our daughter's bed.

'I didn't think this would be possible,' George said. 'I didn't think you'd pull it off.'

'Neither did I,' I admitted.

'That's not true, you knew you could do it. I should never have doubted you.'

347

'It doesn't matter now,' I said, yawning though the words. 'She's going, she's in.'

'Clara, you should get some sleep. You need your strength for the journey.'

'I might have to.'

30TH JULY 2023

1 day until the deadline . . .

FundMyCause™   Menu   Log In   Sign Up   Search 🔍

Help for Tabatha

We are raising money to send our daughter, Tabatha, to the US for
treatment to help her overcome neuroblastoma.

£218,500
raised of £230,000 target

Donate Now

---

1 day remaining to reach required target

Important update

Tabatha is currently in intensive care following a seizure. We have been told
that the treatments available through our NHS will not save her.

OUR DAUGHTER IS NOW CONFIRMED FOR HER FLIGHT!

She leaves in less than a day. We are still a little short of our target, but we
can now manage.

Thank you everyone, thank you from the bottom of our hearts. Tabatha has a
chance now, because of you.

We will update this page with how she responds to the Floxiline treatment.

Keep us in your prayers.

All our love,

Clara, George and Tabatha x

Supporters

Sarah Bentley
£20

Paula Joy
£50

Penny Wright
£30

Giles Murrey
£30

M. Constance
£100

Mum
£7000

G. Goodwin
£1000

C. Goodwin
£1000

FundMyCause™
Terms of Use   Privacy Policy   Cookie Policy

About Us
Careers
Help & Support

SIXTY-THREE

Clara

'Clara, wake up. Clara!'

I opened my eyes to find George standing over me in a panic. I shot up and looked over at Tabatha, but she was still asleep, the heart rate monitor gently passing time.

'Tabatha?'

'She's fine.'

'What's wrong then?'

'The shop.'

'What about it?'

'Clara, something's happened.'

'What?'

'Clara, your Mum just called, it's on fire. The shop is on fire.'

'What?' I said. 'What, no – the money!'

I grabbed my shoes, put them on and ran out of the hospital towards the car. There was £28,000 in the flat. £28,000 we needed as our costs had already risen by £15,000. I needed to save it. But it was an hour's drive. I had to hope I'd not be too late. As I left the hospital, I saw it was a little after midnight, it was the penultimate day to get my baby out of the country, if anything went wrong now, I didn't know what I would do.

Driving as fast as I could, I hurried home and as I approached the town centre, I could see the orange hue taint the night sky.

'No, no, please God no.'

Accelerating, setting off a speed camera on the high street, I raced towards the glow. I was only able to get so close; the road had been closed as firefighters worked to put out the flames. Black smoke billowed out of shattered windows at the front of the shop. Inside, the fire still raged. I ran towards the building, the heat of the flames forcing me back before I could be grabbed by a firefighter and pulled away. Close by, I heard crying, and saw through the gathered crowd Mum sitting on the side of the road, sobbing.

'Mum, Mum,' I said, shaking her. 'Did you get inside?

'No, Clara, I didn't. I couldn't get in. I'm so sorry. I'm so sorry.'

I ran back towards the building, this time avoiding being grabbed. I went round the back and up the external metal stairs to the flat. I touched the front door to make sure it wasn't hot and noticed it had been forced open.

'No, no!'

I pushed it and as it swung freely I looked into my flat, my home, as thick black smoke engulfed everything.

Lifting my top to cover my mouth, I ran. The air was thick, hot, like a smog sauna. Flames licked the walls, the curtains were engulfed, everything was burning. Soon the floor would collapse, soon everything I had would be gone. I didn't have a lot of time. Fumbling, blinded by the smoke, I ran into the bedroom and saw that everything had been flipped, the room was trashed. I prayed that whoever had broken in hadn't found what they were looking for. I opened the wardrobe, to locate the bag that the money that was hidden in. Grabbing it, reassured by its weight, I ran through the flat and back outside, stumbling down the fire escape and rolling down the final few steps onto the gravel. I couldn't breathe, I couldn't see, and I coughed so hard I was sick. I crawled far enough away from the building that I could no longer feel the heat. I was sick again, my body feeling like it was turning inside out as I vomited and gasped for air. I knew I needed help, but before that I needed to make sure it was all there. I opened the bag and looked inside. It was full of books. Upending it, the books fell onto the ground and I was confused – until I found a note at the bottom of the bag.

I suspect this particular 'whodunnit' is easy for you to crack, DI Goodwin.

You shouldn't have taken my money.

If you talk to anyone, if you tell anyone what has happened here, I will come for you, and I will kill you.

Count yourself lucky you're not dead already, but I figured watching you suffer because you cannot help your daughter is a better punishment.

The money was gone, Mantel had worked out it was me, and he had taken it. All of it. All the money I hadn't been able to bank or had been keeping to one side to give directly to the hospital.

And there was no way we could make it back. We didn't have the time.

CHAPTER SIXTY-THREE

Clara

It took the fire fighters another hour to dampen the flames, and all Mum and I could do was stand and watch on helplessly. The clock ticked down. Tabatha was due to be on the flight in twenty hours, and even though it was paid for, the final 10 per cent we promised the hospital we would pay in cash upon arrival was gone. The police, paramedics, even the fire fighters told us, after they checked to make sure I wasn't hurt, to leave, to go back to Mum's. There was nothing we could do and watching the rest of it burn wouldn't help us. But we couldn't move, so we stayed, we watched.

By the time they had managed to gain control and reduce the inferno to smouldering ashes, everything we owned, everything we had worked for, was gone. It wasn't just the money, it wasn't just the books in the shop, it was everything around our daughter too. Her favourite teddy, the outfits we loved to see her in. Her toys and gifts. Family photos on the walls, things that belonged to Dad, books and trinkets that he left me in his will. They were all gone, burnt or so smoke damaged there was no saving them. But as much as knowing everything that connected us to our past was gone, I knew none of those things really mattered. What did was the £28,000 taken before the place burned to the ground. Without it, we were done. Without it, Tabatha's chances of survival were reduced to zero. We couldn't report the missing money to anyone. It was the reason I targeted Mantel in the first place; dirty money didn't exist, and saying otherwise was an omission of guilt. Mantel knew it, and he rubbed it in my face, too, by driving past the shop as the final smoulders faded to witness the aftermath.

A police liaison officer drove us back to Mum's house.

We asked to be left alone there, and the officer understood, handing us a direct contact number to call whenever we needed. He informed us the police would want to talk, take statements. All this I knew, but I asked them to hold off for now, I needed to be back with my daughter.

After the officer left, I sat numbly listening to the clock on the wall. The way it ticked reminded me of Tabatha's heart rate monitor in the hospital. Tick, tick, tick.

I watched, feeling like at any moment it would stop.

'Clara, I . . .' Mum started, before trailing off.

'Mum, don't. I need a minute.'

'Of course,' she said, getting up and leaving the room. A minute later, the sound of a kettle boiling and her crying drowned out the ticking clock. My phone started to ring, and seeing it was George, I picked it up. It felt heavy in my hands, as though at any moment it would fall and crack the floor. I ignored it, and then he rang on the burner.

'Clara?'

'The money is gone.'

'What?'

'Mantel knew we had it, he knew and he took it, and he burnt the place down. He said he would have killed me, but watching me be helpless to save Tabatha was a better punishment. George, we aren't going to have enough.'

'No, Clara, listen, we are close. The shop, the flat, they're insured, we'll get—'

'George, it's over, we can't do this. We've run out of time. Insurance money? She'll be dead before it gets here.'

'Clara, we still have the other money, we are still close.'

'No, George, we're not. I don't know how we can raise thirty thousand in what, eighteen hours?'

'Clara.'

'George, I have to go.'

'Clara, wait.'

I hung up; I couldn't face it. I put my phone on silent and placed it upside down on the coffee table, I looked up at Mum and her expression said it all. We tried to be smarter than a career criminal. We tried to outcrook a crook. We had failed, and Tabatha was going to pay the price. I couldn't stay, I needed air, and without explaining why, I got up to leave.

'Clara? Clara, come back. Clara?' Mum called as I left her house and headed down the street.

I didn't know where I was going or why I was walking, but I didn't care. I just needed to move, to try and outrun what my life had become. I could smell smoke in the air from the fire. I would smell it forever now. On my left, a house had a light coming from an upstairs window. As I passed, I looked up to see a mum holding her baby, winding her and gently rocking her back and forth after an early dawn feed. I stopped and stared. The mother was smiling down at her little one, the baby a little younger than Tabs. I could almost hear her speaking, comforting her, lost in the moment. I hoped she understood how lucky she was to be able to be with her baby without worry, without grief trying to push in and spoil it. The mother looked up from her daughter and saw me staring so I put my head down and walked away, each step heavier than the one before.

Turning right, I recognized the road and realized where I was. I should have turned around, gone back to Mum's, but instead I continued towards the door I had subconsciously found myself drawn to. It was the door of the only person I knew who might be able to prepare me for the blow, the only person, besides Sadie, who I thought had lost a child. I was outside Gary's front door now and before I could stop myself, I stepped up to it and knocked.

Nothing happened for a minute, so I knocked again, and a light was switched on inside. The door opened and Gary stood there in a dressing gown, sleepy-eyed, his hair on one side flattened from where it had pressed into his pillow as he slept.

'Clara? Is that you?'

'Hi Gary,' I managed to say, my voice weak and distant.

'What's wrong?'

'I'm sorry to wake you so early.'

'No, it's fine. What's wrong?'

'I need someone to talk to, I didn't know where else to go.'

'Come in,' Gary said, taking me by the arm and guiding me inside. As we went into the living room, a voice called from upstairs.

'Gary?'

'It's okay, Siobhan.'

'Who is it?'

'A parent from the support group.'

Footsteps, and a woman came in, wrapping herself in a robe.

'I'm so sorry, I don't know why I came here, I should go,' I said, getting to my feet.

'No, stay, please.' Siobhan looked at Gary and he nodded.

'I'll put the kettle on,' she said, leaving the room.

'Clara?' Gary sat opposite me.

'Gary, she's really sick. Tabatha is really, really sick. She isn't going to win her battle.'

'Oh, Clara.' He took my hand in his.

'I don't know why I came here, I'm sorry for waking you, I just, I know you understand what's about to happen to me, and I really needed someone to talk to.'

CHAPTER SIXTY-FOUR

George

Clara wasn't answering my calls. Our home had burned down, our lives had gone up in flames, and I couldn't do anything about it. I needed to stay with Tabs.

All I could do was speak periodically with Mercer, who was now at the bookshop and updating me when she could. I hated not knowing where Clara was, I was worried. She was under so much pressure, and now everything was lost. I rang Jo, too, to see if Clara was with her.

'George, thank God.'

'Is she there? Is she okay?'

'What? No? I thought that was why you were ringing? She left hours ago. I hoped she was with you and Tabatha.'

'No,' I said. 'Where did she go?'

'I don't know, she just took off. I tried to stop her.'

'Stay near the phone, I'll ring someone at the force to help find her.'

'George, I'm worried. I've never seen her like this, she was broken.'

'I'm worried, too.'

'I don't know what to do. I don't know where my daughter is, I don't know how to help save my grandchild.'

'I'm going to make some calls. If you hear from her or she comes back, please call me?'

'Of course.'

I hung up and as I looked at Tabs, my eye was drawn to the tube down her throat. I knew that the image would stay with me forever.

I wracked my brain, trying to figure out something I could do. Another video might help, but I just didn't know if it would be enough. The only thing I did know that would definitely work was if we got that money back from Mantel. He had it back but he wouldn't be able to bank it. The same rules applied as before; it would have to be hidden and then cleaned. But where would he hide it? Opening the list of my recent calls, I hovered over the third down, took a breath and rang Mercer.

'Ma'am, Clara is missing,' I said before she could speak. 'She took off from her mum's, we don't know where she is. She's not in a good way.'

'Right, I'll get a couple of uniformed officers to help out.'

'Thank you, Ma'am.'

'George, are you okay?'

'No, not at all, not even close,' I replied. As Mercer offered words of support, I felt movement behind me, and turned to see Clara walk in.

'Clara! Ma'am, she's here. Don't worry.'

I hung up without saying thank you or goodbye, and wrapped my arms around my wife. She didn't hug me back, but stood with her arms limp by her side. It felt like she had given up. That the fight in her had died.

'Love, where have you been?'

'Sorry.'

'No, don't be sorry. How did you get here?'

'Gary brought me here.'

'Who?'

'Gary, from the group. I don't know why I went to him.'

'It's okay,' I said, holding her tighter. She smelled of smoke, her hair was thick with it. And as she started to cry, I cried, too.

'It's over, isn't it?' she sobbed, her voice muffled against my top.

'No. No. We can still do this.'

'We can't. Look what I've done. I've hurt people, others are dead. I nearly killed a good copper, a father himself. And now the money we needed is gone. It was all for nothing.

'Clara, listen to me,' I said, and the force in my tone made her lift her head to look me in the eye.

'The money you have taken, it's dirty money, you are giving it a real life. You have hurt a bad person, the two others you didn't kill, Mantel did, and Mike is going to be all right. He'll mend, and he will be very well looked after.'

'I know you're just saying this to make me feel like what I've done is somehow justified. I know it's not, it won't ever be, but I hope it's true. I just don't know how we could recover the money in time to help her?'

'We'll find a way.'

Clara nodded and went to sit in the chair by Tabatha's side. Her face was dirty from soot, her clothes stained by dirt and ash from the fire. I couldn't imagine how terrifying that moment was for her, running into the flat surrounded by heat and flames, only to discover the money was gone. And yet she watched Tab's calmly, her breathing deep and slow. It worried me.

'Clara, are you okay?'

'I'm fine,' she said quietly, not taking her eyes off our daughter.

CHAPTER SIXTY-FIVE

Clara

'Please tell me what you are thinking about,' George implored.

'I'm thinking about her fifth birthday,' I lied because I couldn't imagine it any more.

'Clara. We will do this; we will sort it. I'm going to do a video, a public plea, do you want to do it with me?'

'No, love. I don't have it in me.'

'I understand, I've got this one.'

George took out his phone and I returned my gaze to our baby. He recorded a short message, talking about the fire, the urgency of needing to get Tabatha overseas, and he asked for help. Begged for it. When he finished, he uploaded it to social media.

'There, done. The money will come.'

I nodded, but I didn't think it would be true.

'Clara, don't give up.'

'We're supposed to fly in less than a day, George.'

'Clara.'

'We need to speak to Dr Bhari. We need to tell him it's not going to happen, so he knows.'

'Why?'

'So he can do more. I don't know. So we can do something.'

'We are doing something. We're raising this money, Clara.'

'George, unless it comes soon, we won't do it in time. We can't get on that plane without it all being there. You heard what they said, the transfer alone could prove to be . . .'

'Clara, please, you have been the driving force on this, you are the creator. So we've hit a setback—'

'A setback? Our home is gone, the money is gone. This isn't a setback, George, this is the end.'

'Don't say that.'

'I should have listened, you told me we needed to focus on treatment here, but I didn't, did I? And now look. What if I had focused, on that. She might be getting better.'

'You can't change things. We will find the money. The doctors here agreed the US is the best course of action now.'

'How? How, George, how the hell are we going to do it?'

'Just . . . we will.'

I wanted to believe him, I did, but the facts told a different story, one that wasn't of hope, but of failure. I almost said as much, but was interrupted as Dr Bhari came in.

'Mrs Goodwin, Mr Goodwin.'

'Dr Bhari,' George replied.

'Although she will stay sedated, we all agree Tabatha will be able to fly. We need to begin getting ready for you to leave.'

'We don't have enough,' I said.

'Oh.'

'We've come up a little short. Doctor, if we were to travel and not be able to get into the programme, would Tabatha be okay to come home?' George asked.

'Mr Goodwin, I must stress that if you do not have a guarantee you can join the trial at the other end, the travelling will be detrimental to her health.'

'What do you advise?' I asked quietly.

'We will speak to Philadelphia, see if there can be a payment plan or something.'

'Do you think they'll agree?' I asked hopefully.

'I don't know. Their healthcare system isn't the same as ours. But I will try. I will stress again, though, if there is any doubt that she will be able to begin treatment in the trial, you shouldn't go. It would be harmful to your baby.'

'Then what do we do?'

'We will continue to do what we can for her here, with the drugs and surgery we have at our disposal.'

He hesitated again.

'I don't want to give up, not yet, but Mrs Goodwin, Mr Goodwin, she is critically ill. We still have a little time, we still have things we can try. But I want you to be prepared. I'm truly sorry.'

CHAPTER SIXTY-SIX

Clara

Dr Bhari left us to absorb what he had said, but really, how could we do that? Our baby was going to die. George tried to comfort me, but his words were distant and I sensed the same helplessness I felt in his tone. My chest tightened, my heart squeezing, and I got up to leave the room.

'Where are you going?'

'I need a moment,' I said, my words thick and cloying as they left my mouth.

'No, Clara, stay.'

I walked away. He didn't come after me and I was glad for it. I couldn't bear the pity in his eyes. I wandered down the corridor, towards the lift, and getting in, I pressed the button for the ground floor. It wasn't lost on me that not so long ago, George was the one having to leave the room after discovering how sick Tabatha was. It was only two weeks, but it felt longer, a lifetime longer. I wished I could stand firm as I did then, but that part of me was now gone.

I didn't know where I was going, or what I would do but I walked anyway, hoping the world would stop spinning, the floor would open and swallow me whole. But as much as oblivion sounded perfect, I couldn't give up altogether, not yet. Wandering down the quiet corridors, I averted my eyes from everyone who passed, patients, doctors, nurses, porters. And no one stopped me. My grief was there, visible, palpable, and no one passed comment, asked if I was all right. I guessed grief was everywhere in a hospital, death was around every corner, just waiting for the next one it could take into its embrace.

Turning right, I saw in front of me the sign of the cross, the hospital chapel. The one that George had found days before. I wanted to believe so much, but God couldn't be real, not when Tabatha was allowed to die.

The chapel was small, a few pews, a lectern at the front for preaching. I sat there staring, my mind blank for some time. I tried to find a way to focus, to think, but I couldn't, my thoughts were in turmoil. I don't know how long I was there for, but I was snapped back to the present by a message from George.

Your mum is here, whenever you're ready to come back

I stood up to go, though my legs felt too heavy for the task. I didn't want to go back into that room. I didn't want to see Mum because I would have to tell her what Dr Bhari said and saying it out loud would make it real. To my right sat a tray of small tealights, two already lit, prayers for loved ones. I went over, picked a new one up and lit it for Tabatha.

'Have you spoken a prayer?' a voice called out from the front of the chapel. I looked up and saw a woman with a dog collar smiling at me.

'I don't know how,' I answered honestly.

'There's nothing to it,' she said. 'You just give thanks for what you have and ask for what you need.'

'Give thanks for what I have?'

'Yes.'

I scoffed, not caring whether it seemed rude or not. The priest didn't comment but instead came over to where I stood.

'May I join you?'

'I don't care either way.'

'I'm Jessica. Who is the candle for?'

'My daughter.'

'I see,' She said before lighting a candle of her own. 'What is her name?'

'Tabatha,' I replied, feeling the prickle of tears. Jessica closed her eyes and prayed. When she finished, she smiled at me.

'There.'

'You think that will help?'

'Yes.'

'My daughter is dying, what good will a prayer do?'

'I know what you are saying, believe me, I do. And, between you and me, the prayer itself will do nothing.'

'So why bother?'

'Because God listens.'

'But He doesn't perform miracles.'

'No, not directly, the miracles have never come from on high. But they do come.' She smiled in such a way I wished I had faith, too.

'From where?'

'From us.' She looked at me, holding my gaze, and for a split second, I felt she knew every terrible thing I had done to try and help Tabatha.

'What if the miracle won't come because someone has done dreadful things?' I asked.

'It's all relative.'

'I've done terrible things. Is she being punished because of it?' I asked.

'No, she isn't. There are varying degrees of sin. Not all terrible things are truly bad in my opinion.'

'Yet, the Bible—'

'Is a guide, not a law. One of the ten commandments is to honour your father and mother. But what if your father is a drunk who hits you, what then?'

'What if you steal?' I asked.

'Can I tell you a story? I promise to be quick.'

I shrugged my shoulders.

'When I was young, before I found my faith, I fell on tough times. Truly challenging times. I was hungry a lot of the time, too poor to buy food. Do you think God judged me for taking food from a shop to eat? Would you?'

'No.'

'Clara, God understands our struggles, our need to do what we sometimes have to do. The only thing needed from us in return is faith.'

'Faith in what, in God?'

'No.'

'Then what?'

'Yourself.'

'Will it help?'

'You'll be surprised. I'll leave you to your thoughts now. Tabatha will stay in my prayers.'

The priest smiled and touched my shoulder then left me to look at the flickering candles lit for my daughter. Our exchange left me feeling something. It wasn't faith, it wasn't hope, it was something else, something that told me I couldn't give up, that while there was still life in my baby's body, I would fight on. Leaving the chapel, I made my way back towards the lift. When I walked into Tabatha's room, Mum and George were sitting close together and talking quietly. They stopped when they saw me.

'Sorry, I shouldn't have left.'

'It's okay, Clara,' George said.

'George, Mum, I'm not ready to give up yet. I'm not ready to admit defeat. I want to find the rest of the money; I want to save our baby.'

A look passed between Mum and George.

'Clara, sit down, love,' she said. 'We have an idea.'

CHAPTER SIXTY-SEVEN

Clara

'We've lost a lot tonight. Your home, my business,' Mum said.

'Yes.' My voice was small, broken.

'And we will have to deal with that in time, but right now is not the time,' she continued.

'No,' I agreed. 'All I want to talk about is how we save her.'

'Clara, I've learned something from Mercer, something we can use,' said George.

'What?'

'She called me to see how we were. I was scared Mantel would come here, so I asked if she would keep me informed of his movements, just in case.'

'And?'

'Mantel is on his way to the airport. He's going to lie low, I suspect.'

'He's leaving?'

'Yes.'

'Are you sure, he could be going anywhere?'

'Mantel's wife posted on her Instagram. A picture of her

packing. She said they were going on a last-minute surprise holiday. Hashtagging I-have-the-best-husband.'

'Right.'

'Mercer has someone following the car now, making sure they are en-route to the airport.'

'George, where is this going?'

'I was thinking, Jo and I have talked about it . . .' he began, but I couldn't focus, my attention going instead to my daughter. Helplessly lying there.

'You need to listen to this Clara,' Mum said, pulling my focus back.

'We all know Mantel took that money back before he burnt our home to the ground,' George continued. 'And now he's off, but it is very unlikely he is taking the money with him.'

'George, I—'

'He knows the police are watching him; he knows we speak to customs officers. He knows he won't get through without being searched, and if he was to get stopped at customs with that much undeclared cash . . .'

'He'd be in trouble,' I said, sitting upright a little more as what George was telling me began to sink in.

'Exactly. Clara, don't you see, if it's confirmed that Mantel has in fact gone to the airport, is flying somewhere to keep a low profile for a bit, he won't be at home. But I reckon that money will be. Clara, we'll know when that call comes, when Mercer has confirmed he is gone.'

'Why would she do that? Aren't you likely in trouble with her?'

'Yes, I am, but I also told her I was afraid for my family. Which I am. She'll message either way, for my peace of mind, and when she does, we are going to his house, we are going to break in and we are going to get it back. We do it now, and then we bank the money, and we get the hell out of here with our daughter.'

'What if he doesn't go?'

'We have to hope he does.'

'George, he is going to have security cameras.'

'Yes, it's likely.'

'And the police will still be watching, won't they?'

'I can help with that. As long as we are careful.'

'We?'

'Yes, we.'

'Clara,' Mum said, reaching over and taking my other hand. 'I will stay with Tabs; tell the doctors you have both gone for a walk to process what is happening and talk about options. If they need you, I'll fake call you, and then tell them you need a bit more time.'

'It's not a great alibi.'

'No, but it will have to do.' George was firm. 'Meanwhile, we'll go to his, find the money, come back and before Mantel can do anything about it, you and Tabs will be on that plane.'

'What about you? Mantel will know it's you.'

'Yes, probably. I have a plan for that, too,' George said.

'What are you thinking?' I asked.

'Clara, I did have a glimpse of my baby on her fifth birthday but it's fading. I need to see her in her school uniform, I need to see her smile. When we get the call—'

'There is no guarantee we will, Mantel might just be dropping them off.'

'Have faith, Clara,' Mum said. 'I know you're exhausted, I know you feel like you can do no more.'

'I can't.'

'You can, and you will. Because you must.' Mum sounded hard and resolute.

'When we get the call, we go, Clara. What do you say?' George asked.

'It will be broad daylight.'

'So then we move fast.'

I thought about it for all of a second. I didn't think I could go on, but then if I stopped now, I would regret it for the rest of my life. I had asked for a miracle, and it seemed I might actually get one.

'Let's finish this, let's save our baby,' I said.

CHAPTER SIXTY-EIGHT

George

We waited for the call, the clock ticking. I knew if we didn't manage to succeed now, it would all be over. We had almost run out of time. We needed to be able to get on that flight with all of the money. Because if we came up short, if we failed, Tabatha might not survive.

My phone vibrated on the table and we all stared at it. I picked it up to see a message from Mercer.

Call me

I rang her straight back.

'Ma'am.'

'George. The car is parked at Manchester Airport, four people went into departures, two adults, two children.'

'He's gone?'

'Yes, George, he's gone. We'll try bring him in when he comes home, but for now you can rest, be with your family. Take the time you need. You're safe.'

'I will, thank you Ma'am.' I looked at Clara, gave her a nod, and she smiled before standing and kissing Tabatha on the head.

I hung up. Clara and Jo were hugging, Jo clinging on to her daughter.

'You be careful.'

'I will.'

'And you,' she said, grabbing me and pulling me in, kissing me on the cheek and squeezing me tight. When she let go, I took Clara by the hand and we walked out of the room. In a few hours, Clara and I would be back, a bag full of money, and I would pave the way for their escape.

CHAPTER SIXTY-NINE

Clara

It took an hour to get to within walking distance of Mantel's house, and in that time George and I spoke very little. He was focusing on the road ahead, the task at hand, and I spent most of the journey on Google Maps, looking at Mantel's street and working out a way to get in and out without being seen by any curtain-twitching neighbours or people out with their dogs. I had to move fast and be clever. I zoomed in on Mantel's house and satisfied I'd found a solution, I closed my phone and looked out of the side window. George was nervous, I could tell. He tried to engage in idle chit-chat a couple of times to deflect the tension, but I quashed it each time. I needed to ready myself for whatever came. As he stopped the car a few streets down from Mantel's road, I turned in my seat to face him.

'George, we go via the back, over the garden wall.'

'Okay.'

'When we get there, I need you to stay outside, keep watch.'

'What? No.'

'George, two of us in there doubles the chance of something

going wrong. I've done this a few times now, I know what I'm doing.'

'Yes, sorry, you're right.'

'I'll be quick. I'll find the money and we'll get back to the hospital before anyone even knows,' I said, my strength, my courage renewed.

Getting out of the car, we walked away from the direction of Mantel's road, looping around the back of the estate. Mantel's house backed onto a golf course and we climbed over a small fence and walked along the edge of a fairway. Thankfully, it was quiet and I could only see a few people in the distance, facing in the opposite direction. We clambered through a small thicket of trees until we found the wall, and pulling myself onto it, I looked over into Henry Mantel's immaculate back garden. The lawn was so perfect I wasn't sure if it was real. There was a trampoline to my right, a playhouse to my left. Close to the bifold glass doors that ran across the entire wall of his kitchen sat a brick barbeque. It looked like the perfect family home, something George and I would have loved. It made me feel sick that a man like Mantel had all of this and we had nothing because of him. I forced down my feelings of unfairness and focused on the reason we were there. Scanning again, ignoring thoughts of the lavish lifestyle Mantel must lead, I checked all was quiet. Satisfied, I climbed over the wall. George followed, and we moved quietly across the lawn. As we approached, I tried to look inside but I couldn't see much. Once we reached the house, we pressed ourselves against the wall.

'Why have we stopped?' George whispered.

'Wait.'

I strained to listen to anything that didn't sound organic.

The leaves whispered as the wind blew through them. In the distance a dog barked, the hum of traffic on tarmac lulled, somewhere closer, I could hear birdsong, but nothing near to us, nothing alerted by our presence. Gesturing to George to move I kept low and hugged the wall as I crept closer to the back door. Breaking through the bifold wouldn't do, it would be too noisy, too obvious if anyone happened to look. So I skimmed past and turned down the side of the house, knowing, thanks to my online search, there was another door that was sheltered by the wall of the detached triple garage. It was a standard half with double-glazed windows. This was where I would go in.

'It's weird doing this with you,' I said.

'It's weird full stop.'

'Not for me. George, keep an eye.'

'I want to go in with you.'

'No, it's best not. I'll be quick. Okay?'

Leaning in, I kissed him on the lips. 'I love you.'

I smiled, then grabbing the hammer out of the bag, I covered my eyes and smashed the glass.

CHAPTER SEVENTY

Clara

Henry Mantel's house was just as immaculate inside as it was out. I forced myself not to see it as something to aspire to, but rather something to loathe.

I knew the money wouldn't be in the kitchen. That space was for family, for friends and associates. Mantel would keep it somewhere more personal. An office, or his bedroom. I stopped focusing on the expensive furniture and ornaments and gadgets and concentrated on finding that small personal spot that was just for him. As I left the open-plan kitchen I found myself in a long corridor. I struggled to see; all the doors were shut and there were no windows, there was no light to give me angles and edges of doorframes and units. I felt my way, my hands out front to stop me colliding with things as I felt for door handles. Finding one, I opened it to see a living room and daylight spilled from it into the dark corridor. After my eyes adjusted, I saw a deep red rug, a fireplace, a TV mounted on the wall and a coffee table with books scattered across it. He wouldn't keep it here. Leaving the door open to illuminate the corridor, I kept moving. The next door was a playroom, dolls and Lego and games in every space. The walls had pictures and a bookcase full of stories and DVDs. As I backed away, I couldn't help but think this home didn't suit the man. This house was beautiful, full of love. I imagined children playing and people laughing. The house looked like it belonged to someone I would want to know, and yet it was Henry Mantel who owned it. The murderer, the man who spoke through gritted teeth when mentioning my daughter, the man who burned my life to the ground.

I thought about going up to his bedroom, but as I made my way towards the stairs, I tried the third door along and found it was locked. My heart skipped a beat. Why would Mantel lock a door inside his own already locked house? This had to be it. It just had to be. Behind that door was the money, behind that door was my daughter's salvation. Using the hammer, I dug the claw into the lock and began to pull with all my strength. The task seemed too difficult but nothing would stop me saving my baby. Nothing. The claw slipped, and as I had been pulling so hard, I fell into the adjacent wall. I picked myself up and tried again, and despite my hands burning, this time I kept going. Around the lock, the door began to budge, allowing me to push the claw of the hammer further into the gap to give me more leverage. Now the wood began to groan, splinter, and with one final pull it cracked and split and the door swung open.

Breathing heavily, I walked inside. Whereas the rest of the house felt light and open, made for a family, this room was entirely different. The walls were dark, the wood was dark, the carpet was dark. A thick blind hung across the window, making it impossible to see inside. A huge and expensive desk sat in the middle of the room, a lamp on it. Pushing the door shut behind me, I dared to turn it on and I took in the space. Mantel's private office. It was here, in this room, I could feel it.

I started by moving things around his desk, carefully putting them back in place until I realized it didn't matter whether I was careful or not. Mantel would know it was me. I cleared the desk with my arm, sending paperwork scattering and his Mac crashing to the floor. Using the hammer, I prised open his desk drawers and pulled everything out. I turned and eyed the bookcase. Grabbing a handful of spines, I dragged them from the shelf and dropped them at my feet. I cleared the whole row, and the row above, and still nothing. Grabbing his office chair, I dragged it in front of the bookcase so I could reach the top and I pulled the contents down. The books up high were heavy encyclopaedias, old and expensive, and a few of the spines cracked as they hit the ground. I moved the chair, to reach the furthest corner of the top shelf and pulled on one of the books, but it didn't budge. I tried repeatedly but it wouldn't move. Looking closer, I saw that this row of books, seven in all, had no gap between them. They were one solid unit. Just like at the club.

Digging my fingers either side, I pulled harder and this time the box came away from the wall. Holding it above my head, I threw it at the floor as hard as I could and it spilt open. I moved the broken pieces of wood away and found a bag. My hands shook as I tried to open it.

CHAPTER SEVENTY-ONE

George

I felt like Clara was taking too long and with every noise I heard, wind blowing, dogs barking, I thought it was someone coming to catch her in the act. A cold sweat clung to my brow and my hands were clammy. I had no idea how Clara must be feeling but I was glad she had told me to stay outside and keep watch.

From inside, I heard a commotion, banging, knocking and I climbed through the gap in the broken window to try and see what was going on.

'Clara?' I whispered, not daring to call out. 'Clara, is that you?'

More crashing and banging came and I started to move towards the source. I listened out for any voices; if someone were here, Clara would surely shout for help? I heard groaning, and then the sound of a door crashing open. I peered into a corridor in time to see Clara disappearing into a room. Letting out a sigh, I stopped for a moment to catch my breath. And as I heard Clara starting to trash the room, I made my way back towards my lookout post in the garden. Clara seemed to be moving things and dropping things, she must be on to something. I kept an ear on her as well as an ear outside, hoping she would find what we needed and quickly.

My phone vibrated, it was a text from Mercer. Even before I read it, panic set in.

Mantel isn't with the family. The wife and two children went through customs, the other man, his right hand, Tony, was only an escort for them. They knew we were there, the fucker smiled at our officer who followed them as he left. He's up to something, we are going to try and arrest him now. I'm sending officers to the hospital, keep a low profile until they arrive

'Shit.'

I ran back into the house and towards the room I'd seen Clara go into.

'Clara! Clara?'

I found her on her knees, bundles of money in her hands.

'George, I found it,' she sobbed. 'It's all here. All of it.'

'Clara, Mantel hasn't left the country. We need to go, now.'

CHAPTER SEVENTY-TWO

Clara

'He what?' I asked, my elation turning to fear in a single heartbeat.

'He didn't go, Clara, he knows we're here. We have to go, now.'

Getting up, I pushed all the money back into the bag and moved closer to George. I wanted to run for it, but knowing Mantel, I figured he would wait to ambush us. At the doorway, I looked out into the corridor towards the kitchen. I saw movement, someone walking past the door. I backed up out of sight.

'Someone's in the kitchen.'

'Shit. What do we do?' he asked.

'We find another way out.'

George nodded and I reached around him to pick up the hammer. Quietly we moved towards the door and once more I carefully looked out. I couldn't see anyone, but I knew they were still there, waiting for us to make our move. I looked the other way, towards the front door of the house, and began to silently head towards it. George reached for my hand and held it as we crept towards the exit. Reaching the door, I tried to open it but it was locked.

'Shit. Do we go up?' George asked.

'No, if we do we will be penned in. We have to go back the way we came in.'

'Someone's there waiting for us.'

'Then we have to get past them. I am getting this money to our daughter, George. Whatever it takes.'

'Whatever the cost,' he said.

We began to move back towards the kitchen. As we drew level with Mantel's office, a voice called out.

'I know you're here, DI Goodwin.'

We froze, dipping into the office again. George looked at me and something was different; he was no longer afraid, no longer panicked.

'Clara, get our daughter to Philadelphia,' he said, pulling the car keys from his pocket and placing them in my hand.

'George?'

'Hide.'

Before I could stop him, he stepped out into the corridor and closed the door behind him.

'No Clara today, just me,' George said, his voice muffled through the closed door.

'George? Well, what a surprise.'

'My wife might have started this thing, but I am finishing it. Where's the money, Mantel?'

'You've got some balls.'

'I'm not leaving here without it, so I'll ask again, where is that fucking money?'

I heard Mantel laugh, maniacal and dangerous, and then

I heard his footsteps advancing. George continued to goad him, but I could hear he was backing away, towards the front door. At first, I didn't know what he was doing. He knew the door was locked; he knew if he went upstairs, he would be trapping himself. Seconds later, Mantel walked slowly past the study door, pursuing my husband. And then I understood. George was drawing him in so I could run. I waited, I listened. Mantel was toying with George as he started to go up the stairs.

'DS Goodwin, you really think I'm going to let you take my money?'

'I don't give a fuck what you think.'

I heard Mantel ascend and I moved to the doorway. Slowly I began to open it, then looked out into the hallway. There was no sign of anyone. Above me, I heard movement, Mantel reaching the top step.

'You know, DS Goodwin, I've called the police already, told them someone is in my house. I suspect they'll come quickly.'

'You think I care?'

'I can't see what you have to gain, DS Goodwin. What possible good will come from this?'

I opened the door fully, and slowly moved towards the back door. Upstairs, Mantel continue to speak.

'You can't get away with this. I just don't understand; you won't find the money, you'll be arrested, how did you think you would succeed? Unless . . .'

Mantel went quiet, and I suddenly heard footsteps moving quickly.

'Clara, run!' George shouted, and I took flight, running

as fast as I could towards the exit. As I reached the door, Mantel came barrelling into the room.

'You fucking bitch!'

As I began to duck through the broken pane, Mantel caught up and pulled me back, slamming me into the wall. I fought to get free, but his grip was strong, fuelled by his rage. He raised his hand, balled his fist and I waited for a blow to the head. As he began to swing, George grabbed him and pulled him back. Mantel swung for George now, hitting him in the head but as George stumbled, he managed to drag Mantel down with him.

'Get out!' George shouted as he hit Mantel hard enough to daze him and break free.

'George, I—'

'Get out, Clara, finish this,' he said getting to his feet and pushing me towards the door.

'No, George, I won't give up on you.'

'Nor I you, now go help our daughter.' He kissed me before pushing me harder towards the way out.

I ran, tears streaming down my face, and behind me I heard George and Mantel fighting. I hated leaving him, but if it were the other way around, if George were holding the money and I was fighting with Mantel, I would want him to run, too. Tabatha was the priority, both of us knew this. We had experienced the world and all its wonder and sadness and light and darkness and in becoming parents, we had signed an oath to help our child experience all those things and so much more. So I ran, with the money to save my baby in my hands, and I didn't look back.

CHAPTER SEVENTY-THREE

Clara

Seven hours later

As the team of doctors brought in for the transfer strapped Tabatha's bed in, making sure she was comfortable and that she would be safe in case of turbulence, I stood watching. I wanted to help, to do something, but as Mum said, I had done my part.

I hadn't heard from George. I didn't know what happened, or where he was. Seven hours had passed, and I didn't know if he was all right, I didn't know if he was alive. Seven hours was too long to not hear anything, and I was desperate to know, but as painful as it was, I had to push that to the back of my mind and get my daughter out of the country.

As the doctors finished prepping for travel, I was instructed to sit beside her. As I did so, my phone pinged. I looked at the screen and saw it was Mum. Her message was simple, cryptic. It would be read by the police, of that I had no doubt.

All is sorted, have a safe flight. I love you, I love you both

It was done. Mum had banked the money and sent the

rest of what we needed over to Philadelphia. We had done it, Tabatha was going, there was no turning back now, nothing else to block our path. My baby was getting the treatment she needed. We just had to get off the ground, get in the air, out of the UK. They could have me, arrest me, when I got home, but not before.

As I looked at my daughter, tears began to roll down my cheeks. It had taken so much, cost so much, but she had a chance now. The coin that had offered fifty-fifty was different, the odds were swinging in our favour, and even though I felt sick with worry for my husband, I couldn't help but smile.

'Could you put on your seatbelt, please, we are cleared for take off,' asked a steward. I nodded, wiped my eyes and strapped myself in. The plane began to taxi along the runway, and then the engines rumbled, readying themselves for take-off.

My phone, still beside me, began to vibrate. I looked and saw it was an unknown number.

'Could you turn it on to airplane mode please?' I was asked.

'Sorry.'

The phone stopped ringing, and seconds later it started again. Before I could be told not to, I snatched it up to my ear.

'Clara,' a voice said, his voice.

'George!'

'I've got to be quick. It's my one call.'

'Where are you?'

'At the station. I'm okay. Please tell me you are gone?'

'You have to turn off your phone, please,' the steward said.

'One sec,' I replied.

'You're on the plane?'

'Yes.'

'It's all done?'

'They're waiting for us in Philadelphia.'

On the other end, I heard George start to cry.

'What happened?'

'Don't worry, everything is going to be okay.'

'Mantel?'

'He's in custody, too. Even though I was in the wrong, he was assaulting a police officer.'

'Do you think they will keep him in?'

'Yes, Lee Sharman has also been called in. When they searched Mantel's house they found images from his body cam, which he'd given to Mantel. He's with DCI Mercer right now and he's talking. Mantel isn't going anywhere.'

'Are you hurt?'

'I'll live.'

'Madam,' the steward insisted.

'George, I have to go.'

'Go. When I'm allowed home, I'll call.'

There were three beeps in my ear as the time George was allowed was over and then the line went dead. I turned the phone off and flashed an apologetic look at the steward, who quickly forgave me.

'Sorry.'

'It's all right,' he said.

Sitting back in my seat, fresh tears fell as the plane picked up speed and then lifted from the ground. Looking out of the window, I watched as the world became small, I watched as we left England behind. I had done it, and I knew my baby had a chance.

I watched my daughter sleep, her body supported by

machines keeping her alive, and I tried to think about her fifth birthday, but I was too tired. I had nothing left. My body, my mind, had finally given in to the exhaustion that weighed me down and as my eyes began to close, I kept looking at my daughter until my vision blurred and I fell into a deep and safe sleep.

EPILOGUE

Clara

Tabatha's 5th Birthday

I couldn't wait for them to come. I had counted down the days to be able to see George walk through that door, hand in hand with our daughter. I couldn't wait to see my little girl, to hold her, smell her hair. And as I got dressed for visiting hours, I could barely contain my excitement. Seeing Tabatha and George on their weekly visits was the highlight of the week for me. That short hour fuelled me to keep going, ride out my sentence, and I leapfrogged one week to the next because of it. Today was extra special, though. Today was the day I dreamt of back when I was doing what was needed to save my baby. The day I implored George to think of for so long, until he could see it, too. The day I had fought and suffered for.

Today was Tabatha's fifth birthday.

Her fifth as a happy, healthy little girl. Today was the day I nearly died for, that others died for. Today was the day George risked jail for. He was investigated for the assault on Mantel and for breaking into his house, and although he was suspended for

393

it, he avoided charges being drawn against him because they factored in the mental health crisis he was experiencing due to our daughter's ill health. He was lucky. And I was grateful that one of us was.

Today was the day that was the reason I spent my weeks in a prison cell, sleeping when I could over the shouts and cries of other inmates. And as it was that day, the one that gave us hope in our darkest moments, I couldn't help but reflect on that strange and difficult time in our lives. The things I had done, the places I was prepared to go. It was all worth it. I knew as much the day we landed back in Manchester after Tabatha's treatment, where I was met by a reception of several officers waiting to arrest me. I confessed to breaking into Mantel's garage, to almost killing Mike. I couldn't deny it, my blood was at the scene. I had to pay my penance, and I was prepared to. I was questioned about the other break-ins, and everyone knew I was connected to them, but as there was no evidence, I couldn't be charged. But Mike, I couldn't deny. Thankfully he made a full recovery, though he had to leave the force. I was charged with GBH with intent, and burglary. They could have thrown the book at me and given me a heavy sentence, but I got off with only eight and a half years. As with George, Tabatha's health was a factor in my sentencing. My crimes were much more severe than his and I deserved to be incarcerated. If only they truly knew how bad I had been, how I was culpable for so much more.

As for Mantel, he made the huge mistake of calling the police when George and I broke in. In the office that I had trashed they found the link to Lee Sharman, who co-operated fully and drew enough evidence together for both Mantel and Tony to be charged for all three men who had been killed.

No one ever knew about the money, and no one ever would. Everything I stole was dirty, everything I had taken didn't exist. I was questioned about the cash deposits into our bank accounts, but as we were fundraising for Tabatha, we were being gifted a lot of money. They didn't press the matter further.

I've asked myself over and over, was there another way? Could I have done things differently to raise the money, without so much pain? But I didn't think it was possible. Regardless, I would carry it always, and my heart would never heal from this. But today, Tabatha was five. Healthy and well and cancer-free, which is all I'd ever wanted.

Brushing my hair one more time, I tidied my books and then looked at myself in the mirror. Four years in jail was showing. My eyes were more heavyset, my lips thinner, my skin softer and aged through lack of natural light. There was a weight now that wasn't there before, a burden I had to shoulder now and forever. I didn't care. I wore my marks with pride. And the woman who looked back, I knew who she was.

There was a knock on my cell door, and I turned to see Michael, one of the nicer guards on our wing.

'You all right?' he asked in his thick Yorkshire accent.

'Yes, nervous.'

'You'll do fine.'

'Michael, did you manage to, I mean, were you able to get that cake?'

'Yes, love, it's waiting in the visitors' room.'

'Thank you.'

'Pleasure. Shall we? Don't want to keep your little girl waiting on her special day.'

I took one last look at myself. 'No, I don't.'

I made my way along the wing and a few other inmates I had got to know nodded my way as they joined the line to see their loved ones. As we walked into the room to take our seats a few saw the cake on my table and smiled. They knew today was special. They would never know quite how special. Only George would truly understand.

'Just think, Clara,' Michael said. 'If you continue to behave, on her next one you will be home.'

The visitors' door opened and I sat up straight and watched as people filed in, gravitating to their family members for hugs, kisses, smiles and laughter. Right at the end of the line, the last people to come in, were George and Tabatha. My daughter was in a little checked dress, her hair in a pony tail and a big badge sat proudly on her chest. I stood and waited as they came over to me, and bent down to scoop up my girl and hug her tightly.

'Happy birthday, baby.'

'Thank you, Mummy.'

Putting her down, George stepped forward and kissed me on the cheek.

'How are you?'

'Better now you're here.'

'Look, Mummy,' Tabatha said, holding up a teddy bear.

'Oh wow. Who got you that?'

'Nana. Her name is Teddy-Weddy.'

'Teddy-Weddy.' I laughed and saw people at other tables smiling too. 'Well, it's a great name.'

'And Daddy said later, when we're home, we can go for a McDonald's.'

'A McDonald's! Wow, you are a lucky girl.'

'And he said that I have more presents coming later today.'

'Oh, that's amazing.'

'In fact,' George smiled, 'I have one here right now.'

He pulled a small box from his pocket, one he no doubt had to have cleared before bringing it into the room. I didn't know what it was.

'Go on, open it.'

Tabatha tore into the wrapping paper, dropping it on the floor, and pulled out a small red box. She struggled to open it. 'Mummy, do you want to help?' George said, and I did. Prising the box open, I saw two silver chains.

'What is it?' Tabatha asked.

'A necklace,' I said quietly.

'This is from Mummy,' George said, although I'd had no idea about this at all. 'It's two necklaces, making up one heart. See, Tabby, if you wear one half and Mummy wears the other, your hearts will always be close.'

I didn't dare speak for fear I would cry, so I took out the first necklace, the smaller of the two, and I put it around Tabatha's neck. I then kneeled down and helped her put mine on me. I lifted my half and held it towards Tabs, and she picked up hers, putting the two together.

'There, see,' George said.

'Mummy, are we now sharing a heart?' Tabatha asked in amazement.

'Yes, baby, we are.'

'Always?'

'Always.'

I hugged my girl, and as I did, I mouthed a 'thank you' to George. He smiled back, his eyes full of tears.

George and Tabatha stayed the full hour. We sang happy birthday to her, along with most of the other people in the room, George and I singing our hearts out with everything we had. As we smiled and chatted, I thought of everything we did just to be able to have this day.

When the bell sounded telling everyone that visiting time had ended, Michael came over and said we could have an extra ten minutes. As the other visitors and inmates left, Tabatha told me about school and her friends and her teachers, and once the room was empty, with just the three of us and Michael remaining, I knew it was time to say goodbye. Tabatha kissed me and as we hugged, she began to cry.

'I miss you, Mummy. I want you to come home.'

'I do, too. But remember, now we have the same heart, we will always be together.'

'I love you,' she said, holding on to my neck.

As I held my daughter, I looked at George. 'This is so much better than I could have imagined.'

'What is?' George asked.

'This, her fifth.'

'Is it? Even with you here?'

'Yes, even with me here. This is better than I could have hoped for. Look at our daughter, look at our girl.' I squeezed Tabatha tighter.

'All thanks to you,' George said, and even though he smiled, I could see he still wished it was him in prison instead of me. He had told me it a thousand times, but this couldn't have happened any other way, and I had made peace with that.

'See you next week?' he said.

'I can't wait.'

'Say goodbye to Mummy.'

'Bye Mummy.'

'Bye darling, happy birthday.'

George then kissed me on the cheek, and I kissed Tabatha on the head one more time, taking in her smell.

I sat down; my heart ached and I had to fight back the tears. It wasn't all sadness about not being able to go home with my baby. Some of it was joy. I said I'd do whatever it took, and I knew I wouldn't change a thing.

'She's precious,' Michael said.

'She is.'

'Do you need a minute?'

'Please.'

'Take your time,' he said, walking away to give me some space as I fiddled with my necklace, my incomplete heart.

I would do my time without complaint because I promised I would do whatever it took.

Whatever the cost.

Whatever the price.

ACKNOWLEDGEMENTS

Writing *The Price* has been the single most difficult undertaking of my career to date. When I set out to tell the story of Clara, George and Tabatha, I didn't fully understand how challenging it would be to tell the story in the right way. This book made me doubt myself as a writer, but somehow, we got there. Without the help of people in my life, I wouldn't be writing theese acknowledgements now.

First, I need to thank my agent, Hayley Steed at the Madeleine Milburn agency. Hayley, as ever, I feel truly grateful you are in my corner. You're insight, guidance and support has helped me through this journey. Thank you to Elinor Davies too, I'm so glad we get to work together, and I'm thankful for the energy you give.

Thank you to my editor, Katie Seaman, for steering the ship and helping me find the right story when it got muddy. Between us we have examined over a quarter of a million words to find this book. We got there!!!!

Also, thank you to the team at HQ for the work you do behind the scenes in helping me find readers. It is something I'm so grateful for, I just wish I could tell you more often.

Thank you to Cari Rosen for such wonderful work on the copy-edit of this book and thank you to Phil Norton for helping me create the fictious FundMyCause which features in this book.

To my author buddies, John Marrs, Lisa Hall, Cally Taylor, Lynn Fraser, Alice Hunter, thank you for being around, offering advice, sharing stories and helping when things have got tough. How lucky am I to know you guys.

To Darren Maddison and Alex Forster, thanks for listening to me talk about this book incessantly, and for offering ideas when I couldn't see a way through.

And finally, as always, the final thank you is to my amazing son, Benjamin. Without you, there is no motivation, no determination, and no inspiration. And I will forever try to repay you for this.

**Read more unputdownable thrillers from
Darren O'Sullivan – the master of the killer twist**

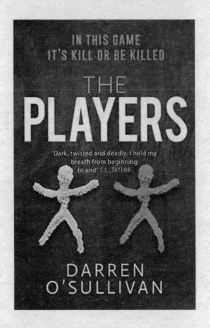

In this game it's kill or be killed . . .

A stranger has you cornered.
They call themselves The Host.
You are forced to play their game.
In it one person can live and the other must die.
You are the next player.
You have a choice to make.

This is a game where nobody wins . . .

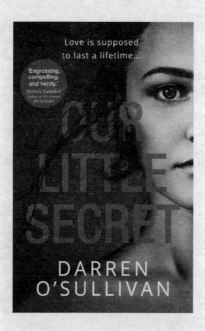

A deserted train station: A man waits. A woman watches.

Chris is ready to join his wife. He's planned this moment for nearly a year. The date. The time. But he hadn't factored in Sarah.

So when Sarah walks on to the platform and sees a man swaying at the edge she assumes he's just had too much to drink. What she doesn't expect is to stop a suicide.

As Sarah becomes obsessed with discovering the secrets that Chris is clearly hiding, he becomes obsessed with stopping her, protecting her.

But there are some secrets that are meant to stay buried . . .

DARREN O'SULLIVAN

CLOSE YOUR EYES

... and count to ten.

He doesn't know his name. He doesn't know his secret.

When Daniel woke up from a coma he had no recollection of the life he lived before. Now, fourteen years later, he's being forced to remember.

A phone call in the middle of the night demands he return what he stole – but Daniel has no idea what it could be, or who the person on the other end is. He has been given one warning, if he doesn't find out, his family will be murdered.

Rachael needs to protect her son. Trapped with no way out she will do anything to ensure they survive. But sometimes mothers can't save their children and her only hope is Daniel's memory.